MYSTERY IN PRIOR'S FORD

The fifth warm-hearted novel of village life in Evelyn Hood's much-loved Prior's Ford series

Cookery writer Laura Tyler arrives in Prior's Ford determined to become immersed in village life – and the village drama group's forthcoming production of *The Importance of Being Earnest* offers her the perfect opportunity. But Laura has cause to regret her involvement when murder calls a halt to rehearsals. Constable Neil White investigates, with help from an unexpected source – American visitor Amy Rose, with her passion for crosswords and mystery-solving, can't resist a spot of amateur sleuthing...

Mystery in Prior's Ford

Evelyn Hood

Severn House Large Print
London & New York

This first large print edition published 2012
in Great Britain and the USA by
SEVERN HOUSE PUBLISHERS LTD of
9-15 High Street, Sutton, Surrey, SM1 1DF.
First world regular print edition published 2011 by
Severn House Publishers Ltd., London and New York.

British Library Cataloguing in Publication Data

Hood, Evelyn.
    Mystery in Prior's Ford. -- (Prior's Ford series)
    1. Prior's Ford (Scotland : Imaginary place)--Fiction.
    2. Villages--Scotland--Dumfries and Galloway--Fiction.
    3. Women food writers--Fiction. 4. Amateur theatre--
    Fiction. 5. Theatrical producers and directors--Crimes
    against--Fiction. 6. Americans--Scotland--Dumfries and
    Galloway--Fiction. 7. Detective and mystery stories.
    8. Large type books.
    I. Title II. Series
    823.9'14-dc23

    ISBN-13: 978-0-7278-9835-7

Severn House Publishers support The Forest Stewardship Council
[FSC], the leading international forest certification organisation. All
our titles that are printed on Greenpeace-approved FSC-certified paper
carry the FSC logo.

MIX
Paper from
responsible sources
FSC
www.fsc.org   FSC® C018575

Printed and bound in Great Britain by the
MPG Books Group, Bodmin, Cornwall.

DEDICATION

In the first Prior's Ford book, *Secrets in Prior's Ford*, when Clarissa tells Naomi, the feisty minister, that she has lost her best friend, Naomi's reply is, 'You can never lose a friend. You only lost someone you had assumed to be a friend.' This, I swear, came directly from Naomi, not from me – this is something that can happen when a character is brought to life fully; they even start thinking for themselves.

Having had a pretty rotten time over the past two years, which entailed losing a few people I had thought of as friends, I was deeply impressed by Naomi's comment. So I started counting up my true friends, and discovered that if true friends can be compared to wealth I'm a veritable Paris Hilton.

So this book is dedicated to all the wonderful friends I will never lose, who have gossiped, laughed and cried with me every step of the way, and also to the wonderful readers who, during my writing career as Evelyn Hood, Louise James, and Eve Houston, have taken the trouble to tell me how much they've enjoyed my writing.

I am so grateful to you all.
Evelyn Hood

5

Acknowledgments

My thanks and my gratitude to the following people for their generous assistance during the writing of this book:

The Reverend Alison Burnside, who throughout the series has patiently answered my questions regarding the work of one of my favourite characters, the Reverend Naomi Hennessey.

Charlotte Peck, landscape architect, who has provided invaluable advice on the restoration of the Linn House estate.

Beryl Shaw, who offered to proofread chapter by chapter.

Steve O'Brien and Mary Hackett, who kept me straight when it came to police procedure and life in the police force.

Main Characters

The Ralston-Kerrs – **Hector Ralston-Kerr** is the Laird of Prior's Ford and lives with his wife **Fliss** and their son **Lewis** in ramshackle **Linn Hall**. **Lewis** is engaged to **Molly Ewing,** the mother of his baby daughter, **Rowena Chloe**. **Fliss** wonders, secretly, if Lewis is really Rowena Chloe's father, and if flighty **Molly** is the right person to take over the reins of Linn Hall when Lewis inherits it.

Ginny (Genevieve) Whitelaw – is helping to restore the Linn Hall estate, which **Lewis** hopes to open to the public to raise much-needed income.

The Fishers – **Joe** and **Gracie Fisher** are the landlord and landlady of the local pub, the Neurotic Cuckoo. They live on the premises with their widowed daughter **Alison Greenlees** and her young son **Jamie**.

Clarissa Ramsay – lives in Willow Cottage. A retired teacher and a widow. Although some twenty years his senior, she has strong feelings for **Alastair Marshall**, an artist who has been living in a small farm cottage on the outskirts of the village. Alastair has strong feelings for Clarissa.

Sam Brennan and Marcy Copleton – live in Rowan Cottage and run the local Village Store together.

The Reverend Naomi Hennessey – the local Church of Scotland minister, part Jamaican, part English. Lives in the manse with her godson, **Ethan Baptiste**, Jamaican.

The McNairs of Tarbethill Farm – **Jess McNair** and her younger son **Ewan** are struggling to keep the family farm going, following the suicide of Jess's husband. **Victor**, her elder son, has deserted the farm for a life in the nearby town of Kirkcudbright and is about to be married. **Ewan** is in love with the local publican's daughter, **Alison Greenlees**, but since his father's death, he has had to face the fact that he will never be able to afford to marry. The farm's future must come first with him from now on.

Jinty and **Tom McDonald** – live with their large family on the village's council housing estate. **Jinty** is a willing helper at Linn House, and also cleans the village hall and primary school, while **Tom** is keen on gambling and frequenting the Neurotic Cuckoo.

Kevin and Elinor Pearce – Kevin, a former journalist, runs the local drama club.

Amy Rose – Clarissa's American friend, who composes crossword puzzles and loves solving problems, puzzles and mysteries.

One

'I must be getting old,' Marcy Copleton announced. 'I hate change, and too many changes have been happening in this village recently.'

'Oh, come on – it's exciting,' Helen Campbell argued as she hoisted her basket on to the counter. 'I enjoy seeing new people around the place, and changes like the Gift Horse becoming Colour Carousel.'

'That's because you've got plenty to write about in the Prior's Ford column of the *Dumfries News*. And as for Colour Carousel, you're surely not saying that you don't miss Ingrid and the Gift Horse and the coffees we used to enjoy there.'

'Of course I miss Ingrid and Peter and the girls, but Anja's like a breath of fresh air,' Helen was saying when the village store's door opened and Anja Jacobsen swept in. With her black and white patterned top, crimson cropped trousers and blonde hair, cut short and dyed a vibrant purple around her elfin face, she seemed to flood the village store with colour and vitality.

'Hello, I am looking for chocolate biscuits,' she said in her sing-song Norwegian lilt. 'Jenny has been working hard all morning and she

11

needs sustenance.'

'Chocolate digestives are her favourite. Second top shelf, right over there. How are things coming along?' Marcy asked.

'Very well. We'll be all finished for the opening next Wednesday,' Anja assured them as she put the packet of biscuits on the counter. 'Done and dusty, as you say.'

'Dusted,' Helen corrected her without thinking.

'That too,' Anja assured her, producing payment for the biscuits from a tiny scarlet soft-leather purse slung like a pendant from a silver chain about her neck.

'That's pretty. Where did you buy it?' Helen wanted to know.

'This? I made it.'

'Are you planning to sell purses like that in the shop?'

'No, but if you want one I can make it for you.'

'I have two daughters, Gemma and Irene. Could they each have one?'

'Of course. In different colours?'

'Yes please – you choose them.'

'It's as good as done,' Anja assured her, scooping the biscuits up. 'Goodbye!'

'I wish we'd been brave enough to dye our hair amazing colours when we were her age.' Helen's voice was envious. 'Doesn't just looking at that girl give your spirits a lift?'

'I suppose so – but I still miss Ingrid.'

'We all do.' Marcy, Helen, Norwegian-born

Ingrid MacKenzie and Jenny Forsyth were all close friends, and Jenny had helped Ingrid to run the gift shop she had opened in the village some seven years earlier. But almost a year ago, Ingrid, her husband Peter and their daughters Freya and Ella had gone to Norway when Ingrid's father developed Alzheimer's and his wife was unable to cope with the family hotel on her own.

The original plan had been for Ingrid and Peter to find a new manager for the hotel and then return to Dumfries and Galloway, but that had turned out to be more difficult than first expected, and Ingrid had brought bad news for her friends when she returned on a flying visit at Easter with her two girls and her niece Anja.

'My father still thinks that he's perfectly able to manage the hotel, and it would be difficult for a new manager to understand how to work with him. He trusts Peter, and Peter's wonderful with him. But it looks as though we'll be away from home for more than the year we first spoke of,' she told her friends with regret. 'My mother needs us so much.'

'So do we,' Jenny said, and then, to the others, 'I've had to tell Ingrid that I don't enjoy running the Gift Horse on my own. I'm happier as an assistant than a manager.'

'And that's why Anja's come to Scotland with me. She's just finished college and now she's a qualified interior designer, yearning to travel and meet people and set up her own business. So Peter and I thought that she could take over the

Gift Horse with Jenny's help, selling paint and wallpaper to people who want to decorate their homes, and also offering advice and her own services as a decorator. And she can live in our house. She's so excited about it all.'

'So am I,' Jenny chimed in. 'I'll keep the shop going, selling paints and wallpaper and various things for the home like pictures and mirrors, to leave Anja free to visit people in their own homes. She's decided to change the name to Colour Carousel.'

Ingrid nodded. 'This is a good time for her to come to Prior's Ford; I see that people have begun to move into that new housing estate across from the farm.'

'Clover Park,' Jenny said.

'Sam must be pleased at the prospect of getting new customers.'

'Oh, he is,' Marcy's voice was dry, and the others chuckled. Sam Brennan, Marcy's partner and owner of the village store, liked nothing more than the sound of money dropping into the till.

'So we're not going to see much of you and Peter and the girls for a while.'

'Don't worry, Helen, we'll be back to stay eventually. I need to be with my Norwegian family just now,' Ingrid said, 'but the Scottish part of me misses Prior's Ford and you three so much!'

Three days later she and her daughters were on their way back to Norway and a sign writer was busy changing the name of the Gift Horse to

14

Colour Carousel.

'It's the village's character I'm concerned about.' Marcy reverted back to the original topic as she helped Helen to pack her purchases. 'Twenty one pounds and thirty pence, please.' Then, as Helen began to fish around in the depths of her shoulder bag, 'New housing means growth and that pleases Sam, but I like this place just as it is. As I said earlier, I hate change! I even miss old Ivy McGowan's sharp tongue – and I never thought I'd hear myself say that.'

'Sometimes I wish some clever person could invent tiny helium balloons to fasten to the contents of handbags so that they float to the top when you need them,' Helen fretted, and then, producing the large shabby purse she had used for more years than she could recall: 'At last! I miss Ivy more than I thought would, too,' she went on as she began to count out notes and change. 'She was so determined to outlive Doris Thatcher and so pleased when Doris went first and left her as our oldest inhabitant. And within a year she was gone too, six years short of getting her telegram from the Queen, poor old soul. We don't even have an oldest inhabitant any more.'

'We must have – we just don't know who it is.'

'Sometimes,' Helen said as she tucked her change into the purse, replaced it in her shoulder bag and gathered up her shopping, 'I feel as though it might be me.'

'So, how's your love life comin' along?'

Clarissa Ramsay winced. 'Amy, that's no question to ask of a mature woman in her fifties.'

'Forget the mature, and forget the fifties.' Even though Amy Rose was at home in America her voice travelled the miles with ease; it was as though she were standing in the hall with Clarissa. 'You're a woman, and love strikes at any age – as you well know. Come on, how are you and Alastair managin' with all that distance between you?'

'I've spent a week in Glasgow since I last spoke to you,' Clarissa admitted. 'It was lovely to see him. He's enjoying working in that art gallery.'

'I hope you stayed with him?'

'Amy, he shares a small flat with a work colleague. I booked into a hotel.'

'On your own?' Amy's voice rose a good half-octave.

'Yes, on my own. It's ... difficult, with Alastair being so much younger than I am.' Clarissa shuddered at the thought of walking into a hotel, even a small one, with Alastair and booking a double room. 'Imagine the looks we would get!'

'Oh, tosh! I bet he said let's go for it and to blazes with what other people think,' Amy retorted, and then, taking her friend's silence for agreement, she went on: 'Look here, Claris-sa, you've finally admitted that you're mad about the boy – remember that song? I still love it –

16

and he's clearly mad about you, so for goodness' sake will the two of you do somethin'
about it? If you wait until he comes back to the
village it'll only be worse because then you'll
have to face everyone. If the two of you are a
real couple by the time that happens, it'll make
the facin' a lot easier because you can do it
together.'

'Maybe you're right, but—'

'You're darned right I'm right. Listen,' Amy
said, 'one of the reasons I phoned is to say that
I fancy another trip to Scotland. Are you up for
it?'

'That would be lovely. You know that you'll
always be welcome here.'

'Good, that's settled. I'm all booked up to
arrive some time in June. I'll buy myself a run-
around automobile same as last time and get in
a bit of travellin' while I'm in Scotland. Why
don't you arrange a week's holiday for you and
Alastair for just after I get there? A cottage
somewhere quiet, without anyone else around?'

'But—'

'Or a tent, even. I'll hold the fort while you're
gone. It'll be great to catch up with what's goin'
on in Prior's Ford. Can't wait,' Amy Rose said,
and hung up, leaving Clarissa to gape at the
receiver in her hand.

It wasn't possible, she told herself once she
had remembered to close her mouth and put
the receiver back on its rest. She and Alastair
couldn't just ... she felt her face grow hot at the
thought, while butterflies began to flutter around

17

in her stomach.

She had allowed herself to get into the most terrible mess. A short while after she and Keith, the man she had married in her late forties, retired to Prior's Ford he had died suddenly, leaving her alone and among strangers. The discovery, while going through his papers, that Keith had been unfaithful to her throughout their marriage, and with her closest friend, had been a terrible shock. She had wandered from the house and was found by Alastair Marshall, an artist in his thirties, sitting on a stile in the pouring rain, soaked to the skin. He had rescued and befriended her, and helped her to gain the strength of mind to rediscover herself. Ridiculous though it was, they had fallen in love with each other.

Amy, on a visit to Clarissa the previous year, had forced the two of them to accept the truth they were trying to deny, but by that time Alastair had accepted a job with an art gallery in Glasgow.

They missed each other badly, phoned almost every day, and Clarissa had been to Glasgow two or three times. It had been wonderful, spending the evenings and weekends together, but she was still afraid to make the final commitment. Amy was right; Alastair had begged her to book a double room, but she had refused.

'I'm ... you might not...'

'Clarissa, I love you for being the person you are, and for your mind and your warmth. I want you, all of you, not some brainless bimbo with a

18

beautiful body. I will never ever let you down; I just want us to belong to each other, completely. What else can I say?'

The whole situation was ridiculous, but the simple truth was that she wanted Alastair as much as he claimed to want her. She longed to be with him, but still saw the age difference as an insurmountable barrier. Perhaps, she thought, Amy had the right idea. Perhaps they should rent a cottage in some quiet place where nobody knew them. It would take all her courage, but they couldn't continue the way they were. Her middle-aged body might repel him, but if she kept refusing to take the final step she would probably lose him anyway.

Eventually, if all went well between them, she and Alastair would have to present themselves to everyone as a couple. She winced at the prospect, then tried to take comfort in the thought that at least they would be facing the music together.

Two

Ginny Whitelaw had never been happier in her entire twenty-eight years, and it was all thanks to Prior's Ford. She had come to the village with reluctance some three years earlier as companion to her mother, Meredith, who had rented a cottage for a year in order to get over the shock and humiliation of being written out of a top television soap opera. Although she and her mother were as different as chalk and cheese, Ginny had felt obliged to be a dutiful daughter in Meredith's hour of need.

Ginny's parents, both actors, had divorced when she was a child. Her father moved almost at once to Australia, where he still lived with his second wife and their children, leaving Ginny to be raised by a succession of housekeepers while her mother concentrated on her career.

To Meredith's annoyance her one and only child lacked the looks, talent and desire to follow her into the world of theatre, preferring instead to work in a flower shop and then in a garden centre.

Village life had done them both good. For several months Meredith savoured the pleasure of being the most famous person for miles around, and enjoyed throwing the local drama group, run by former journalist Kevin Pearce, into total disarray. Ginny's life had been completely turned around when she met Lewis Ralston-Kerr, who lived in Linn Hall with his parents, Hector and Fliss. An unexpected windfall had given the Ralston-Kerrs the chance to start making the rundown manor house wind-and-water-tight, while Lewis took on the task of restoring the extensive gardens to their former glory with a view to opening them to the public.

Ginny immediately volunteered her assistance and was given the task of restoring the Hall's old kitchen garden. With the help of young Jimmy McDonald, who shared her passion for gardening and whose late grandfather had been Linn Hall's head gardener, Ginny threw herself into the task of locating vegetable beds, fruit bushes, trees and flagged paths beneath a thick tangle of weeds and undergrowth. When her mother, having been offered a part in a television play, cut her stay in the village short, Ginny opted to stay on. By the autumn she and Jimmy had restored the walled garden to the useful and attractive place it had been in the days of Lewis's grandparents and great-grandparents.

She had returned every year since then, and between them she, Lewis, and the one and only gardener, Duncan Campbell, had, with the help of Jimmy and the young backpackers who came to Linn Hall every summer – willing to work in the house and garden in return for bed and board – made a big difference to the estate.

The old stable block, used for many years as a depository for unwanted, useless or broken items from the house and grounds, was now a shop selling home-grown produce. Polytunnels had been brought in, and with Hector Ralston-Kerr's help Ginny had begun to study old account books and photographs in an attempt to find out exactly what the grounds had looked like in the days when the family was wealthy enough to employ a team of gardeners.

She and Lewis had tracked down several of the original plants, removing the weeds that had been hiding them for years and lavishing much-needed care on them. It was Ginny's idea to have every plant, bush and tree labelled and the gardens photographed every year in a bid to encourage visitors to return each summer to see for themselves the progress that had been made. The photographer was Cam Gordon, a villager who had been Lewis's closest friend when they were young, and knew the estate well. Cam, who worked for a building company, was an excellent amateur photographer and some of his pictures of the Hall and estate had sold well in the stable shop.

Ginny had also discovered that the stagnant lake and the small pond in the rose garden, which had been drained and turned into a flower bed, were originally fed from a stream running down the hillside behind the Hall. The stream was choked by rubbish at the top of the hill and her new project was to clear it and fill the lake and pond with fresh water once more.

The previous year she had bought herself a camper van and parked it in the kitchen yard so that she could spend every waking hour working on the estate. When Lewis found that there was enough money from opening the gardens to the public and selling goods from the stable shop to employ her over the autumn and winter, she was in seventh heaven.

With the extra time she had been granted, and assistance from a team of local helpers, she had cleared out both lake and pond, relined the lake with sand, traced the old water pipes and used a small hired JCB to reopen channels that had once kept the water flowing. The JCB had also been used to rough-dig the area round the lake. Now that all the rubbish had been cleared, Ginny was busy forking over the ground and visualizing how it would look in a year's time, once it had been replanted.

'Hi Ginny!'

She glanced up and waved, putting on her best smile while at the same time muttering a mild curse behind her bared teeth. Every garden had its thorns and red-haired Molly Ewing, Lewis's fiancée, was definitely the thorn in Ginny's side. She was emerging from the tree-lined path linking the lake and the lawns at the side of the house, hand in hand with her small daughter.

'Hello, Molly,' Ginny said as enthusiastically as she could, and then, with genuine warmth: 'Hello, Rowena!' Nobody could resist three-year-old Rowena Chloe.

'Look, Ginny, look what I got!' The little girl

pulled away from her mother and dashed ahead, waving a handful of wilting weeds. 'Flowerth!'

'Any idea where Lewis is?' Molly wanted to know.

'He might have gone to the garden centre in Kirkcudbright, but I'm not sure.'

'But we're only here for the weekend and we wanted him to spend all his time with us, didn't we, Weena?'

'Thith,' Rowena Chloe announced, ignoring her mother, 'ith for *you*.' She carefully selected one of the weeds and presented it to Ginny, who tucked it behind one ear.

'Thank you. Do I look nice?'

'Yeth,' Rowena Chloe decided, then, her hazel eyes caught by a movement on the ground, she dropped the rest of the weeds, pounced, then turned to face the adults. 'Look what I found,' she said happily, holding out a squirming pink earthworm. 'Can I take it to show Gran?'

'Agghh! Put that down at once, Weena,' Molly shuddered.

'It doesn't like houses, Rowena, it likes grass. Put it over there carefully,' Ginny suggested, pointing to a grassy patch below a tree, 'and then it can go and find its own mummy.'

Rowena obediently scuttled off to lay the worm down then stayed bent double, presenting her blue-denimed little backside to the others as she watched it carefully.

'Mum and I had a great time watching your mum's new television sitcom,' Molly said. 'It was brilliant. I hope it's coming back.'

24

'She's filming the second series just now and it'll be on-screen early next year, as far as I know.'

'I'd love to have a famous mum. You're so lucky!'

'Yes,' Ginny agreed, pasting a polite smile on her lips. If she had a pound for every time she had been told how lucky she was to be Meredith Whitelaw's daughter, she'd be a millionaire by now. Little did the envious ones realize that she would have given anything to have run-of-the-mill parents.

'What Mum and I can't understand is you turning out to be an ordinary gardener when you could have been a famous actress like her,' Molly surged on. Ginny's smile began to waver, but fortunately Rowena Chloe saved her mother from receiving a handful of soil in the face by straightening, dusting her chubby hands together, and rejoining the adults. 'All gone.'

'Give me your hands. Ugh!' Molly's pretty face was screwed up in disgust as she pulled a handkerchief from the pocket of her jeans. 'How could you touch a dirty thing like that?'

'It wath all clean,' her daughter protested, pulling away. 'Ginny holdth them.'

'Ginny's a gardener,' Molly retorted. 'You're a little girl and little girls don't pick worms up.'

'Not little!' Rowena Chloe shook her head, covered in bright red curls inherited from her mother, and stamped her tiny trainer. 'I'm a big girl!'

'Big girls don't pick worms up.'

'But Ginny'th a big girl an' she—' Rowena Chloe started to argue, then as Cam Gordon came swinging along the path, his camera slung over his shoulder, she screamed 'Cam!' and ran to meet him.

'Hello, Trouble.' He picked the toddler up and tossed her in the air. As he caught her again she threw chubby arms around his neck and landed a smacking kiss on his cheek.

'Cam, have you seen Lewis?'

'Nope. How's it going, Ginny?'

'Not bad.'

'So where are you off to this year, Moll?' he asked. Molly spent every summer travelling. She and Lewis had met when she spent a summer working in the Linn Hall kitchen for bed and board. Despite motherhood she continued to follow her normal routine, spending the winter and spring months at home in Inverness with her parents, sister and Rowena Chloe, taking whatever job she could find in order to save money so that she could travel in the summer.

'Portugal,' she said now. 'There's a group of us going, but not till the end of June. I can't wait. Weena's staying here with her daddy, aren't you, precious?'

'Wish I was going,' Cam said, and she raised her eyebrows at him.

'Why don't you? We're only young once.'

'Too much work on. Get thee behind me, temptress.'

She pouted at him. 'Spoilsport! Fancy a coffee?'

'That sounds like a more reasonable sort of temptation. What about you, Ginny?'

'I'd like to get this bit finished first.'

'Let me help!' Rowena Chloe struggled to get down. As soon as she started toddling Lewis had bought her a little plastic gardening set, and she loved 'helping' in the gardens.

'Want an ice lolly?' Cam suggested.

'Yah!'

'Then let's go get one, and leave Ginny in peace.' With one easy movement he lifted the little girl up to sit on his shoulders, where she grabbed two handfuls of his curly dark hair and drummed her heels against his chest, shouting, 'Go, go!'

'See you, Ginny.' Molly swung round to walk by his side, slipping her hand through his arm. Today her hair was confined in a single thick plait reaching halfway to her waist. It bounced lightly against her back as she walked, glowing ruby red in the sunlight.

'See you.' Ginny chewed her lip as she watched the three of them move from sunlight into the dappled shadow of the trees, their voices fading as they turned a corner and disappeared from her sight. The last thing she heard was a peal of laughter from Molly. They looked for all the world like a family group, and there were those in the village, she knew, who suspected that they might be.

She had been told by Jinty McDonald, young Jimmy's mother, that with her gorgeous hair, sparkling green eyes, slender body and cheerful grin, Molly had captivated Lewis almost as soon as she first arrived at Linn Hall. Cam and Lewis had come to blows over her in the local pub that summer when Lewis discovered that Cam already knew Molly, having met her when they were both on holiday abroad.

'Apparently Cam hinted that he and Molly had been more than good friends, but that lad's always been a joker,' Jinty said, 'and he was probably just trying to rattle Lewis's cage, as they say nowadays. Unfortunately Lewis believed him, and the two of them had a right go at each other. But on the other hand, Molly's a very friendly girl; it does make you wonder if she isn't too friendly too often, know what I mean?'

By the following summer, the summer Ginny and Lewis met, he and Molly were engaged and Rowena Chloe had arrived. Lewis adored her and was never happier than when she was staying at Linn Hall. As the entire Ewing family loved holidays, Rowena Chloe spent the best part of the summer with the Ralston-Kerrs. Having inherited her mother's cheerful nature as well as her bright red hair, she was happy wherever she happened to be.

For Lewis's sake, Ginny hoped that he was right in his belief that Rowena Chloe was his daughter, but for her own sake she wished that Molly had never found her way to Linn Hall and into Lewis's life. What chance did a sturdily built young woman with an uninteresting, weather-beaten face and black hair, cut short so that wind and rain couldn't do it much damage,

28

have against the likes of Molly Ewing?

None at all, and it hurt more than Ginny would admit even to herself.

'I have decided,' Kevin Pearce announced to the assembled members of Prior's Ford Drama Club, 'on *The Importance of Being Earnest* for our October production.'

The murmur of interest and, in some cases, concern, was drowned out by Cynthia Mac-Bain's hearty approval. 'What a splendid idea, Kevin. Absolutely perfect for this club!'

'Who wrote that?' someone wanted to know, and was told:

'Oscar Wilde. It's the play with the handbag woman.'

'Lady Bracknell.' Gilbert MacBain corrected the speaker sternly. 'It's a very well-known play, and very humorous.'

'A classic. How clever of you to think of it, Kevin,' Cynthia purred.

'I've wanted to direct that play ever since I played the part of Algernon Moncrieff years ago. It was my first principal role and the local newspaper gave me a very good review,' Kevin told the group proudly.

'Are you sure we can do a full length play for October?' Pete McDermott asked.

'Of course. We'll stage the play in mid October and still have time to do the pantomime in early January.'

'What I mean is, this is almost the end of May and some of us have booked summer holidays.'

'Anyone planning a holiday of more than two weeks?' Kevin asked, and when there was no reply: 'There you are then. We'll rehearse over the summer and work around holidays. We've got at least four months; professionals can do it in less time, and this,' Kevin said, 'is a semi-professional group.'

'I don't know about that,' Pete's wife Cheryl said nervously. 'Pete and I haven't had much acting experience. We were too busy running the ironmonger's shop to have any hobbies, and when we sold up and retired here we joined the drama club more for fun than hard work.'

The McDermotts, both in their fifties, had thrown themselves enthusiastically into village life on their arrival. Pete was on the Prior's Ford Progress Committee while Cheryl was an active member of the local WRI. In the past they had both played small parts in the drama club as well as helping out with backstage duties.

'Under my guidance this club has attained the level of semi-professionalism,' Kevin insisted. 'If you remember, Meredith Whitelaw was most impressed with us when she stayed in the village, and she knew what she was talking about, being a well-known stage and television actress.'

'I can't say I think much of her performance in that sitcom she's in now,' Cynthia said dryly, and her husband nodded vigorous agreement. During her stay in Prior's Ford, Meredith had managed to persuade Kevin to give her the part that had been Cynthia's in their current play, and had then left him in the lurch when offered professional work.

'The reviews have been good.' Kevin still treasured memories of the special friendship he liked to believe that he and Meredith had shared.

'Over-generous,' Cynthia corrected him.

'I think she's excellent in it. I was pleased to hear that another series has been commissioned,' Jinty McDonald said.

'The cast is as follows,' Kevin called them back to business. 'Two young men and two young women, the butler and the minister, both older men, and Lady Bracknell and the governess, both ... er ... mature ladies.'

'And guess who'll be Lady Bracknell,' someone was heard to mutter, and Cynthia, the club's leading lady, turned to glare in the direction of the voice.

'I have here copies of the script as well as photocopies of the audition pieces,' Kevin hurried on. 'The auditions will be held two weeks tonight.'

Three

'Kevin, are you sure you can cast that play and have it ready for mid October?' Elinor Pearce asked as she and her husband walked the short distance between the village hall and their home in Adams Crescent, overlooking the village green.

'Absolutely. It'll take hard work, but that's what the theatre's all about. I've always wanted to do an Oscar Wilde, and casting shouldn't be too much of a problem. Cynthia as Lady Bracknell, of course. She'll be perfect for the part.'

Elinor couldn't argue with that. Cynthia, who taught English at Kirkcudbright Academy, was an adequate actress with a voice that hit the back wall of the hall with ease. She was good at learning lines, but a bit of a prima donna.

'Gilbert as the minister and Charlie Crandall in the part of the butler.'

'Charlie's only just joined the group.'

'I know, but beggars can't be choosers and it would be a good way to test his acting skills'

'Shouldn't you wait for the auditions before making those decisions?'

'As you said yourself,' Kevin reminded his wife, an exasperated note creeping into his voice, 'there isn't much time, or a lot of talent to choose from. The girls are easy: Steph Mc-Donald and Alison Greenlees. The two young men might be more difficult to cast, but I have ideas. D'you think Ewan McNair might be available? He has the making of a good actor.'

'I very much doubt it, dear. Now that his father's dead Ewan's had to take on responsibility for all the farm work with only one man to help him.'

'Mmm. There's Cam Gordon, and the oldest McDonald boy, Steph's twin.'

'Grant McDonald won't have time to rehearse now that he's training to become a professional football player.'

'Is he?'

'He's signed up for one of the big local clubs. From what I hear he's very talented.'

'That's a nuisance. I wonder if any of the people moving into that new housing estate would be available. I'll draw up a leaflet and get copies to put through the letterboxes.'

'We'll need to hire some of the costumes. Jinty and I will never manage to do all the outfits in the time we have.'

'Are you sure?'

'Can you see Cynthia playing Lady Bracknell in home-made costumes?'

'I suppose not.'

'And there are the men's outfits ... they'll have to be hired. I think Jinty and I should concentrate on the costumes for the two girls and the governess; she'll only need one costume.

They'll keep us busy enough.'

'I wish you'd mentioned this before, Elinor. It costs a fortune to hire costumes.'

'I did try, dear, but you were so taken with the idea of doing *The Importance of Being Earnest* that you didn't listen.'

They had reached their house, and Kevin bustled up the garden path to open the door, leaving his wife to follow. Elinor smiled at his rigid back, well aware that Kevin hated to be criticized, even gently. He was a somewhat self-centred man who always overestimated his own abilities. Most people in the village were under the impression that he had been editor of a national newspaper when in fact he had started his career as one of the reporters in the small office of a weekly paper, fully intending to end up in London's Fleet Street, but had never got there.

Elinor, originally from Moffat, was running her own dressmaking business when they met, and when Kevin retired she persuaded him to move back to her home ground, where the money from the sale of her successful business had paid for the nice little detached villa they now lived in. Prior's Ford suited Kevin, for it gave him the chance to be a fairly large fish in a small pond.

'Horlicks, dear?' she asked when they got into the house, as she did every evening at that time.

'I think so,' her husband replied as he did every evening. 'Bring it into the living room when it's ready, would you? I need to go over

34

the stage moves again.'

'Of course, dear,' said Elinor, and went into the kitchen, where everything needed for their nightcaps had already been laid out. Her only regret in her fairly uneventful life was that she and Kevin had never been blessed with children. But as she had once said to Naomi Hennessey, the village's minister, when Naomi said that Elinor would have made a wonderful mother, 'I have Kevin.'

He may not be much but he was hers; she loved him in her own way, and knew that he loved her too – in his own way.

'I've been on the Internet and I believe,' Laura Hunter announced, 'that I've found us the perfect holiday home.'

'I've told you already that I don't see the necessity for a holiday home,' her husband grunted without looking up from his newspaper.

'Allan, I think it's just what we do need, both of us. It's far from the madding crowd, an old cottage in a lovely little village. Peace and quiet for me to work on my next book, and you to get started on those memoirs you keep talking about.' Laura moved behind his chair and put her hands on his shoulders, her slim strong fingers massaging the taut muscles beneath his shirt. 'I've been thinking about this for the past year, ever since you retired. After a lifetime in the police force you need to find a way of relaxing.'

'I can relax where I am.'

Laura looked down at the top of his head, where the cropped grey hair was just beginning to thin. It had been many years since she had seen Allan relax; even in his sleep he twitched restlessly. When they first married she was teaching domestic science in a good school and he was a police constable. They had both done well over the years, Laura publishing popular recipe books and appearing in several televised cookery programmes while Allan worked his way through the ranks, ending up as Chief Superintendent.

Sadly, ambition and the ongoing stress of the job had changed him from the fairly easy-going man she had married to a career-concentrated perfectionist. When he was at home the very walls seemed to vibrate with tension, and even when he was out she felt that both she and their large and comfortable flat awaited his return with nervous apprehension. He was hard on himself and on others, and when he retired, Laura, who had given up teaching a few years earlier, found life difficult with him around all day. For years he had been talking about writing a book about his time in the force, but had been unable to settle down to the task. It seemed to her that he needed a change of scene, and so did she.

'The village is called Prior's Ford, and it's in beautiful countryside.'

'Whereabouts?'

She moved to sit down opposite him. 'Scotland. Dumfries and Galloway, near the border.

There are three golf courses within easy access. Scotland's known for its golf courses, isn't it? You could take the game up again,' she went on, then as he grimaced: 'We could fill our lungs with clean country air, go for lovely walks together, and both write in peace with no city noises to intrude. I've always wanted to live in a village. The south of Scotland isn't impossibly far from Leeds so we wouldn't have a lot of travelling to do.'

'Never heard of the place. Where did you come across it?'

'In a magazine to begin with. I was reading an article about scarecrow festivals – apparently they've become very popular – and this village I'm talking about holds one every year. There was a picture of the people who won prizes for the best scarecrows, and the background looked lovely. They even have a little village green. So I looked it up on the Internet and there were quite a few photographs. They have a village pub called the Neurotic Cuckoo – isn't that a fantastic name? – and it's got guest rooms. We could stay there when we go to view the cottage. And guess what? There are nesting peregrine falcons in an old quarry just outside the village.' She knew that he had been a keen birdwatcher in his youth. 'The birds have attracted a lot of visitors to the place; can't you just picture those magnificent birds of prey wheeling across a blue sky?' Then, as he turned a page of his newspaper with a great deal of irritable rustling, his way of showing that he wanted to be left in peace: 'As a matter of fact, I phoned the pub earlier, and the nice man I spoke to said that a double room's available.'

'You've booked it, haven't you?'

'It made sense to grab it before someone else did.'

'I don't see the sense in going to see this place, since I've no intention of buying a holiday cottage.'

Laura had thought the entire conversation through step by step before approaching him, so she was prepared for the rebuff.

'That's all right, dear, I'll go on my own.'

'What?'

'I don't mind. And if I like the cottage I'm going to buy it. I can afford it,' she went on as she finally got his attention.

'You ... buy a house? Don't be ridiculous!'

'There's nothing ridiculous about it. We haven't had a decent holiday for years because you've always been too busy. My books have earned enough money to allow me to indulge myself for once. I really like the idea of having a holiday home in a village nobody's heard of. I'll have time to stock the freezer and fridge before I go, so you won't starve.'

'You don't need to. I'll come with you.'

'Are you absolutely sure?'

'If you're going to be rash enough to spend a fortune on a country cottage,' he said, 'I want to check it out first.'

Laura loved the cottage from the moment she

saw it. It stood on its own with a short driveway down one side, a path leading off it to the front door. The garden consisted of a small lawn edged with flower borders filled with daffodils, narcissi, crocuses and snowdrops. A forsythia hedge on the far side of the lawn was massed with yellow blossoms.

'There's a vegetable garden at the rear. The long-time owners won a lot of prizes with their flowers and veg,' the estate agent told them, producing a key. 'Shall we go inside?'

'Let's look at the back garden first,' Laura decided, and led the way. The garden, slightly larger than at the front, was efficiently divided into sections: a drying green with clothes poles, a small garage, and several vegetable beds. At the far end, one corner held a greenhouse and the other, behind the garage, had a little grassy area shaded by a tree covered in white flowers.

'A magnolia – how lovely! And the River Dee below, just on the other side of the hedge,' Laura enthused as the sound of running water came to her ears. 'Why doesn't this place have a name?'

'It's always been known officially as Number Five, Riverside Lane. The locals call it Thatcher's Cottage because Mr and Mrs Thatcher owned it for over fifty years.'

'It should have a name, not just a number. If we buy it,' Laura said firmly, 'we'll call it Thatcher's Cottage in memory of its long-term owners.'

Already she was picturing herself, with or without Allan, sitting in the back garden in the summer evenings, enjoying a drink before dinner and listening to the birds and to the soft music of water in the river below.

All at once Allan's grumpy reluctance to buy Thatcher's Cottage became totally unimportant. She wanted it, and she was going to have it.

'It's not very roomy,' Allan said an hour later, when they were having lunch in the Neurotic Cuckoo.

'A holiday home doesn't have to be roomy. All we need is enough furniture to make it comfortable. The second bedroom can be turned into a study for you to write in, and I'll use the living room.'

'The kitchen's far too small. We've already spent a fortune remodelling the kitchen in the flat without starting all over again here.'

'I don't need a working kitchen here because this one will only be used to make meals for the two of us, eaten outside when the weather's good. I've already perfected all the recipes for the new book. I'll have this one modernized a little but that can be done in a few weeks. Later, if necessary, it can be extended. And the food in this pub's very good. We'll eat here often.'

'You're talking as though it's all decided.'

'It is, as far as I'm concerned. I'm going to put in an offer this afternoon.'

'Without consulting me?'

'I don't see any point in consulting you because you'll only try to make me change my mind. I'm not one of your subordinates, Allan;

as far as I'm concerned you're my life partner, not a high-ranking police officer. I want that cottage, and I'm going to have it with or without your agreement. Thank you, that was delicious,' Laura said sweetly as Gracie Fisher arrived to clear their empty plates away. 'Can we have two black coffees, please?'

And when Gracie left them: 'After we've had our coffee, let's go and look at this quarry where the peregrine falcons nest.'

Four

For years everyone in Prior's Ford had known everyone else. Even outsiders, once they had settled in, grew to love the place and stayed put.

Events were held in the well-used village hall, children aged from five to eleven years were educated in the village school, a successful and popular Scarecrow Festival was held every July, and the Ralston-Kerrs at the big house, Linn Hall, held a summer fête every August.

In the early nineteen eighties Slaemuir, a small council housing estate, had been built, and ten years later came Mill Walk, some fifteen private houses. Divided by Riverside Lane, they both fitted snugly into the village and swiftly became part of it.

But change was coming to Prior's Ford. A small private housing estate had just been built on land opposite the entrance to Tarbethill Farm. Ten smart semi-detached villas and four detached villas, each two-up two-down with its own garage, tiny driveway, front porch, pocket-handkerchief-sized front garden and slightly larger rear garden complete with patio had been completed to deadline. Now, Clover Park's front gardens were landscaped, one of the semi-detached villas was furnished as a show house and potential buyers were driving in between the handsome stone pillars marking the entrance.

Many of the villagers, however, mourned the loss of the small field they had once held fêtes and galas on. The prospect of a flood of incomers unsettled them.

'Come on,' Cam Gordon appealed to those predicting horrendous change to the village over their pints in the Neurotic Cuckoo. 'You're makin' it sound as if we're goin' to be attacked by a plague of locusts. They're only people like us.'

'The main street'll be choked with cars,' someone countered. 'Probably those great big off-road things with grills in front to protect 'em from wild beasts.'

'Most of 'em'll shop in Kirkcudbright and that means they'll be drivin' away from the village, not into it,' Cam pointed out and then, realizing that Sam Brennan was present: 'Sorry, Sam. I'm sure that lots of them'll use the village shop. It'll be no worse than when the Mill Walk Estate was built; *that's* private housing right in the middle of the village, and most of the folk who live there have settled into village life, haven't they?'

'That's different,' a voice spoke up from a corner table. 'Once buildin' starts on farmland it spreads like measles. Before we know it we'll be no more than a suburb of Kirkcudbright.'

'We won't!' Cam scoffed. 'Another half in

43

there please, Joe.'

'To my mind it's a shame to see trees and bushes torn up and the land covered with boxy houses,' said an elderly resident. 'It feels as if part of my childhood's been taken away.'

'Your childhood disappeared a good while ago,' someone else pointed out. 'When was the last time you rolled your painted Easter egg down that wee hill?'

'It wasn't just *my* childhood, it was my youngsters' as well; and I'll never see my grandchildren enjoy an Easter egg day in that field now.'

'And I hear that the cottage where the Thatchers used to live's goin' to be a holiday house again, like last time.' Bill Harper owned a small garage near to the cottage.

'I hope they're not like the last pair, him lookin' as if he felt he was too good for the likes of us, and her turnin out to be a high-class tart,' someone said, and there was a murmur of agreement.

'It's nothing like last time,' Gracie Fisher put in from behind the bar. 'Last year's folk were going to tear the garden apart to make the cottage larger but the new people seem happy to leave the place as it is from what I've heard. It's Laura Tyler and her husband; she does cookery programmes on the telly. They stayed here overnight when they came to see the cottage, but it wasn't until they were leaving that I realized who she was. I plucked up the courage to ask if I was right and she couldn't have been nicer.

Imagine someone like her eating food that I'd prepared! And she was very complimentary about it, too. She'll be a feather in our caps. The Rural's all excited about her coming to the village.'

'But it still means that Doris's cottage's a holiday home again.'

'I grant you that that's a shame, Bill,' Gracie's husband Joe agreed. ''Specially when your Tricia was so set on buying it. But she and Derek are going to be cosy enough in Ivy McGowan's place. It's good they found somewhere local to live. When's the wedding to be?'

Bill Harper and Doug Borland, the local butcher, both sighed heavily into their pint glasses. 'September,' Doug said, 'and we'll both be glad when it's past, won't we Bill?'

'We will that. The womenfolk are goin' mad over it. At least you don't have to bear the cost, Doug, bein' father to the groom.'

'We're paying for the changes being made to Ivy's house, though, and I reckon that'll come to as much as the wedding, if not more.'

'Life goes on and things change,' said Gracie. 'Some for the better, some for the worse. We just have to soldier on. As for the new housing estate, it's the McNairs that've suffered the most from that.'

There was a general murmur of agreement, followed by one final comment from a corner table. 'Mark my words, it can get very difficult when a wee place like Prior's Ford has a sudden rush of new folk. Who knows what we might be gettin' among us?'

'Decent ordinary folk like ourselves,' Cam retorted, picking up his drink. 'You wait and see.'

Two years earlier everything in Police Constable Neil White's life had been coming up roses, as the well-known song put it. He loved his job and he had recently married the most perfect woman in the world, who also happened to be a police constable – a beautiful, shapely, blonde police constable at that.

Sadly, Gloria White, née Frost, was as ambitious as she was beautiful. She was aiming for the very top of the tree as far as promotion went, and no sooner had the happy couple returned from an idyllic honeymoon spent in the Maldives and exchanged bikinis and skimpy bathing briefs for uniforms than Gloria began to work on becoming a sergeant.

Almost before their all-over tans were gone she began to feel that marriage had its drawbacks. For one thing, she was no longer being looked after by her mother and therefore free to concentrate on her studies. It hadn't occurred to her to make sure before she walked down the aisle that Neil was a good cook who delighted in shopping and housework when off duty. Unfortunately he turned out to be more of the 'if we had eggs we could have bacon and eggs if we had bacon, so let's eat out tonight' variety, and although he had no objection to her hunger for career advancement he also expected that they would enjoy a busy social life together, other than visiting or entertaining alternate sets of parents on alternate weeks, depending on shift patterns.

He tried hard to fit in with her demands for her own space, but it quickly got to the stage where Gloria decided that her space was more important than her husband, and not long after their first anniversary she was back in her family home, free to concentrate on promotion, while Neil had moved into his brother's flat.

'You've been too soft with her,' his brother, a confirmed bachelor, told him. 'You have to show her who's boss.'

'Believe me, she already knows who's boss.'

'Find yourself a better woman, mate, as soon as possible. When you fall off a horse you should get back on again.'

'Gloria isn't a horse and I still love her. Maybe once she makes sergeant she'll ease up on the ambition and we can get back together.'

'Dream on,' his brother said.

Nobody other than the senior staff at the station where they both worked knew of their separation. Had it become common knowledge, one of them would have been transferred to another station, and as neither wanted a move they had assured their bosses that the split was amicable and they had no problem when it came to working together.

Recently, a glimmer of light was beginning to show at the far end of the dark tunnel Neil had been living in since the marriage ended. A premium bond, one of a hundred he had bought years before and forgotten about, had suddenly paid off handsomely. Between the bond and his half share of the sale of the marital bungalow he was able to put down a reasonable deposit on one of the new semi-detached villas in Clover Park, which was doubly convenient because his confirmed bachelor brother had just become engaged.

'I never thought I would meet the perfect woman,' he bragged to Neil over a celebratory drink in his local pub. 'Never thought she existed. But she does, and she's all mine!'

'Well done,' Neil said kindly, not wanting to pour cold water on the poor man's excitement. He himself had once believed that he had found the perfect woman, and look how that had turned out. The truth was that there was no such animal as the perfect woman, but it was probably best to let the deluded fool find that out for himself in due course.

Now, he walked around his new home, opening the doors in the built-in wardrobes, admiring the view from every window, trying the taps in the bathroom and the downstairs cloakroom, stepping through the kitchen's single French window into the back garden and generally getting the feel of the place – his very own bachelor pad.

He and Gloria had divided the furniture from the bungalow between them and his share was in storage. He was working out what should go where and what he would have to buy when the doorbell rang, announcing his very first visitor.

He opened the door to see a small blonde vision standing on his doorstep.

'He–lloo,' she said, or rather, sang as two notes, the second lower than the first. 'My name is Anja Jacobsen, and I have recently come from Norway to Prior's Ford to run my own business.' A small hand with purple fingernails the same colour as the front of her hair proffered a card. 'I am a qualified interior decorator and my business is called Colour Carousel. I sell paint and wallpaper and can obtain and advise on fabrics for curtains, ornaments and anything else you may need for your new home. You and your wife are very welcome to come and look around my shop.'

'I'm ... er—' Neil cleared the frog from his throat. 'I'm on my own, actually.'

Her long-lashed blue eyes widened. 'You are going to live here all on your own? So it could be that you will need help to plan your colour schemes?'

Her eyes were the same shade as the drifts of bluebells filling Neil's parents' garden every spring. His mother loved bluebells and had planted them everywhere. 'I expect I will,' he heard himself say.

'Then I am here for you whenever you want me to be,' Anja Jacobsen assured him warmly. 'May I come in and look around? I will take photographs and measurements, and I also need to get to know you, so that I can make sure that you have a home that suits your personality,' she

49

went on briskly as she stepped into the hall, slipping a large bag from her shoulder. 'I have everything I need in here. And then you must come to the shop and find out what I have to offer. I have to get to know you very well. That is important,' she went on as Neil blushed, 'because I must find out what sort of person you are before I can give you the home that best suits, you know? Would that sound good for you?'

'I think that that sounds very good for me.'

'I'm glad. Together we will make a lovely home for you,' said Anja, and as she beamed up at him, Neil White began to feel that at last his luck was turning.

Five

The field buried for ever beneath concrete and bricks had not in itself been of any great value to the McNair family, for it was more of a small hill than field, with straggly clumps of bushes, a few stunted trees and boulders scattered beneath a thin covering of soil that could only support undernourished grass.

While three generations of the McNair family worked the larger, lush fields on the opposite side of the road leading into Prior's Ford, the little field had become a playground for the local children, occasionally used for village events, but a few years earlier its role had changed, leading to bitter strife among the McNairs.

Victor McNair, a young man with ambitions far beyond toiling on the farm, had persuaded his father Bert to sign the useless land over to him. His idea was to turn it into a small caravan park, but once he discovered that planning laws required a vast amount of money to be spent on piping in water and electricity for the proposed holidaymakers, as well as making provision for showers and toilets, he secretly sold the field to a builder.

When Bert found out he disowned his first-born, banishing him from the farm. Now Victor lived in the nearby town of Kirkcudbright with his fiancée's family and worked in her father's garage.

Once work began on the field Bert was unable to leave his own land without being confronted by machinery tearing up the trees and bushes and gouging the boulders from the ground that had held them close for centuries. That, and the unrelenting struggle that he, his wife Jess and their younger son Ewan faced every day, with Victor gone and only Wilf McIntyre, who had come out of retirement to help his former boss, had broken Bert. Coming in from the fields one day to find that his favourite sheepdog, Old Saul, had died, Bert took the animal's body and his shotgun to the barn and killed himself.

Ewan, as passionate about the farm as his father, was now struggling to keep it going. His hopes of marriage to Alison Greenlees, the widowed daughter of Joe and Gracie Fisher, landlord and landlady of the Neurotic Cuckoo, had crashed about his ears when his father died. Now he spent every waking hour working to keep the farm going, and trying at the expense of aching muscles to overcome the far greater pain of a broken heart.

'It took a long time to get him to start courting me,' Alison was saying to Jess McNair in the farm kitchen round about the time the men in the pub were shaking their heads over the new housing estate. Jess was doing her week's supply of baking while Alison had dealt with the ironing and moved on to the pile of darning in Jess's sewing basket.

'Ewan was always the shy one, nothing like his brother. If I could've divided Victor's confidence and Ewan's love of this place equally between the two of them, it would've made all the difference.' Jess flipped a round of pastry over deftly, scattered it liberally with flour, and picked up the rolling pin again.

'I like Ewan just as he is. I love him for his shyness and his determination to do the right thing by you and his dad, and Jamie thinks the world of him. He'd make a great father for Jamie—' a tremor came into Alison's voice as she went on – 'and for the brothers and sisters I hoped we'd give Jamie in time.'

'Ye've no' given up on the lad already, have ye?' Jess asked, alarmed. For the past year she had allowed herself to dream of the day when Ewan made Alison and her young son, at present hauling a wooden truck up and down in the yard outside, part of the McNair family. It was one of Jess's secret sorrows that Alice, her only daughter, lived on a farm in the Lake District with her husband and three children. Jess, who belonged to the local Women's Rural but didn't often find the time to attend meetings, was hungry for the company of other women and for the joy of seeing children running about the place.

Victor's fiancée was a town girl with no desire for the farming life and although she and Victor were to marry soon and take up residence in one of the smart little houses that had just been built on what had once been Tarbethill land, Jess knew that she would see little of her new daughter-in-law. That left Ewan as her only chance to see children about the place again, and have another woman to talk to. And knowing that Ewan was happy again would go a long way to filling the huge hole Bert's death had torn through her heart and soul.

To her relief Alison said firmly, 'I'll never give up on Ewan. I thought when Jamie's father died that nobody could ever replace him, then I met Ewan and knew that I was wrong. I've lost one good man, Jess, and I've been lucky enough to meet another. I don't want to lose him as well, but at the moment it's him who's given up on me. He treats me like a stranger now; he never comes to the pub unless it's to deliver the eggs, then he's off as quickly as he can. And I know he'd prefer it if I stayed away from the farm.'

'Has he told you that?'

Straight fair hair swung just above the girl's shoulders as she shook her head. 'Not in so many words, but I see it in his eyes if he has to look at me, and hear it in his voice if he has to speak to me. You know what I mean, don't you?'

'Aye, I do. He's changed since we lost Bert.' Ewan scarcely spoke to his mother when he came in to eat and sleep, and any mention of Alison was met with a stubborn refusal to discuss her.

'I've tried to tell him how much you want to

help, but he'll not listen. The most I've got out of him was that he'll not let this place do to you what it's done to me. Why can't he see,' Jess suddenly burst out, abandoning the baking and collapsing on to a chair by the table, 'that there's no point in keepin' the place goin' if there's nob'dy to hand it on to? An' why can't he see that I've never once grudged a minute of the hard work of livin' here? I did it for Bert, because he meant the world to me, even though he could be a thrawn bugger a lot of the time. An' it wasnae just for Bert and our sons. I love Tarbethill, but not if it's goin' to rob Ewan of his right to happiness! It's only land when all's said an' done, and if Bert heard me say that he'd be mad at me, but I don't care.' She used the skirt of her apron to mop the tears on her weathered cheeks.

Alison set the darning aside and hurried to put her arms about the older woman. 'Don't upset yourself!'

'I'm not upset,' Jess choked out. 'I'm furious! Furious with Bert for leavin' us the way he did and furious with Ewan for bein' as stubborn as his father. God forgive me, Alison, but there are times when I think Victor did the right thing when he put his own needs before us and the farm!'

'Don't give up,' Alison urged her. 'Not yet. There's surely ways and means of you and me and Ewan getting what we want. It might not be perfect, and we might all have to settle for less than we'd wish for, but as long as you and me can work together, we can manage to change Ewan's way of thinking!'

Ewan McNair was dog-tired when he came in for his supper; so tired that hungry though he was, he almost fell asleep twice while eating. To his relief his mother, who had eaten earlier and kept his meal hot for him, didn't say a word about how late it was and how little sleep he would manage to get before it was time to rise again for the early morning milking.

Looking at her as she moved about the kitchen, always finding something for her hands to do, he felt a twinge of guilt. A year ago, when his father ran the farm, they ate at a set time and went to bed at a set time to allow as much sleep as was necessary, but such luxuries were no longer possible.

'Go to bed, Mum,' he urged her as she put a mug of hot tea and a plate containing a large slice of home-made dumpling before him. 'I can wash the dishes before I go up.'

'Indeed I will not.' She was insulted. 'The day you do my work's the day I go out and do yours, and I doubt if you'd like that any more than I would.'

He grinned at her despite himself as he picked up his spoon.

The plate, spoon and mug were removed as soon as they were emptied and Ewan got to his feet, stretching and yawning. 'Is there anything you want done before I go up?'

'You could take that pile of ironing with you,

it's all yours anyway. Alison was here this afternoon,' Jess went on casually, turning from the sink to watch her son pick up the neatly folded clothes. 'She did the ironin' for me, and darned those socks on the top of the pile. She's very good with a darning needle, is Alison. Just as well, because those socks of yours are more darn than sock now.'

Ewan's broad shoulders, stooped with exhaustion, stiffened noticeably but he said nothing other than: 'See ye in the mornin', then.'

'You always do,' Jess responded, turning back to the sink.

Once in his room, Ewan put the ironed clothes on top of the shabby big wooden dresser, too tired to bother putting them into the drawers.

Four pairs of thick work socks were on the top, each neatly rolled into a snug ball. He took a pair in each hand, and sat down heavily on the bed, staring at them, holding them close within carefully curved fingers and savouring the softness of them against his calloused palms.

Then he put them to his face, inhaling the wool as though seeking a trace of the light flowery scent Alison always wore. It was the nearest he could allow himself, now, to Alison.

But it wasn't enough. It would never be enough.

Six

Once Neil had met Anja Jacobsen he found it difficult to get her out of his mind. She had bustled around his new home on that first day, taking photographs and measurements everywhere before announcing that the next step was for him to visit her shop, Colour Carousel.

'There, I can show you pictures and samples, and tell you about my plans for your new home. I must be sure to make you happy,' she said firmly.

On his first day off duty he went to the village, parking his car outside his new home and walking the rest of the way, past the school on one side and the village hall on the other before turning right into Adams Crescent, which curved round the half-moon shaped village green with the Mercat Cross in the middle.

The first building in the crescent was Colour Carousel, each letter of its name painted in a different colour over two windows holding paintings, ornaments and photographs of room interiors, all backed by pleated swatches of material in a rainbow of colours.

A musical two-tone bell reminiscent of Anja's 'Hell–oo' chimed as Neil opened the door to find the shop's interior just as colourful and well laid out as the windows. To his left and right shelves held tins of paint while facing him on the wall behind the counter, paintings were grouped on either side of a bead curtain leading to the back shop.

'Won't be a minute,' a woman's voice – not Anja's, he realized with disappointment – called from behind the curtain.

'That's all right.' He picked up the top leaflet from a pile on the counter and saw that the village drama club was about to start rehearsals for *The Importance of Being Earnest*, and new members would be made very welcome at the Monday and Thursday meetings in the village hall. There was something warm about belonging to a community with a village hall and a drama club, he thought as the curtain of coloured glass beads chimed softly.

'Good morning, welcome to Colour Carousel.' The woman smiled warmly. 'What can I do for you today?'

'I'm looking for Anja – Miss Jacobsen. She's helping me to organize the house I've bought at Clover Park.

'Oh, you must be Mr White.' She reached across the counter to shake his hand. 'I'm Jenny Forsyth, Anja's assistant. She's out at the moment but she shouldn't be long. Come into the back room. Can I get you some tea, or coffee? Or perhaps a glass of wine?'

'Tea would be nice.'

One half of the back shop was a small neat

workshop with a sewing machine and shelves stacked with books of samples, the other a small kitchen with a round table, four chairs, stove, sink and counter.

'Anja told me you would be coming in to see her,' Jenny said as she brought cups and saucers, cutlery and a plate of biscuits to the table. 'She's looking forward to helping you settle into your new home.'

'I'm glad she offered because I'm useless at that sort of thing,' Neil confessed.

'You're in good hands, I can assure you.' Her fair hair was feather-cut, shaping an attractive face. 'Until quite recently this was a gift shop and tea shop combined, run by Ingrid Mac-Kenzie, Anja's aunt, with my help. But last year Ingrid and her husband and their two daughters had to go to Norway because of Ingrid's father's poor health.'

'So they're not coming back to Scotland?'

A shadow crossed Jenny's face. 'Not in the foreseeable future, it seems. Her parents own a hotel and she and Peter have more or less taken it over for the time being. Ingrid thought that their absence would give Anja the chance to start her own business and live in their house while they're away. So – Anja tells me that you're a police officer. What made you decide to settle in Prior's Ford?'

'I came to the village last year to deal with a couple of incidents and I liked the look of the place.'

'Were you here when poor Bert McNair killed

himself?' Jenny asked, and then, when he nodded: 'That was a dreadful business.'

'Yes.' The memory came back to him of the
dim light in the barn, and the two bodies – the
farmer and his old dog, the shotgun lying beside
them. He recalled, too, the anguish in the sons'
eyes and the quiet dignity of the farmer's wife.
'How are his wife and sons?'

'Still trying to come to terms with what
happened. Mrs McNair's an incredibly brave
woman. She and her son Ewan are trying hard to
keep the place going. The older son, Victor,
lives and works in Kirkcudbright. The field
where Clover Park stands now was his; he sold
it to a builder. He and his fiancée are getting
married soon, and moving into one of the houses
there,' Jenny was saying when the doorbell
chimed and quick, light footsteps came round
the counter. Neil scrambled to his feet as the
curtain was drawn aside.

'Neil, how good to see you!' Today Anja was
wearing a sleeveless green tunic over matching
trousers, with silver bracelets on both wrists and
a silver chain about her throat. 'Jenny, is there
any more tea in that pot?'

'Of course.'

As Anja set down her shoulder bag she noticed
the flyer Neil had brought in with him. 'You're
interested in the drama club?'

'Might be. It was the play that caught my eye.
The Importance of Being Earnest was perform-
ed during my final year at school, and we all had
a great time working on it. I played the part of

61

Jack Worthing. I still have happy memories of that production.' He didn't mention that the happy memories included a brief but passionate fling with a pretty girl called Marion, who had played the part of the elderly governess, Miss Prism, but was nothing like an elderly governess in real life.

'Really? You should join us, Neil. The play hasn't been cast yet but I know that Mr Pearce is in need of more men.'

'Are you a member of the group?'

'I'm going to help Mrs Pearce with the wardrobe. There are a lot of lovely dresses to be made, and I think it's important for newcomers like you and me to mix in. That's why I came to Scotland, to improve my English, and to get to know lots of people. They're holding auditions a week on Monday in the evening. Why don't you come to them?'

'I will, if I'm free.'

'Then I will hope that you are free,' Anja said, and went to the workroom area to take a blue folder from a pile on one of the shelves. 'Now, let me show you my ideas for making your new home beautiful for you.'

Amy Rose arrived almost halfway through June, zooming into the village in a little red car on a sunny day when the gardens were ablaze with colour.

Clarissa was weeding in her front garden, and by the time she opened the garden gate Amy had clambered from the driving seat, tipped it forward, and was halfway into the back seat. She emerged breathless but triumphant, parcels spilling from her arms.

'Hi, I stopped off and got some things. Hold these.' She deposited her load on Clarissa, stooped to pick up a bundle that had fallen to the pavement, and managed to balance it on top. 'You take them in and I'll get my bags.'

Clarissa wobbled her way carefully up the path, glad that she had had the foresight to leave the front door open, and managed to keep her burden from spilling over until she reached the bottom of the stairs, where she put everything down with a sense of relief.

'What have you got here?' she wanted to know as her guest arrived, carrying two suitcases and with a large bag slung over one shoulder.

'The garage I bought the car from met me at the station with it, so I took the chance to do some marketing before I set out,' Amy said casually as she set the cases down. 'Cookies and so on – stuff I thought you might need.'

'There's enough here to feed a WRI meeting.'

'It there's too much for us, we'll do just that.' Amy slid the bag from her shoulder and ran the fingers of both hands through hair that, though cut shorter than it was on her last visit, and back to its usual russet colour rather than the green shade she had been flaunting when last seen, was still an unruly mass of curls. 'That's better!'

She shook her head vigorously, then hugged Clarissa. 'Great to see you! So how are you? How about coffee? I stopped off somewhere for a cup and it was so good that I got them to sell me a packet of the stuff.' She burrowed among the parcels on the stairs and found what she was looking for. 'You have to try this. I'll see to it,' she said over her shoulder as she headed to the kitchen.

Clarissa felt suddenly cheered as she piled the parcels neatly on the hall table before carrying the cases up to the spare room. Amy, with her bouncy nature, ridiculous hair and erratic dress sense, was better than any tonic. Being small and slight, she claimed that she was always overlooked until she decided to dye her hair and fill her wardrobe with brightly coloured clothes. Today she was wearing a white and green checked blouse over flared blue trousers patterned with big yellow sunflowers.

The kitchen was filled with the rich aroma of coffee when Clarissa returned downstairs, and a plate of biscuits she had never seen before sat on the table.

'You have to try these.' Amy waved a hand at the plate. 'They melt in your mouth and reappear almost at once on your hips, but hey, it's worth it. We should all live dangerously. Try the coffee.'

Clarissa sipped cautiously, then nodded. 'It's delicious.'

'I thought so. Just one final thing,' Amy said, and before Clarissa could stop her, she had whipped out a small bottle from her bag, unscrewed the top and tipped half the contents into Clarissa's mug and the other half into her own.

'What's that?'

'Whisky. I need to get you nice an' mellow, honey,' Amy went on when Clarissa began to protest, 'because you an' me have got some serious talkin' to do.' She clinked her mug against Clarissa's. 'Down the hatch.'

There was no doubt that strong coffee, a good dash of whisky and Amy Rose made a splendid combination. By the time the mugs were empty Clarissa had agreed to phone Alastair and arrange a week's holiday in a rented cottage that Amy had already found for them.

'Right on the banks of Loch Lomond, and what could be more romantic than that? All you have to do is to phone Alastair – right now, while the whisky's still runnin' through your veins – an' find out when he can get time off. Then we'll get on to your computer and sort out the cottage. Phone him now,' Amy insisted. 'I want to say hello to the handsome hunk.'

In less than two hours after her arrival it was all arranged. It had happened so swiftly that it took an hour or two before the reality of it sank into Clarissa's head. 'Amy, I don't know if I can...'

'D'you have anythin' important in your diary for that week?'

'Not really.'

'You do now. An' I'll be here to look after the house.'

'If anyone asks about me, you won't say I'm with Alastair, will you?'

'Course not, I'll tell 'em you had to rush off to

65

help out a sick friend.'

'All my friends are here in Prior's Ford!'

'I'll say a friend from where you used to live. Who's to know it's a lie?'

'I couldn't bear it if people found out about us,' Clarissa panicked.

'Well now, that's somethin' the two of you'll have to work out for yourselves. That is, if you decide that bein' together's what you want, which I think you will.'

'Why did I let you rush me into this?'

'That's not what Alastair said on the phone a while ago. That boy's just so pleased that you're finally goin' to have some time to get to know each other. Clarissa, you're too intelligent and independent to allow me to rush you into anythin' you don't want to do. What I'm sayin' is that deep down you can't wait to get some quality time alone, just you an' Alastair an' nobody else around to spoil things. So now you're goin' to do it.'

'It's the age difference that worries me.'

'It doesn't worry him. An' talkin' about age, honey, we all go to bed older than we were when we got up in the mornin'. You don't have time to waste.'

'What if I regret it?'

'If you do, *I'll* go to that nice romantic cottage by Loch Lomond with Alastair. But we both know it's you he wants and I don't think you'll regret anythin'. Now then, I bought us a couple of nice steaks for dinner, an' a bottle of wine...'

* * *

66

Amy, as always, was right. Clarissa awoke next day to another sunny morning, and lay in bed for a good ten minutes thinking of what it would be like to be in a secluded cottage by the loch, with nobody else around but Alastair.

And when she finally got up and looked in the mirror she saw that she was smiling.

Seven

The usual group of backpackers seeking bed and board in exchange for work arrived at Linn Hall in good time for the gardens' opening to the public. This year they were to be open from the middle of June until the end of September, the longest stretch yet.

The new stable shop had proved to be popular and Ginny's idea of opening the gardens while in the process of being restored had attracted quite a few serious gardeners, happy to wander around talking to the workers, asking questions and sometimes offering advice. Many of them had written in the visitors' book that they intended to return each year to follow the progress of restoration.

'I can't wait to see the water gushin' down the hill into the pond an' lake,' Jimmy McDonald said as he and Ginny ate their lunch in the shade of a tree.

'You and me both, kid. The sooner I can get Lewis to go up there with me so that we can have a good look at the water situation the better. At least the lake and the pond are ready now.'

'D'you think...' Jimmy began, and then fell

silent, head bent, plucking at the grass where he sat.

'Yes, sometimes, but probably not as much as I should.'

'That's not what I meant. I was goin' to say, d'you think...' he hesitated again.

'Go on then.'

'It's daft.'

'Try me.'

'D'you think I might get a job as a gardener here when I leave school?' The words came out in a rush and when he glanced up at her, Ginny saw that the boy's face was almost as red as his carroty hair.

'When will that be?'

'I'm sixteen now but my mum's got this bee in her bonnet about us all stayin' at school as long as we can manage it, even Grant, though everyone knew he was goin' to be a football player. Mum says a good education's more important than anything.'

'She's right. So you're OK about staying on, then?'

He shrugged. 'I don't mind and anyway, when my mum says you're goin' to do somethin' you do it, no questions asked. She's brilliant, but she's got a velvet hand – no, that's not right.'

'An iron hand in a velvet glove?'

'That's the one. I mean, I don't need a load of schooling to become a gardener.'

'D'you get Latin at school?'

'Uh-huh.' He chewed at a piece of grass.

'Stick at it. The best gardeners have to be able

to reel off the Latin names of all the plants.'

'I never thought about that. I'm goin' to have to listen more in Latin class. D'you know all the Latin names?'

'No, but I'm not one of the best gardeners.'

'I think you're ace. Look what you've taught me.'

'It's easy to teach someone who's keen to learn. You're a natural, Jimmy.'

'I got it all from my grandad. He was the head gardener here and when my gran died he moved in with us. I was helpin' him in the garden at home when I was Rowena Chloe's age, and he talked about Linn Hall a lot. I was the only one who wanted to listen. It was great, hearin' him talk about what this place used to be like.'

Ginny's ears pricked up. 'D'you remember anything of what he said?'

'Oh yes, because the way he described things was so good that I could see it in my head, know what I mean? I mind him sayin' once that there are a lot of valuable plants here.'

'If there are, I've not seen them. I wonder what he meant by "valuable"?'

'Some of 'em had come from abroad, I mind him sayin' that.'

'I wish he was still alive. I'd love to be able to find out which plants he was talking about. The pity is that they've probably all been smothered to death by the ivy and nettles and thistles we're still clearing out.'

'I wish he was still here too,' Jimmy agreed. 'So d'you think I might be able to get a proper job here when I leave school, as a real gardener like my grandad? One day I'd like to be head gardener like him, with my own team to boss around.'

'I think, Jimmy McDonald, that you can be anything you want to be as long as you work hard and don't lose sight of what you're aiming for.'

'But could the Ralston-Kerrs ever afford proper full-time gardeners again?' he fretted.

'They might, once the estate's been put back to the way it was, with people flocking here in the summer to enjoy it. But that won't be for a few years yet. So you've got time to stay on at school and learn to enjoy Latin. Although it's called a dead language it's still very much alive in a lot of careers, not just gardening. If you can manage to do a college course in horticulture after school that would further your chances even more. By the time you finish college Lewis may be in a position to offer you a proper job. And I'm sure he'd be delighted to employ someone local, especially someone who's already been such a help to him.'

Ginny threw her final crust to a thrush that had been eyeing them both hopefully before scrambling to her feet. 'But for now – back to work!'

'You're really filling in the map,' Lewis marvelled that evening. The two of them were in Ginny's camper van, poring over the large map she had been working on for months. She had rescued an old roll of wallpaper found in a cupboard and destined for disposal. Now it was spread patterned side down over the small table, giving her the space she needed to mark out each part of the estate. Every detail she could extract from the account books and photographs Hector Ralston-Kerr had unearthed for her was recorded in a determined attempt to find out how the estate had looked in its heyday.

Lewis frequently helped her with the map, but when Molly was around she claimed all his spare attention. On those occasions, Ginny usually gathered up the map, books and photographs and went to visit Lynn Stacey, headmistress of the primary school. Two years earlier, when Ginny showed the local schoolchildren round the kitchen garden, presenting them each with a small plant and encouraging them to start growing their own herbs, Lynn's interest in the restoration work was fired, and she and Ginny had become good friends.

But this evening Molly had gone out with a village friend and Lewis had wandered over to the camper van, much to Ginny's delight.

'I'm beginning to get a fairly good idea of what a few areas were like,' she said now. 'The good thing is that some of the plants, trees and shrubs are still there, just waiting for us to rescue them from undergrowth and give them a bit of tender loving care. It would be an idea to ask Cam Gordon to photograph each section we've located from the old photos, so that we would have then and now illustrations to compare. Would that be all right with you?'

'Go ahead.' Lewis was more relaxed about Cam now that Molly was gone. 'Then and now photographs could look good on the walls of the stable shop, and Cam's photographs of the estate sold well last year.'

'I'm also thinking of starting to do more detailed sketches of each area. That would make it be easier to see what we're aiming for.'

'I didn't know you were an artist.'

'I'm not, but I could probably manage to get the idea across, then with any luck we'll find someone who could do them properly. It's a pity Alastair Marshall's not living in the village, he'd have been ideal. Lewis, do you ever talk to Jimmy McDonald?'

'Now and again when we meet up, but we've never got down to a proper conversation if that's what you mean.'

'You should have a proper conversation some time. He's been telling me about his grandfather, the last head gardener here; he was the one who instilled a love of growing things in Jimmy, and apparently he talked quite a lot about Linn Hall. Even though Jimmy was just a kid, he says he can remember pretty well everything the old man said. If that's true, he could be really useful to us.'

'Old Norman Cockburn – I remember him, but only just. Cam and I preferred to keep out of his way because our main passions involved scrumping for apples and eating fruit off the bushes in the kitchen garden, and playing with catapults and bows and arrows and air guns. We tended to run away from old Cockburn rather than towards him,' Lewis recalled nostalgically.

'So you wouldn't know of the whereabouts of special plants? Valuable ones, probably from abroad, according to what Jimmy heard.'

'No, but I know a man who might.' He removed the various mugs and ornaments holding down the wallpaper and began to roll it up. 'We'll go and ask Dad, and have some hot chocolate while we're about it.'

'I heard something about a great-uncle,' Hector said thoughtfully, 'who had itchy feet, travelled a lot. I believe he was a keen botanist who collected plants for several estates as a way of financing his journeys; he probably brought some of them back here as well. He died before my time.'

'So you wouldn't have any idea where the plants he brought back to Linn Hall were placed?' Lewis asked. His father shook his head.

'Not the foggiest. Being from foreign parts, they probably died of neglect once the grounds started to go wild. But I'll have another hunt upstairs for books that might mention them.'

'There could be letters too,' Ginny suggested. It was almost bedtime, and the backpackers were probably all in the pub. There were only the four of them, the Ralston-Kerrs and Ginny, in the butler's pantry that now served as the family's private living room and Hector's study.

Fliss was sewing loose buttons back on to one of Hector's shirts while the other three studied

Ginny's wallpaper chart, held down by their mugs of hot chocolate. Every time one of them had a drink someone else had to anchor the paper down with a hand or an elbow.

It was a cosy, happy domestic scene, Fliss thought as she watched and listened. Her days were spent in the kitchen, usually with Jinty McDonald, her friend and support, cooking for the hungry young people who poured in three times a day for food and twice a day for tea or coffee breaks, and she treasured the peaceful evenings in the long narrow high-ceilinged pantry. The day was coming when they would be able to use one of the reception rooms that had been closed for many years, but she wasn't in a hurry for that.

It was good to see shy Hector so animated and excited about the prospect of returning the estate to something resembling the grandeur he recalled from his childhood. Although he was given to avoiding outsiders, he got on well with Ginny, who was beginning to seem like the daughter they had never had.

Sadly, Molly terrified him, and Fliss didn't know how he would cope if Lewis ever married her and brought her to live in Linn House. She tugged at a button, found it to be secure, and bit off the thread. Molly scared her too, but not because of her chattering and the way the very air around her seemed to crackle with electricity. Fliss couldn't visualize active, travel-loving Molly settling down to become mistress of Linn Hall and her secret fear, which she daren't mention to Hector or even Jinty, was that one day the young woman would manage to persuade Lewis to sell the place so that Molly could exchange boredom for wealth.

Deep down, she knew and had always known that Lewis loved the place as much as she and his father did. She had come to ramshackle, leaking, cold Linn Hall as a bride, willing to live there because she loved Hector and knew that he wouldn't be happy away from the place. Over the years – years of scrubbing, painting and grouting, of wearing layers of shabby clothing in an attempt to beat the draughts from warped window frames, of rushing to the top floor every time it rained to lay down a motley collection of vases, basins, buckets and chamber pots to catch the drips – she had come to love the place for itself, not just for Hector's sake.

Their struggles had eased in the past three years or so, following a surprise windfall. The roof had been made watertight, the windows replaced, and now there was talk of opening the ground floor rooms to the public as well as the gardens. Linn Hall was slowly heading back towards its better days, but would it ever be enough for Molly?

Fliss gave a sudden shiver, noticed by Hector. 'What's wrong?'

She smiled at him. 'Nothing,' she said. 'Just someone walking over my grave.'

Eight

Neil White and Anja met at the Neurotic Cuckoo for a quick drink before going along to his first drama club meeting. Anja had a tomato juice while Neil, who was nervous, ordered a whisky and downed it quickly, then wished he had brought some peppermints to freshen his breath. When he said so, Anja delved into her tiny bag and produced a tube of mints.

'But there is nothing to be nervous about,' she said as he popped one into his mouth and blinked in surprise at the strength of it. 'They'll be delighted to see you. There are a lot of men in this play, and you know it well.'

'I *did* know it, quite a long time ago.'

'Not to worry, a leopard never changes its spots,' Anja assured him enigmatically, and then, as he was still puzzling over the remark and coping with the eye-watering effect of the mint: 'We should go, we don't want to be late.'

They arrived to find almost everyone there, apart from the MacBains, who made their entrance just as Neil was being introduced.

'Have you heard the news?' Cynthia burst out at once. 'The cottage where Doris Thatcher used to live has been sold again.'

77

'I think we all know that,' Hannah Gibbs said.

'But do you know who's bought it?' Cynthia said, as Hannah shook her head. 'Laura Tyler!'

'Who's Laura Tyler?' Kevin Pearce asked.

At the same time, Jinty McDonald said, 'I know, Gracie Fisher told me. Isn't it exciting? But they're only going to be holiday visitors.'

'Oh dear, that's what most of the villagers don't want – the place being invaded by holiday home owners.'

'But it's Laura Tyler, Elinor!'

'Who's Laura Tyler?' Kevin said loudly.

'A well-known cookery expert, dear,' his wife told him. 'She's written some excellent recipe books and done some television programmes as well.'

'She's been on television?' Kevin began to show some interest.

Cynthia nodded. 'Gilbert and I were in the Cuckoo last week for a pre-lunch drink, and there she was, having lunch on her own. I went over to speak to her and she invited us to sit at her table. She's a charming woman, isn't she, Gilbert?'

'Charming,' her husband agreed, apparently just as excited as Cynthia by the meeting.

'And they're not like those dreadful previous owners; they're not going to tear the cottage apart and enlarge it. It's only the kitchen that's being modernized slightly. Laura confided to us that she's about to start work on another book, and her husband's planning one as well. He was a high-ranking police officer and now that he's retired he wants to write his memoirs. They bought the cottage because they both need peace and quiet for their writing. She was here to organize furniture and carpets and to see how work on the kitchen's getting on.'

'When are they moving in?' Hannah Gibbs asked eagerly.

'Within the next few weeks as far as I know.'

'Could I have everyone's attention please?' Kevin demanded. 'Our task at the moment is to begin work on the play we're performing in October. Time's short, so I've decided that rather than hold proper auditions we'll read through the play and I'll call a halt here and there to give everyone a chance to read different parts. Steph, pass the books out, please.'

'One moment, Kevin.' Cynthia held up a hand. 'I see a stranger in our midst. Please introduce us.'

If she doesn't get the part of Lady Bracknell, Neil thought to himself as Kevin made the introductions and Cynthia dazzled him with a gracious smile and a few words of welcome, *I'll eat my uniform hat with salt, tomato sauce and possibly a dash of Thousand Island dressing in front of the entire police station tomorrow.*

As soon as they began to read the script he knew that his hat was in no danger. Although Kevin allowed several people to read for all the other parts, only Cynthia read Lady Bracknell's lines, thundering each one out in a deep, dramatic voice.

Throughout the reading Kevin struck a

dramatic pose, sitting with his left elbow propped on the table and his left hand spread across his forehead as though in deep thought or possibly in pain. Every now and again he scribbled a note on the writing pad before him.

'An excellent read-through,' he said when the last line had been delivered, 'and I'm delighted to say that on this very night, without further ado, I am in a position to announce the cast list for our play.'

'Good, because we don't have much time to rehearse,' Pete McDermott said.

'I think it's wonderful that Kevin can cast the play after only one reading,' Cynthia responded. 'Clearly, he has a very quick mind.'

'Thank you, Cynthia, for your understanding. I did originally intend to give myself a few days to mull matters over, but already I feel that I can put together a cast with the ability to work together to—'

'Kevin, time's moving on,' Charlie Crandall pointed out.

'And the Cuckoo awaits us,' Cam Gordon added, earning a glare from Cynthia.

'Do put us out of our misery, Kevin,' she said sweetly.

'Of course.' He positioned the writing pad before him, put his elbows on the table, steepled the fingers of both hands and said, 'The part of Lady Bracknell goes to our very own Cynthia MacBain who, I know, will give us and our audiences a magnificent performance.'

Gilbert started to applaud, nodding to the

others to follow suit, while Cynthia smiled, bowed and waved, every inch the arrogant noblewoman.

'Thank you, Kevin, for your faith in me. I shall not let you down.'

'You never have, Cynthia, and I know that you never will. The part of Algernon Moncrieff goes to...' He paused, looking round the group before him, face by face, before announcing, 'Cameron Gordon.'

Cam smirked an acknowledgement of the smattering of applause. Kevin waited until it had died down before going on. 'John Worthing will be played by–' again he took a long pause, oblivious to the shifting of feet – 'our new member, Neil White.'

Neil felt his face redden as he was applauded and Anja gave him the thumbs-up. 'Thank you very much, but there's just one thing – I work shifts, so I might not be able to get to every rehearsal. But I played that part years ago and I still remember a lot of the lines, if that helps.'

'You read very well, young man. We'll be rehearsing twice a week, every Monday and Thursday evening, so I'm sure you'll be able to keep up even if you can't be with us every time.' Kevin made it sound more like an order than an assurance. 'The part of the Reverend Canon Chasuble goes to...'

'For pity's sake, Kevin, you're not Chris Tarrant and this isn't a quiz show,' Cam burst out. 'Just get on with it!'

'Gilbert MacBain,' Kevin said through set

teeth, and then, rapidly, 'Merriman the butler, Charlie Crandall; Gwendolen Fairfax, Alison Greenlees; Cecily Cardew, Steph McDonald; Miss Prism, Hannah Gibbs, and you're Lane the manservant, Pete. Everyone got that?'

'Just about,' Charlie said.

'Good. Now we've only just got time for another read-through.'

'It's great to be in a famous play like this, isn't it?' Steph McDonald said when the reading was over and they were preparing to leave the hall.

'Lovely,' Hannah agreed. 'I'm looking forward to being the governess. Wasn't Margaret Rutherford wonderful in that part in the old film?'

'I've only seen the play on television and I can't wait to wear those lovely costumes! What about you, Alison?'

'Sorry, what did you say?'

'I said, I love the costumes we're going to wear in this play. Is anything wrong? You look very serious tonight.'

'No, I'm fine. Just got things on my mind.' Alison, who loved acting, looked down at her script without enthusiasm.

When she first joined the village drama group she and Ewan had played opposite each other in a one-act play. It was during rehearsals that they fell in love with each other. But now that he was no longer part of her life, nothing seemed worth the effort.

'A quick word, dear.' Cynthia drew Elinor

Pearce aside as the others began to leave the hall. 'I'm planning to hold a small party and I hope that you and Kevin will be available; have you got any holiday plans?'

'We usually spend a week in Edinburgh during the Festival so that Kevin can catch some of the plays, but he's decided against it this year in order to concentrate on this play. Are you celebrating something special?'

'Gilbert and I thought that it would be a good idea to hold a little party to welcome Laura Tyler to the village.'

'But you said she and her husband are looking for peace and quiet to work. Will they want a welcoming party?'

'Of course they will! With her being a celebrity they're probably expecting someone to arrange a proper welcome to our little village. It's only for one evening, and it's the best way for them to meet their new neighbours. You'll agree, surely, that the sooner they integrate with the local community the better, especially since some people are opposed to holiday homes.'

'I suppose so. When's it likely to take place?'

'Laura told us that she thinks the cottage will be ready in about three weeks' time, so Gilbert and I thought the welcoming party could be held about a week later.'

'Thank you, Cynthia, I'll pass your invitation to Kevin when we get home.'

'Tell him that for the meantime we'd like to keep it quiet, dear.' Cynthia laid a cautionary hand on Elinor's arm. 'We want to make it a select little gathering – the right people, as you might say.'

'I wish we'd known about this woman coming to Prior's Ford before Cynthia got wind of it,' Kevin said as he and his wife walked home, 'then we could have been the ones to hold the party. Isn't there any way we could...'

'I think we should leave it to Cynthia, dear. She wouldn't be very pleased if we ruined her plans, and she's much better at social events than I am.'

'I suppose you're right,' Kevin said reluctantly, to his wife's relief. She hadn't forgotten the fuss he had made of Meredith Whitelaw's brief stay in the village, when he had handed over Cynthia's leading role in the current play to the well-known actress, only to be let down at the last moment when she was offered a part in a television play.

Cynthia had, rightly, been furious, and if Kevin succeeded in stealing her thunder with yet another celebrity, Elinor was convinced that he may well go in danger of his life. That, she wouldn't like.

He may not be the most wonderful man in the world, but he was *her* man and she didn't want anything to happen to him.

Nine

'It's good to see you back in Prior's Ford,' Lynn Stacey said warmly when she met Amy Rose in the village shop.

'It's good to be back.'

'How long have we got you for this time?'

'I'm aimin' to be around for a while. I want to see a bit more of Scotland before I go home and Clarissa doesn't mind me usin' her as a base.'

'I asked because the school's about to close for the summer holidays, but if you're still in the village when the new term starts you must come and talk to the children again. They loved your visit last year.'

'That would be my pleasure.' They had both arrived at the checkout, where Amy hoisted her full basket on to the counter.

'I haven't seen Clarissa for a few days,' Marcy remarked as she began to empty the basket and scan each item. 'Is she all right?'

'She's more than all right,' Amy said without thinking, and then, as the other two shot puzzled looks at her: 'I mean – she's fine, but she's not here at the moment. Her stepdaughter contacted her just a few days after I arrived to ask if she could go to England – some sort of family thing that needed her attention. Lucky I was here to keep an eye on the house for her.'

'Oh dear.' Cynthia MacBain had joined the short queue. 'I hope that Mrs Ramsay hasn't been called away because of an emergency.'

It only took one glance at Cynthia's bright, interested eyes to warn Amy that here was a woman who enjoyed gossip. 'I don't think so,' she said airily, 'when we spoke to on the phone last night she was fine. Said she'd be back at the weekend. How much do I owe you, Marcy?'

Recalling Cynthia's inquisitive face as she carried the shopping across the village green, she realized that it was women like that who were worrying Clarissa, should she and Alastair decide to live together openly.

'Well, we can't let gossip-mongers spoil our lives,' she said aloud as she opened the front door. 'We have to learn to stand strong against them.'

The question was – could Clarissa find that sort of strength?

At that moment, Clarissa was telling her reflection in the small bathroom mirror, 'Good grief, woman, you look ten years younger!'

She and Alastair were halfway through their holiday in the little cottage on Loch Lomond's shore, spending every day exploring the hills above the loch and every night asleep in each other's arms. She had never been as happy in her entire life, and it showed.

She ran both hands through the short brown hair that had until fairly recently been worn in a spinsterish loose bun on the nape of her neck, then smoothed them down over her face. Closing her eyes tightly she counted to five and opened them again to find that she still looked years younger than she had a mere week earlier. Clear brown eyes sparkled back at her and even in repose her mouth lifted at the corners in a way it never had before. Her skin, lightly tanned from hours in the fresh air, looked smoother and almost wrinkle-free. None of the people who had known her in England as a dedicated and contented schoolteacher and then, in middle age, as the quiet and obedient wife of a headmaster would recognize her now. She scarcely recognized herself, which was surprising for a woman nearer to sixty than to fifty.

There was only one explanation, and that was the love of a good man. A really good man, she thought, blushing and laughing at the same time. It had taken her a long time to recognize that she loved Alastair and, even more surprising, that he loved her. And he and Amy had been right when they said that the age difference didn't matter. Somehow, Alastair had banished the prim and proper rules she had lived with until now and taught her that life was for living at any age. Not only for living, but for taking and giving. The phrase rhymed nicely, and she was wondering if anyone had ever put it into a song when she heard Alastair call from downstairs. 'Breakfast's ready!'

'Coming,' she trilled, and went eagerly to join him.

On the morning after the Hunters moved into Thatcher's Cottage Laura woke to a beautiful day. Sunlight flooded the small bedroom and the muted sound of rush-hour traffic they were accustomed to had been replaced by birdsong.

'This,' she said, stretching her legs luxuriously down the length of the bed, 'is the first day of the rest of our lives.'

Allan, never at his best in the mornings, grunted in a non-committal way.

'I'll nip into the bathroom first to give you time to settle into the day, then I'll go down and make us a nice breakfast.' She got out of bed and opened the curtains. 'It's such a beautiful view, Allan; houses and gardens and trees instead of blocks of flats, and not a traffic jam in sight. We'll have breakfast in the back garden,' she went on as she shrugged into her dressing gown.

Poor Allan, she thought as she started to prepare breakfast in the tiny kitchen, so unlike the large, modern kitchen at home. He had moped around the flat like a bear with a sore head ever since retiring. The police force had been his life and he was lost without it.

'I'm going to the village this morning to stock up on supplies and have a wander around the place,' she decided as they ate breakfast on the small patio by the river. 'Fancy coming with me? We could have morning coffee in the local pub.'

He shook his head. 'I want to start sorting out the files I brought with me.'

'I thought we might meet some of our new neighbours.'

'Meeting strangers isn't my idea of having a good time. We'll have to meet them soon enough, at this dratted party we've been invited to.'

'Oh yes, the MacBains,' Laura said without enthusiasm. She would far rather get to know the villagers on a one to one basis than at a prearranged party. 'D'you remember that block of flats we lived in when we were newly-weds? And the couple on the floor below who brought us a bottle of horrible home-made wine the day we moved in and invited us to their fancy-dress party the following week?'

'Remember them? How could anyone ever forget that party?'

'I went as a twenties flapper and you were a pharaoh...'

'And our hosts were dressed as Adam and Eve. If you could call it "dressed".'

'Everyone there spent the entire evening staring into their glasses of home-made plonk in an attempt not to look at them.'

They were both laughing now. 'I'll never forget their wine either,' Allan said. 'It was the only time I ever felt my teeth try to take refuge in my gums.'

'I wonder where that couple are now. They were quite nice, really.'

'Older than us, so perhaps they're enlivening

some old folks' home with their fancy dress antics.'

'With cocoa instead of home-made wine.'

'I'll drink to that.' Allan took a sip of orange juice.

'Anything you want from the village store?'

'The *Guardian*, if they have it. Or the most decent newspaper they do have.'

'Right. I'll put in a daily order for the *Guardian*, shall I?'

'Thanks.'

It had been good, Laura thought as she went into the village store an hour later, shopping basket over her arm, to see Allan laugh. He had been a first-class, hard-working police officer who deserved his quick rise through the ranks, but somewhere on the way the job had taken him over. She missed the carefree Allan she had met and instantly loved all those years ago.

'You're Mrs Hunter who's bought Doris Thatcher's cottage, aren't you?' the woman at the checkout asked as she keyed in Laura's purchases.

'That's right.'

'I'm Marcy Copleton. My partner, Sam Brennan and I run this place and live at Rowan Cottage, just along from the pub.'

Laura held out a hand. 'Hello, Marcy, my name's Laura. My husband and I are looking forward to living in a village. Although we've still got our flat in Leeds we intend to spend a lot of our time here.'

'I'm very glad to hear that.' Marcy began to pack the basket deftly. 'You got off to a good start; the Thatchers were well thought of and people are pleased that you've named the cottage after them. Doris was a widow when I came here so I never knew her husband, but by all account he was a lovely person, as was Doris.'

'I loved the cottage from the moment I first stepped into it. It felt – contented.'

'That was because the people who bought it after Doris died only stayed for a very short time, thank goodness,' put in a woman who had just joined them at the checkout.

'Didn't they like it?'

'Jinty, Mrs Hunter – Laura – doesn't want to hear local gossip.'

'Actually, she does,' Laura assured them both, and Jinty McDonald lifted her basket on to a clear area of the counter and settled down to her story.

'They never fitted in from the start. They had loads of money and liked folk to know it, and they had twin teenage daughters who were a right pair of flirts. The two of them caused a stir among the local lads, I can tell you – including my sons. Then the family suddenly up and left and the For Sale notice reappeared. It turned out that most of their wealth came from her secret job. She was moonlighting, as you might say.'

'Moonlighting?'

'She was what's sometimes called a lady of the night. And her husband knew all about it. He even approved.'

91

'Good gracious! I can assure you that we don't have any dark secrets like that.'

'Oh, we all know who you are, and I can tell you now that the Rural are already planning to ask you to give us a talk about how you came to write such good cookery books.'

'It was all down to my mother; she was a fantastic cook, and adventurous with it. I'll be happy to give a talk.'

'I'll tell our president. She'll be upset when she hears that I met you before she did,' Jinty said with a grin.

Heading towards the Neurotic Cuckoo in search of coffee, Laura saw a library van parked on the road curving round the village green. Curiosity, since she had never been in a mobile library before, turned her steps towards it.

The interior consisted of shelving packed with books from floor to ceiling on either side with a middle aisle leading to a desk at the far end. Two people were browsing at the shelves, an elderly man and a small woman with a head of short curly hair of a russet shade that surely must have come out of a bottle.

'Good morning, can I help you?' The librarian had a shy but welcoming smile.

'My husband and I have just bought a holiday cottage here and I wondered if I could get tickets to use when we're staying in the village.'

'Of course.' The woman produced a form and a pen. 'If you fill this in and produce proof of identity you can join immediately. The van

92

visits this village every Wednesday morning, Mrs...?'

'Hunter.'

'You've bought Doris Thatcher's cottage,' the red-haired woman suddenly appeared by Laura's side. 'I'm Amy Rose, how d'you do?' Her accent was American, her handshake surprisingly strong for a small person. 'And this is Stella Hesslet, our very helpful librarian, who also lives in the village. This gentleman is Charlie Crandall.'

'Welcome to Prior's Ford.' The man reading a book further down the van looked up and gave Laura a friendly nod.

'It's very nice to meet you – all of you. I was about to go to the public house for a coffee,' Laura said to the librarian as another two people came into the library. 'Can I fill this form in there and bring it back later? It'll save me getting in everyone's way.'

'Yes, of course. I'll be here until three o'clock.'

'I'm going for a coffee once I've chosen my books,' Amy Rose said. 'If you can wait for five minutes we'll go over together.'

Ten

'You're American, aren't you?' Laura asked as they walked the short distance to the Neurotic Cuckoo.

'I was born in England so technically I'm as English as a cup of tea, but my folks emigrated when I was a kid and I took to America the minute my little sandals landed on its concrete.'

'So you don't live in the village?'

'Just visitin' my friend Clarissa. That's her cottage we just passed. I first came here last year and enjoyed myself so much I'm back again. Clarissa lets me use her cottage as a base to explore Britain. I guess you could call it catchin' up with my roots.'

'Wouldn't your friend like to join us for coffee?'

'She's away for a few days, but you've got to meet her when she comes back. You two will get on well together, I promise you. Here we are.'

The lounge bar was empty other than three young women chatting at one of the tables. 'Hi,' Amy greeted them. 'I've brought a newcomer to the village. Mind if we sit with you?'

'We'd love it.' The woman from the village store smiled as Laura. 'I've just been telling the others that I met you.'

'That's right – you're Marcy, from the village store.'

Extra chairs were brought, coffee ordered, and Laura was introduced to Jenny Forsyth and Helen Campbell.

'This is nice,' she said happily. 'I've been looking forward to getting to know people.'

'Jenny works part time in Colour Carousel with Anja Jacobsen, who's a very good interior designer if you're in need of one,' Marcy told her, 'and Helen's a writer.'

'Really?'

Helen blushed. 'More of a housewife and a mum – and would-be writer.'

'Don't be so modest,' Jenny scolded her friend. 'She writes the Prior's Ford column for a weekly newspaper and she's working on a novel.'

'Good for you,' Laura said warmly. Then, as Joe Fisher brought the coffees: 'Can I get you three another coffee?'

'I've got to get back to the store,' Marcy said.

'And I've to get back to Colour Carousel, alas.' Jenny picked up her bag, while Helen added that she had to get home before her children came out of school.

'They're nice people,' Laura said when she and Amy were on their own.

'It's a nice village, I think you'll enjoy it. Aren't you a writer too?' Amy asked.

'Three cookery books.'

'I love cooking. We must talk about food some

time. I used to be a midwife, but now I'm a cruciverbalist and I bet you don't know what that is.'

'You compose crosswords.'

'Hey, you're good! What does your husband do?'

'Allan recently retired from the police force. That's why we bought the cottage here, to give him somewhere quiet to unwind and work on his memoirs while I put together another recipe book.'

'My husband was a cop too – there's a co-incidence. So how does a cop meet a midwife, you're wonderin'. Well, he'd no sooner arrested this woman for shoplifting than she went into labour so he had to rush her to hospital. It was a riot. When I undressed her, I kept finding lipsticks and packets of pantyhose and heaven knows what tucked away. The baby came quickly, with me at the business end and him gettin' his hands mauled every time the pains came. She called the baby Gordon after him. How did you meet your husband?'

'At an archery contest. Archery was my passion at the time.'

'Were you any good?'

'I won a few cups.'

'You must be strong – remind me not to arm-wrestle with you. My Gordon was a great guy. It's hell bein' a widow, I can tell you. If we'd had kids it might have helped, but although I delivered hundreds of 'em in my time we were never blessed ourselves.' Amy hesitated, eyeing

96

her companion closely, then said, 'You don't have any either, do you?'

'One, years ago, but he died when he was only months old. How did you know?'

'It was the way you winced when I talked about deliverin' hundreds. I hit a nerve, didn't I?'

'After all those years that particular nerve's still raw. You're very perceptive.' Laura found this American fascinating. 'Tell me about the friend you're visiting.'

'Clarissa's one in a million. She moved here from England with her husband when they both retired. She was a school teacher an' he was her school principal. He up and died not long after they came here and after that she wasn't sure whether to stay or go back where she came from. She was in a bit of a state from what I gather, but then she met this young man, Alastair Marshall, an artist and one of the nicest people I know. He helped her to get over her problems an' she decided to stay here. But first, she went off travellin' all on her own, and that's when I met her in America.'

'So you haven't known each other for long?'

'Not long, but very well. I took to Clarissa right away, so when she invited me to visit some time I did. Would you like some more coffee?'

'Why not?'

'Good. Joe, could we have another two cups of coffee here? Thanks. The thing is, I knew when I first came here that Clarissa needed me, though she didn't know it. That's why I'm back again, 'cos she still needs me.'

'In what way?'

'That,' Amy Rose said, 'I can't tell you just yet, but maybe soon. I hope soon, but I've got to wait until Clarissa's ready to make a big change in her life. She's one of those folk brought up never to do anythin' other folks might disapprove of.'

'But you believe she should stop worrying about what other people think.'

'You've got it in one, Laura. For the first time in her life she's goin' to have to let go of the rule book and put herself first. Though when she does, there's goin' to be a bit of an explosion in this little village and I want to be here to help her get through the fallout. Thanks, Joe,' Amy said as the coffee arrived. 'This is Laura Tyler, by the way, a famous cookery expert. She and her husband have bought the cottage down by the river. Joe and his wife Gracie run this pub.'

'Joe and I already know each other. My husband and I stayed here when we came to look at Thatcher's Cottage.'

'Yes, I remember.'

'Gracie's off on a shopping trip with our daughter today; she'll be disappointed to hear that she missed you.'

'I'm sure we'll be seeing a lot of each other from now on,' Laura assured him, and then, when he had returned to the bar: 'I'm looking forward to meeting Clarissa. Am I right in thinking from what you say that her life's been lived within a fairly strict framework and yet once she

98

got over the shock of being widowed she went off to America on her own?'

'Not just the US of A – she went all over before she came to us.'

'She sounds courageous.'

'She is, more than she knows.'

'Sometimes,' Laura said, stirring her coffee, 'we start life as a certain type of person, then something happens that forces us to become someone else, whether we like it or not.'

'That sounds interestin'.'

'Not necessarily,' Laura said, and changed the subject.

'I wish you weren't going to be away for so long,' Lewis said.

'Don't start that again, babes,' Molly protested. 'Some of my best mates are going to be in Portugal this summer and we always have a terrific time together. I'd hate to miss it.'

The two of them were in Lewis's bedroom, and, unknown to them, Jinty, her arms filled with fresh bed linen for his parents' room, loitered outside the door, which was slightly ajar.

'I'll miss you, and so will Rowena Chloe.'

'You're a big boy now, Lewis, you can manage without me and Weena loves being here with you and your parents. She won't miss me one bit.'

'She will.'

Jinty could almost hear Molly shrug. 'Only for the first few hours, and it's good for her to get used to being with different people.'

'I bet your parents didn't go off and leave you and your sister Stephanie when you were her age.'

'Now you come to mention it, they didn't.' Her voice was suddenly cool. 'They went everywhere together and they always took us with them. I got my love of travelling from them. My dad didn't spoil things for everyone by insisting that he had to stay home and work in the garden.'

Fliss appeared at the top of the stairs, and Jinty frantically signalled her to keep quiet.

'What are you...?' Fliss began, then stopped as she heard her son's voice.

'Your dad's garden's not like the estate. Once the grounds are properly organized we'll be free to travel together – you, me and Rowena Chloe.'

'But when will that be? Now that Ginny's here all year round, surely she and Duncan can cope while we take Weena abroad?'

'I can't afford holidays just now.'

'You're getting lots of money from the bank, aren't you?'

'We're borrowing lots of money and it all has to be paid back. In any case, the loans are for the house and the estate, not for us.'

'Is it always going to be like this, Lewis? Because if it is, I don't know if I want to live here. I don't want to be like your mum, having to work hard all the time, and making do instead of enjoying life.'

'I promise you that things will improve once everything's been put right.'

'And how long will that take?'

'Only a few more years now, if our plans work out.'

'A few more years of this?' Molly's voice rose. 'A few more years of living in a kitchen and sleeping in a cold bedroom and you talking about this place non-stop? Can you wonder at me being desperate to get away for a break in the sun?'

'Molly, Linn Hall's been in the family for generations and my parents can't save it on their own. I have to help them.'

'You mean you *want* to help them, even when it means that I'm being left out in the cold!'

'Just hang on for a bit longer and I promise I'll make it up to you.'

'Oh, don't worry,' Molly snapped, 'I'll make sure of that. One day this place'll belong to you and by that time it'll be put right and worth a lot of money. Think how much you'd get if you sold it, Lewis. We could have a wonderful life, you, me and Weena with no more worrying about Linn Hall.'

It was then, just as things were getting interesting, that Jinty realized Fliss was shaking like a leaf. She put her free hand beneath the other woman's elbow and steered her hurriedly along the corridor to the room she shared with Hector. As she closed the door quietly behind them she heard Lewis's bedroom door bang shut, indicating that either he or Molly had stormed out.

Fliss sank down on to the bed. 'We shouldn't have been listening.'

101

'I quite agree, Mrs F, but I'm glad we did. Imagine her trying to get Lewis to sell the Hall off when he inherits it – which I hope won't happen until she's out of his life!'

'She won't be, if they get married.'

'Marriages don't necessarily last these days, and if you ask me, that Molly's too flighty to settle down forever with one man. In any case, I can't see Lewis selling this place, not after the work he's put into it.'

'Are you sure about that, Jinty?' Fliss suddenly looked old, fragile and frightened.

Jinty dumped her armful of bed linen down and sat on the bed, putting a comforting arm about her employee's shoulder. 'Yes I am! He loves this place as much as you and the laird do, and if he ever has to choose between Molly and the Hall I'm certain he'll choose the Hall. Molly's not the right girl for him – or the right mistress for this place.'

'He loves her, and Rowena Chloe. We all love Rowena Chloe.'

'She's like a little ray of sunshine,' Jinty acknowledged, 'and a lot easier to love than her mother.'

'Hector would be heartbroken if we lost her.'

'You wouldn't lose her altogether, if she's Lewis's heir.' Jinty put a slight emphasis on 'if'.

'That's another thing; I'd love her to be my grandchild, but we don't know for sure, do we? And I doubt if Lewis would agree to one of those whatsit tests.'

'DNA. It could come to that yet, whether he

102

likes it or not. But that's all in the future,' Jinty went on briskly, seeing the other woman's eyes fill with tears, 'so let's stop worrying ourselves and get this bed changed. It's almost time to start making the lunch.'

'Not a word to Hector,' Fliss said as they began to strip the bed.

'Not a word to anyone as far as I'm concerned,' Jinty assured her.

When they got back to the kitchen Molly was down on her knees, playing with her daughter and Muffin, the Ralston-Kerrs' large and very hairy mongrel.

'Gran,' Rowena Chloe squealed, rushing to Fliss, who picked her up and hugged her. Molly sat back on her heels and watched the two of them, smiling, while Muffin, feeling left out, bounded over to Jinty to be petted.

It made a pretty picture for Hector to see as he emerged from the pantry, where he had been reading the newspaper in blissful solitude.

Eleven

'It's been such a perfect week, but now I feel like the condemned man eating his last meal,' Clarissa said sadly. Alastair had moved the small kitchen table outside so that they could have breakfast in the warm July air; the sky was blue, with only a few cotton-wool clouds and the sun made the loch, only yards away from where they sat, sparkle as though strewn with diamonds. A light breeze rustled through the trees overhead, birds sang and bees buzzed around the tiny flower-packed garden where they sat.

'Me too. No regrets, then?'

'Only that I wasted so much time facing the truth. This week has been the happiest in my entire life, thanks to you.'

'My pleasure, ma'am.' He reached across the table to touch her hand. 'My very great pleasure. And there'll be other weeks – lots of them.'

'I'll drop you off at Balloch and you can get a train into Glasgow from there.'

'D'you want the last piece of toast?' Alastair asked, and when she shook her head, he picked it up and began to butter it. 'No need to stop in Balloch, I managed to get two weeks off, so I'm going to Prior's Ford with you.'

'To Prior's Ford? To *Willow Cottage*?' Clarissa's voice shot up an octave.

'Your home would be more comfortable than the farm cottage I lived in – which I no longer pay rent on, incidentally – so it has to be Willow Cottage.' Alastair bit into his toast.

'But you can't stay with me! People will find out that...'

'That we're a couple? Clarissa, the time's come for everyone to know the truth. We've got nothing to hide.'

'I don't know if I'm ready for this,' she said feebly.

'No need to be scared. Yes, there's going to be talk, but who cares? The only person who ever frightened me was Ivy McGowan, the woman with a tongue as sharp as a Samurai's sword, but Ivy's gone. I think you'll find that most of the villagers will look on us as a three-day wonder and then wish us well. Even if they don't wish us well, who cares? So let's get it over with, shall we?'

Clarissa swallowed hard, then nodded. 'I suppose you're right. We've got to face the world some time.'

'And we'll do it together. Well begun, half done,' Alastair said cheerfully. 'More toast?'

Lewis was less than happy as he drove home from Dumfries after seeing Molly off at the bus station. They'd had a blazing row over his refusal to even consider the possibility of selling

Linn Hall once he inherited it, and although they had both made the effort to appear happy in front of the others, she had spent the journey in an angry silence.

'Kiss Weena for me every day and tell her that Mummy loves her to bits,' she said as she boarded the bus. Then she found a seat on the opposite side and all he saw as the bus pulled out was the back of her red head.

The sun was shining, but he drove home feeling that a heavy cloud hovered above his shabby old car. When they first fell in love she had seemed excited at the thought of being the next mistress of Linn Hall, but now her change of attitude to the home he loved and never wanted to leave horrified him.

If they could only hold on for a few more years, each free to pursue their own interests, surely she would begin to understand his point of view, he told himself. In another two years Rowena Chloe would be ready for primary school, and Lewis hoped that, like him, she would attend the village school. By then, if the bank continued to stand by them, the house and estate could well be completely refurbished and making enough money to pay off the loans and provide them with a decent lifestyle.

With any luck Molly would have sown her wild oats by then and be ready to settle down as a wife and mother, with no more talk of selling his family home. They would be a proper family at last.

The cloud began to lift, then came down again

when he recalled a single sheet of writing paper folded until it was an eighth of its original size and hidden at the back of a drawer in his bedroom where nobody would find it.

During the previous year the village had been swept by a series of poison pen letters that had caused a lot of grief and anger. The letters had stopped once local minister Naomi Hennessey spoke of them during a Sunday service, and nobody had found out who the writer was. Lewis had received a letter, and he had read it so often that he knew it off by heart.

'A fool and his money are soon parted. You should ask that flighty girlfriend of yours for proof that you're the wee one's true father. Most of the village think otherwise. There's talk going round and it's time you either made it all legal or called an end to it.'

He had told no one about it, but had read the few words so often that they were burned into his brain and refused to go away. If Molly would only marry him it would surely stop any village chatter. But he knew that that was like papering over cracks. The main problem was the hint that he may not be Rowena Chloe's father and the best way to deal with that was to speak to Molly. Once or twice since the letter arrived he had almost summoned up the courage to do just that, but if she refused to give him a straight answer he would then have to revert to a DNA test. He couldn't bear the prospect of it. Perhaps, a tiny voice whispered somewhere in the recesses of his mind, he was afraid to seek the truth in case he discovered that the child he adored wasn't his.

'Shut up!' he said aloud, and saw that his fingers gripped the steering wheel so tightly that the knuckles gleamed bone-white.

His black thoughts began to melt away as he neared Linn Hall. The stone pillars on either side of the entrance had been repointed and now that the shrubbery was trimmed back the long avenue leading to the house looked wider. The Hall itself was recovering its original appearance too; the golden stonework glowed softly in the sunlight and the wide gravel sweep before the house was weed-free for the first time in years.

Following a lifetime's habit, he drove along the side of the house, making for the kitchen entrance.

Ginny and Rowena Chloe were coming out of the kitchen garden when he stopped the car in the stable yard, both carrying baskets and accompanied by Muffin.

'Daddy!' Rowena Chloe launched herself at him as he got out of the car. 'Look what I got for your dinner!' She held the basket up to display some tomatoes.

'That looks good.' He scooped her up, hugging her to him, relishing the feel of her sturdy little body and the smell of her soft curly hair. 'Yes, I see you, Muffin, but you're too big to pick up.'

'Come here, Muffin,' Ginny ordered. 'Rowena Chloe's been helping me to get vegetables for

108

the kitchen. She picked those tomatoes all by herself.'

'In the polywobble,' the little girl added.

'You were in the polytunnel? Good girl.' He kissed her sun-warmed cheek and smiled at Ginny. 'Thanks for keeping her busy.'

'She's great company.'

As he led the way into the kitchen and set Rowena Chloe on her feet it occurred to him that his life would be perfect if only Molly loved Linn Hall as much as Ginny did.

'I'll book into the Neurotic Cuckoo for a week,' Amy said when Clarissa phoned to tell her of their change of plan.

'You don't have to.'

'Oh, come on, you don't want a gooseberry in your spare room, now do you?'

'It might be better if you're there as well as Alastair. I don't think I'm ready to face the village yet and I need all the support I can get...'

'No arguments, I'm movin' out, and you've got all the support you need 'cos I won't be far away. OK?'

'I suppose so.'

'Clarissa...'

'Yes?'

'Good for you!'

Amy had gone by the time Clarissa and Alastair arrived at Willow Cottage that evening, leaving a note on the kitchen table: *Fridge and freezer well stocked, so you don't even have to go out if you don't want to. Stella's invited me to stay with her for the next week.'*

The house was filled with flowers, rose petals had been scattered lavishly over the bed in Clarissa's room, and a bottle of champagne awaited them in the refrigerator, a white bow tied around its neck.

Clarissa awoke in the morning to the usual village sounds drifting through the open bedroom windows: birdsong, cars passing along the main street, children's and adults' voices. The bedroom was filled with sunlight, and she lay still for a moment as she always did on awakening, enjoying the sounds of home and watching the curtains lift slightly then fall back at the whim of the breeze.

She turned her head on the pillow and saw that Alastair was still sound asleep, lying on his back with one tanned arm thrown above his head and a lock of brown hair over his forehead. She longed to smooth it back, but didn't want to disturb him, so she got out of bed slowly and carefully, her eyes widening as she saw the clock on the wall. They had both slept late, but on the other hand the day was theirs. She picked up her dressing gown and went to the bathroom, her bare feet stepping on rose petals scattered across the carpet.

She had showered and was back in the bedroom, almost dressed, when his hazel eyes blinked open.

'What time is it?'

110

'After ten, and it's a lovely morning. I'm going down to start on breakfast now.'

He stretched a hand towards her. 'Later.'

'I'm starving. Time you got up.' She leaned over to kiss him then went downstairs, hoping that they might manage to stay out of sight in the cottage and the garden for the day.

It was a vain hope. Alastair was still upstairs when the doorbell rang. Clarissa started to leave the kitchen then hesitated, biting her lower lip. If she stayed where she was and Alastair stayed where *he* was, the person at the door might go away.

The bell rang again and it occurred to her that it could be a delivery, or perhaps Amy, reluctant to use the key she had. And if she did nothing, Alastair might come down to find out what was going on, which would be worse.

So she went into the hall and opened the door, then stared in disbelief at the caller standing on the doorstep.

'At last! I was beginning to wonder where on earth you were. Did you get my phone message?' asked Alexandra. 'Obviously,' she went on as her stepmother said nothing, 'you didn't get it.'

She advanced into the hall, driving Clarissa before her, and put her small suitcase down before picking up the phone and listening. 'It got through all right.' She stabbed at a number before holding the receiver out to Clarissa.

'Clarissa, it's me.' Her crisp, unmistakable voice crackled briskly down the line. 'I'm

111

attending a four-day conference in Edinburgh, standing in for a colleague at the last minute, and it ends tonight. I don't have to be back at work until Monday so I thought I'd fit in a day or two with you before going home. I should arrive mid-morning tomorrow.' Then, as a bell rang and a surge of voices was heard in the background. 'Must go, see you tomorrow.'

'I was out yesterday. I must have forgotten to check for messages,' Clarissa heard herself say as she put the phone down. Absurdly, she recalled a T-shirt she had once seen in a shop window, showing a cartoon mouse crowded into a corner and menaced by the looming shadow of a cat. Now she knew just how the mouse felt.

'You should get a mobile, they're very useful.' Alexandra picked up her case. 'I'll take this up to the spare room.'

She had set one foot on the stairs when Alastair called from above, 'Fancy a Buck's Fizz before breakfast? There's still some champagne left.' Then, appearing at the top of the stairs: 'Oh, I didn't realize we had a visitor. Hello, Alexandra.'

She took time to look him over, from his tousled hair, still wet from the shower, to the towel looped about his neck, his open shirt, jeans, and down to bare, bony feet, then turned to Clarissa. 'Just what is going on here?' Her voice was level, her face stony.

'Alastair's staying with me for a few days,' Clarissa's voice sounded rusty to her own ears, but strengthened as he continued down the stairs towards her. 'Staying ... *with* me, which means that the spare room is available and you're welcome to use it, of course.'

Alexandra, normally very quick on the uptake, blinked at her. 'The spare room's available? But...' And then her eyes widened. 'You don't mean ... you can't possibly mean that the two of you...'

Alastair was at the bottom of the stairs, reaching out to drape an arm about Clarissa's shoulders. 'The two of us,' he said blithely, 'are an item and very happy about it, aren't we, darling?'

His touch gave her the strength to say, 'Yes, *very* happy about it.'

'Oh my God...'

'There's enough champagne for three glasses of Buck's Fizz if you'd like to join us for breakfast.'

'No ... this can't be real!' said Alexandra, backing away from them towards the front door as though they were contaminated. 'It *can't* be!'

Twelve

'You knew that Alexandra of all people would find this hard to take,' Alastair said as they stood at the living-room window, watching Clarissa's stepdaughter throw her small suitcase into the hired car and drive away with a teeth-tingling crashing of gears. 'It was bad luck that she had to be the first to find out.'

'I'd planned to call Steven and ask him to break it to her. He'll understand, but Alexandra's so like her father. I just wish she'd given us time to explain instead of rushing out like that.'

'You were marvellous.'

'I was terrified!'

'But you stood up for yourself.' He put his arm around her. 'Facing Alexandra was always going to be your worst scenario. Now that that's over we can go out and face the good people of Prior's Ford together.'

'Perhaps I should phone Steven...'

'Let her break the news to him, then wait for him to get in touch with you. If she finds that you contacted him first she'll only accuse you of trying to get him on your side.'

'There are no sides!'

'I know, my love, but she might not see it that

114

way. Do nothing. Let her be the one to tell Steven. If, as you say, he's all right about us, he might help to cool her down.'

'You're probably right. But if we must face the villagers I'd like to start with Naomi.'

'Good choice. And tonight I'm going to take you to the Cuckoo for dinner. But first things first – let's enjoy our Buck's Fizz.'

'I'm pleased for both of you,' Naomi said warmly. 'And not entirely surprised to hear your news. There's been a bond between the two of you from the start.'

'You're not shocked? You don't think we're doing something wrong?'

'Why would I be shocked or disapproving, Clarissa?'

'Well, you're a minister of the church.'

'I'm still a human being, and in any case, the man I work for – or, perhaps, the woman,' Naomi added, with a grin and the suspicion of a wink, 'believes in love. You're two very nice people who have never to my knowledge judged or harmed anyone, and I believe you have every right to happiness together.'

'That's not what Alexandra thinks, and there are plenty of people who'll agree with her.'

'Again, everyone has the right to their own opinions, but equally, nobody has a God-given right to criticize others. We can hope that Alexandra will come to terms with what she's just discovered, but if she can't that's up to her and nothing to do with you. So, are you coming back to the village, Alastair, or is Clarissa moving to Glasgow?'

'I love living here, and Alastair loves his new job, so we're leaving things as they are.'

'Clarissa will come to Glasgow now and then, and I'll visit her here when I can. We've no intention of living in each other's pockets.'

'I see. I hope you're coming to the church service tomorrow? That's the best way to get the inevitable buzz over and done with quickly,' Naomi added as Clarissa began to shake her head.

'I don't know if I can.'

'Of course you can. You faced Alexandra this morning, and nothing's more frightening than that!' Alastair took her hand in his. 'I'll be with you.'

'So will I,' Naomi said, 'and I intend to help to make your path easier. See you tomorrow.'

After her visitors had gone she hurried upstairs to her small study, burrowed through overflowing files until she had located an old sermon based on 'love thy neighbour' and settled at her desk.

When her godson, Ethan Baptiste, arrived home from afternoon football he found her writing busily.

'What's for dinner?' sixteen-year-old Ethan asked, as he did every time he came home.

'I don't know yet. I'm working on my sermon.'

'I thought you'd finished tomorrow's sermon.'

'I did, but I've changed my mind. I'm reworking one I used a couple of years ago.'

'If there are burgers and frozen chips in the freezer I'll make dinner.'

'There are, but I tell you what,' his godmother said, typing busily, 'give me half an hour and we'll drive to Kirkcudbright and have a Chinese.'

'Cool!' Ethan said happily, and went off to organize a large cheese sandwich to keep him going.

'There's more to those two than friendship, if you ask me,' Gracie Fisher nodded at the corner table, where two of the pub's diners were enjoying a pre-dinner drink.

'Young Alastair and Mrs Ramsay? Don't be daft,' her husband scoffed.

'I'm tellin' you, Joe. Mrs Ramsay's glowin' like a youngster in love, and so's he.'

'But she's old enough to be his mother.'

'What's that got to do with it? Just because we women get older it doesn't mean we've lost interest in men – though most of us have to make do with dreams. But from where I'm standing I'd say that Mrs Ramsay's got more than just a dream right now.'

'Dreams!' Joe said. Then, with a sidelong glance at the woman he had been married to for more than thirty years: 'Do you have dreams, then?'

'That's for me to know and you to wonder about. Though to tell the truth,' Gracie confessed, 'any dreams I might have just now are all about our Alison. The lassie's pining for Ewan McNair and he seems to be turning away from her just when he needs her most.'

'He's got a lot on his mind, has Ewan, with all that's happened at the farm.'

'Alison could help him – she's desperate to help, but he's too shy or too stiff-necked to let her. Could you not have a word with him, Joe, next time he delivers the eggs?'

'Me?' Joe almost dropped the glass he was polishing. 'What could I say? He'd give her up altogether if he thought I was doing the heavy-handed father act!'

'One of us has to do something. I'm going to have a word with Jess – mother to mother. I'd best see how Alison's doing in the kitchen.' Gracie hurried off, reappearing a few minutes later to tell Clarissa and Alastair that their table was ready in the small dining room.

During her sermon on Sunday, Naomi concentrated on the many aspects of love. At its close she said, her wide, warm smile embracing each and every person looking up at her, making them all feel, as she always did, the special love she had for every single one of them, 'I would like to welcome a very good friend of ours, Alastair Marshall, back to the village. Alastair has settled into his new job in Glasgow, but he will always be one of us, especially now that he has a very good reason for keeping in contact with this community.'

'Oh, no!' Clarissa whispered, suddenly realizing what was coming. She bent her head, colour flooding into her face.

Alastair's hand closed tightly about hers. 'Hang on and we'll get it over with all at once,' he murmured. 'Good for Naomi!'

'During his short time here—' Naomi's rich voice flowed on – 'Alastair is staying with Clarissa Ramsay, and will do so on every visit from now on. I trust that I speak for us all when I say how delighted I am that Clarissa and Alastair have found love together.' Then, as a murmur began to spread through the congregation: 'Let us sing our closing hymn.'

'You could have warned us,' Clarissa said at the door, her face still burning.

'You've nothing to hide and the gossip will be over and done with by the end of the week. Bless you both.' Naomi gave her a kiss on the cheek then took Alastair's hand in both of hers as Amy rushed up to them, her face glowing.

'Well done, you two. There's someone I want you to meet.'

As she led them between the groups of people standing before the church, some, like Marcy Copleton and Sam Brennan, smiled at them as they passed while others, such as Cynthia and Gilbert MacBain, averted their gaze and lowered their voices. To Clarissa's horror, Amy halted before the MacBains, who were talking to strangers, a middle-aged couple.

'Good mornin', everyone,' Amy said cheerfully. 'Forgive me for breakin' in, but when we had coffee the other day. Laura, you said you were lookin' forward to meetin' my friend Clarissa.'

'I did indeed,' the woman agreed warmly. 'How do you do? I'm Laura Hunter, and I'm so pleased to make your acquaintance.' Then, turning to Alastair: 'And you're Alastair Marshall; I've been looking forward to meeting you as well because we have one of your paintings in Thatcher's Cottage – I saw it in Colour Carousel and fell in love with it on the spot. This is my husband, Allan.'

Allan Hunter shook hands, looking as though he would rather be anywhere other than where he was at that moment.

The MacBains had started edging away, but were forced to stop when Laura caught at Cynthia's arm. 'You both know the MacBains, don't you? They have very kindly offered to hold a party to introduce us to the local community. The last Saturday of the month, wasn't that what you said, Cynthia?'

'Yes, that's right,' Cynthia's mouth was in such a straight line that the words were almost posted through her lips like stamped envelopes.

'I do hope you can both manage to be there ... I know that you work in Glasgow, Alastair; but please try to come back on that weekend.'

He grinned at her. 'I wouldn't miss it for anything. Thank you, Cynthia – Gilbert.'

Cynthia couldn't bring herself to speak, but her head bobbed helplessly while Gilbert muttered, 'Yes – right.'

'What a friendly, welcoming village this is,'

120

Laura went on. 'Amy and I took to each other as soon as we met, didn't we?'

'Indeed we did, and we're goin' to see a lot more of each other,' Amy agreed. 'You'll have to excuse us; Stella Hesslet's expectin' the three of us for lunch.'

'And we must have a word with the minister before we go, Allan.' Laura took her husband's arm. 'That was an excellent sermon, so true and so wise. I look forward to attending this church regularly.'

'Why on earth did you agree to Mrs Ramsay and Alastair coming to the party?' Gilbert demanded as he and his wife were abandoned.

'I didn't – I don't know how it happened. How could I say no?' Cynthia wailed.

Steven Ramsay phoned his stepmother that evening to say cheerfully, 'You've got Alex in a real tizzy this time.'

'Oh, Steven, it was terrible! I meant to find a way to break the news to you both gently – why did she have to arrive this weekend of all times? If I'd only had the sense to check the phone for messages when Alastair and I got back from Loch Lomond I would have been prepared; I might even have been able to put her off...'

'Relax, it's no big deal; you know what a prude she is. It might have helped if she'd been forewarned, but I doubt if she'd have been very gracious about your news even then. Tell me this – are you happy to have Alastair in your life?'

'Of course I am!'

'Then that's all that matters, isn't it?'

'So you don't mind?'

His laughter flowed along the phone line. 'I'm hardly in a position to criticize anyone when it comes to relationships, my love. Dad never really got over me and Chris living together, and Alex still finds it hard, though to give her her due, she's civil to him when they meet, which isn't often. Chris and I are both delighted for you. In fact, we'd like to visit you next weekend, if that's all right – or is Alastair still going to be there? If so, you'll probably want to be on your own together.'

'He's leaving for Glasgow on Sunday, but it would be wonderful to see you both. Please come! I need all the support I can get at the moment.'

'Great. We'll leave early and be there for Saturday lunch. Book a table for dinner in the local pub. We'll celebrate in style.'

Kevin and Elinor Pearce had spent the weekend with Elinor's sister, who lived in Moffat, and knew nothing of the relationship between Clarissa and Alastair until Cynthia phoned first thing on Monday morning. When they arrived at the village hall for the Monday evening rehearsal, Cynthia was holding the floor.

'I think it's disgraceful,' she was saying. 'A woman of her age and a man young enough to be her son – it's not natural!'

'I think it's romantic,' Jinty McDonald disagreed. 'They're both nice people, and so happy

together. Didn't you see the way they were looking at each other yesterday after church? They
really are in love.'

'How can a woman in her fifties be in love?'

'You speak for yourself, Cynthia. I'm pushing
forty and I only watch *Doctor Who* because
David Tennant makes me go weak at the knees.
I fully intend to feel the same way about men I
fancy when I'm in my nineties.'

'Mum!' protested Steph, blushing.

'Well, it's true, but don't tell your father.'

'I think we all have to live and let live, and
what other people do is none of our business,'
Hannah Gibb said quietly.

'Unless it's something illegal, which isn't the
case with Mrs Ramsay and Alastair,' added
Charlie Crandall. Hannah and Charlie, both in
their early sixties, lived in the row of little ter-
raced houses that had once been the village
almshouses, and had become firm friends. They
had joined the drama group only months earlier.

'I agree with Jinty and Hannah,' Elinor spoke
up. 'I don't see that Alastair and Mrs Ramsay
are any of our business.'

'At the moment,' her husband broke in
irritably, 'our business is getting to grips with
this play. Time's short, so let's get started.'

Thirteen

Neil White's new home was almost ready. Carpets, blinds and curtains were in place and his furniture was due to arrive at the end of the week.

The kitchen was fully equipped and with Anja's help he knew exactly where each item of furniture would go. She had also advised him on the purchase of paintings, mirrors and a few ornaments.

'And now,' she said as they toured the house together, 'all you need to do is to move in and live happily ever after. Are you content with what I've suggested for you?'

'Absolutely. You're a miracle worker. It's been like having a fairy godmother to look after me.'

'Sadly, no. Fairy godmothers don't charge for their work, but I'm afraid that I must. When do you plan to move in?'

'Next Saturday.'

'I'll bring the account to you that afternoon.'

'How about helping me to celebrate the move on Saturday night?' Neil heard himself say. 'Dinner at the local pub?'

'That would be very nice.' She gave him a smile that made him feel as though he were swimming through a warm, transparent sea towards the shores of a tropical island.

It was a delicious sensation.

'This is certainly a cute little cottage you've got,' Amy Rose said as Laura Tyler ushered her two guests into the living room. It was simply furnished with two chairs and a two-seater sofa, all small but comfortable, a television set, a corner cupboard, a filled bookcase and two occasional tables, one with photographs, the other holding a vase of flowers from the cottage garden. A second vase of flowers stood before the empty fireplace; the room was bright with their colours and filled with their delicate scent.

'I loved the place from the moment I first saw it. It has such a peaceful aura, don't you think?'

'It certainly has,' Amy agreed.

'Tea or coffee?'

'Coffee would be lovely, thank you,' Clarissa said, and Amy nodded agreement.

'Won't be long.' Laura hurried off.

'She's such a nice woman.' Clarissa settled down in a comfortable chair while Amy went straight to the photographs. 'I like the way she's chosen furniture that suits the size of the room.'

'That's a nice wedding photograph – a really handsome couple, and they look so happy. There's one of her husband in uniform; he's still handsome, but he looks pretty severe too. Look at this,' She brought a large framed photograph to Clarissa. 'Laura told me the two of them met at an archery competition. If it was this one I bet he fell for her at first sight.'

'He probably did,' Clarissa agreed. The woman in the picture was clearly Laura; the all-encompassing smile was still the same though her shoulder-length hair was black rather than the soft pewter shade of today. Her short-sleeved top and trousers were white and an arrow quiver was slung around her slim waist. She was holding a longbow.

They were still looking at the picture when Laura returned, pushing a small hostess trolley.

'That should have been put away ages ago, but I like to look at it now and again.'

'That bow looks quite alarming,' Clarissa said.

'I've still got it in our flat in Leeds – I never use it but I'd hate to lose it. I started off in Scarborough Archers Club with borrowed equipment, then when Alan and I married he bought me all the gear I needed including my lovely bow. We were in Leeds by then, and I joined a local club and won quite a few contests. Happy memories! Sorry, I'm neglecting you. Milk and sugar?'

'Neither for me, thanks, I like my coffee black and strong.' Amy put the photograph down and picked up another one, a family group. 'That's you, isn't it? With your mother and your brother?'

'That's right. My brother's farming in New Zealand now, married with four children and a host of grandchildren.'

'You look so like your mother. Where do your parents live now?'

Laura's face clouded. 'My father died from cancer not long after I left school and my mother died fairly soon afterwards. I still miss them – her in particular. She was a wonderful person and a wonderful cook and baker. She taught me everything I know about food. When my first recipe book sold to a publisher I decided to adopt her maiden name, Tyler. I saw it as a way of making her part of my new career.' Then, briskly: 'But enough about me – tell me all about Prior's Ford.'

Alison Greenlees strode into the farmyard, swinging a briefcase. The kitchen door was open to the warm August afternoon and she walked straight in to find Jess McNair sitting at the table, peeling potatoes in a basin of water. As always, the room was filled with the smell of baking.

The older woman's face lit up. 'Alison lass, I was just thinkin' that I could do with a bit of company. Cup of tea?'

'Not at the moment, thank you.'

'Is wee Jamie with you?' Jamie often lagged behind his mother to study a dandelion growing by the side of the lane, stroke one of the farm cats or have a chat with the hens pecking around the yard.

'He's waiting for you at the pub, and so's my mother. You've been invited for afternoon tea.'

'Me? But I can't leave the farm just now! There's Ewan and Wilf comin' in half an hour for their afternoon break, and tonight's dinner to

127

get ready and—'

'You said you could do with a bit of company, and so can my mum. And I promised Jamie he'd see you soon.' Alison put her briefcase down on the table. 'I'm here on business.'

'What sort of business?' Jess asked nervously.

'The sort that Ewan's not going to like, which is why you'd be best out of the way. I'll make up sandwiches and butter scones for them, and I'll peel the potatoes and keep an eye on the soup and see to whatever needs doing for the dinner.'

'I'd need to get changed – and my hair's a mess...'

'There's time, if you're quick. Off you go,' Alison said, holding out her hand, and Jess meekly put the potato peeler into the girl's palm before scurrying to her bedroom.

Twenty-five minutes later she was being welcomed rapturously by Jamie and smilingly by Gracie Fisher.

'It's high time you took a break.'

'I don't like tae leave your Alison with all the work tae do.'

'She's not afraid of hard work, never has been. Sit yourself down.' Gracie busied herself with the teapot while Jamie clambered on to Jess's lap. 'She'd make a grand farmer's wife, my daughter.'

'I know, and there's nothin' I'd like more than tae see her an' Jamie livin' at Tarbethill.'

'Me too. She's mad about your Ewan, Jess.

128

Joe and me thought she'd never get over losing Robbie. They were so happy together, and we just couldn't see her ever meeting anyone as right for her as he was.' The Fishers had moved to Prior's Ford in search of a quieter life after Alison's husband, who worked in their Glasgow pub, was murdered by a group of young thugs he had thrown out earlier that night. 'We were so pleased when she started going out with Ewan.'

'So was I. He's not like his brother, he's the shy one but Alison brought him out of his shell. I'm sure they'd be makin' wedding plans by now if my Bert hadn't died.' Jess's voice trembled, and Jamie, concerned, patted her face with a small hand.

'I think that too. She's been breaking her heart at the way Ewan seems to have turned against her.'

'He'd never do that,' Jess said quickly. 'He's desperate for her, but he's watched his father bein' beaten down year after year by the struggle tae keep the farm goin', specially when Victor left, and he's determined that he'll not let the same happen tae Alison.'

'It wouldn't – she'd make sure of that. And if there's any way to get him to see sense she'll do that as well. Ewan might be stubborn, but my daughter can be stubborn too, when it comes to getting what she wants. She's determined not to give up on him.'

'What's this business she wants tae see him about?'

'Drink your tea and try a slab of that fruitcake,' said Gracie, 'and then I'll bring out the business plan she left for you to look at.'

When Ewan walked into the farm kitchen and saw Alison pouring tea into big sturdy mugs his heart turned a complete somersault and then began to bang so hard against his ribs that he was convinced she could hear it.

'Hello, Ewan.'

'Where's my mother?'

'Having a cup of tea at the pub with *my* mother. I said I'd stand in for her – she needs an afternoon off. Hello, Wilf.'

'It's you, Alison – mebbe I should take my tea outside.' The farmhand glanced from one to the other of the young people.

'Not at all! It's true that I want to talk to Ewan, but you need to be here too.' Alison's heart, too, was misbehaving at the sight of Ewan, now washing his hands at the big sink with much splashing, but as she'd had foreknowledge of the meeting she was able to cover it up well. 'I put a dry towel out, and I've made sandwiches and buttered scones.'

She waited until the two of them were seated before opening her briefcase. 'I've taken the liberty of drawing up a possible business plan for Tarbethill.'

Ewan had just bitten into a sandwich, and now he choked and spluttered, reaching hurriedly for one of the paper napkins Alison had thoughtfully laid within his reach. 'A *what*?'

'A business plan.'

'Tarbethill's no' a business, it's a farm, or had you not noticed?'

'Farms are businesses nowadays, and what I *have* noticed is that Tarbethill's a failing business.'

'It is not!' He banged a fist on the table, glaring at her.

'It is. If you keep trying to run it with only Wilf to help you, you're bound to fail, Ewan. I'm not criticizing your ability to work, I'm just stating facts. Two men can't keep this place going for long. It's physically impossible.'

'It's my land now and I'll be the judge of that.'

'Tarbethill,' Alison said calmly, 'has to be brought into the twenty-first century. It's happening to farms all over the country and there's no shame in it. Farming's going through big changes, you have to admit that.'

'If you're talkin' about sellin' off land for buildin' you'd best speak tae my brother. He's the businessman of the family, and look what it did to my father!'

'For pity's sake, Ewan, I'm trying to help you to save your land, not lose it. Look–' she pushed a set of papers across to him, and another towards Wilf – 'it's all laid out there. Farmers throughout the country are looking at all sorts of ways to hold on to their land, and I want to help you and your mother to keep Tarbethill going.'

'Would you like to know what *I* want?' Ewan pushed the papers aside and got to his feet. 'I want to be left to work *my* land *my* way, the way my father did, and his father before him. Why

131

don't you stick to pullin' pints an' mindin' your own business?'

'Ewan, that's no way tae talk tae the lassie when she's just tryin' tae help ye,' Wilf protested, but in vain.

'I'll see you back in the barn, Wilf, when you've finished.' Ewan snatched up a few sandwiches and a scone, pushed them into his pocket and grabbed the mug of tea before storming out, causing the hens pecking around the door to flutter and squawk in outraged protest.

'I'm sorry, lass, he didnae mean it the way it sounded; he's still missin' his dad.'

'It's all right, Wilf, I knew it would be difficult, but I'll get him to listen to me eventually.' She got up and fetched the big teapot simmering on the stove. 'Best to let him have some time to himself. But I'd like you to look through the papers I brought. I need to hear your thoughts.'

She poured tea for them both and sat nursing her own mug, watching his face as he read slowly and carefully, mouthing each word. Eventually he laid down the last page, took a long drink of tea, then said, 'You're askin' a lot o' Ewan, lass. Bert wouldnae like this, and neither'll the lad. He's set on runnin' Tarbethill the way his father an' grandfather did.'

'Farming's changed a lot since their day, Wilf. In order to keep things as they are just now Ewan would have to bring in more help, and we both know he and his mother can't afford to do that. If he carries on the way he's going at the moment he'll work himself to death and that won't solve anything. My plan doesn't involve getting rid of any land, just putting it to better use and making it earn its keep.'

'I suppose so,' Wilf agreed doubtfully. He stuffed half a scone into his mouth and helped it on its way by draining his mug, then pushed his chair back. 'I'd best go, we've got a power of work to get through before dark.'

'Take the plan with you and have another read at it tonight. If you think it might work, you could try talking to Ewan about it.'

'Aye.' The farmhand's voice was heavy with doubt as he folded the two pages and stuffed them into the pocket of his overalls. He made for the door then turned to say awkwardly, looking everywhere but at Alison, 'I'm awful sorry, lass, about the way young Ewan's taken against ye. It's all outward show, ye know, just because he cannae see himself makin' enough from the farm tae consider marriage. I've known him since he was born and I can tell that it's tearin' him tae bits – that, an' losin' his father the way he did. He's a good lad and I wouldnae want ye tae think he doesnae care for ye, because he does.'

She smiled warmly at him. 'I know that, Wilf, I've not given up on him.'

'Good,' he said, and left.

As soon as he was out of the door Alison's smile disappeared and without warning tears filled her eyes then overflowed. She grabbed a handy dish-towel and buried her face in it.

In the barn, Ewan was sitting on a bale of hay,

staring out into the yard but not seeing the hens strutting around, the farm cat sunning itself in their midst, or the wall of the milking shed. All he could see was Alison standing in the kitchen, a ray of sunlight coming through the window to touch her fair hair, smiling at him when he went in. Then her wide brown eyes filling with hurt when he advised her coldly to stick to pulling pints and minding her own business.

Why couldn't she do as he wanted, and leave him alone? He had enough on his plate without her hanging around, reminding him of what might have been if only ... there were so many if onlys. If only Victor had returned to the farm when their father died; if only he had been content to stay on the farm in the first place; if only he hadn't talked their father into signing over the useless field across the road over to him; if only he hadn't then sold the land to a builder. It would have been so different if only these things hadn't happened. Their father would still be alive, the three of them keeping the farm going, Ewan free to marry Alison...

He was so caught up in 'if onlys' that he didn't notice Wilf's arrival, and jumped when the older man touched his shoulder.

'Ewan—'

'Not a word,' he said savagely. 'I'm not in the mood for talkin'. Come on, we've got work to do – we've wasted enough time as it is!'

Fourteen

Early on Saturday afternoon Neil drove through the entrance to Clover Park, pressed the button that opened the garage door, and parked his car.

He took two suitcases from the boot and carried them to the house. His very own place, he thought with pleasure as he unlocked the front door. No more being squashed into his brother's tiny spare room. A swift memory of the home he had shared with Gloria stabbed at him like a jolt of toothache, but he managed to push it away. This was his bachelor pad, his retreat. This was where his life was going to change for the better.

Half an hour later he had hung his clothes in the built-in wardrobe and packed shirts and socks neatly into the drawers. Going out to collect another case from the car he called a cheery: 'Afternoon,' to a man passing by his gate.

'Good afternoon to you. Just moving in?'

'I am.'

'The wife and I've been here for two weeks. Nice place. We must have a neighbours' get together some time soon,' the man said. As he went on his way a car came along, heading towards the entrance; Neil, filled with the joyous prospect of a new life with new friends, raised a hand in a neighbourly greeting then froze. He knew that car. It screeched to a sudden stop outside his gate and the driver was out almost before the wheels had stopped moving.

'Neil! What are you doing here?' his wife snapped.

'I live here.' He indicated the house. 'What are you...' Then he stopped, a dreadful suspicion beginning to form. 'You haven't bought one, have you? Not here, in Clover Park?'

'I've just got the keys for Number Nine. That's why Mum and I are here, measuring for the curtains. This is awful! Why didn't you tell me you were thinking of moving into this estate?'

'I didn't expect you to be interested in my plans. And you didn't tell me that *you* were considering this place.'

'Why should I? We're not living in each other's pockets any more – thank goodness.'

'My point exactly.'

'You'll have to leave.'

'In your dreams! First in stays, and I've already moved in. *You* leave.'

'You've spoiled enough of my life and I'm not letting you spoil any more. I *will not* start looking for another house,' Gloria said through gritted teeth.

'I don't see anything wrong with us being neighbours.'

'It's out of the question!'

136

'It'll make it easier when we have to drive in to work together,' Neil was pointing out when the passenger door of Gloria's car opened and a voice called:

'Hello, Neil, how lovely to see you!' Rosemary Frost was a svelte, older edition of her daughter but with silver-grey hair feather-cut in a style that took years off her age. 'I thought it was you! I said to Gloria, isn't that Neil, and she braked so hard that I really thought the air bag was going to blow up in my face,' she went on as she hurried into the garden to kiss him.

'Hello, Rosemary.' Neil hugged her. He had been told once that a man should always check out his intended bride's mother before taking the plunge, and he had adored Rosemary from their first meeting. Unfortunately, although Gloria had her mother's looks, her temperament came from her father, a man who could be quite difficult at times.

'Don't tell me that you live in this nice little estate!'

'Moved in today.'

'Isn't that a coincidence?' Rosemary said, and then, to her daughter: 'Or is it?'

'Of course it's a coincidence – it's bad enough having to work with him without living practically next door to him!'

'You're looking well, Neil.'

'We ought to be going, Mother, I have a lot to do,' Gloria said from the pavement.

'It's exciting, isn't it, moving into a new home. I hope that you'll be very happy here.

137

You and Gloria both,' Rosemary said with heavy meaning, looking deep into his eyes. She had been as upset as Neil when Gloria decided that marriage wasn't for her, and her straight gaze told him clearly that she hoped things would change. 'So convenient,' she added now.

'What on earth do you mean by that?' her daughter wanted to know.

'Only that you can continue to travel to and from work together as before.'

'That's what I was just saying.'

'I gather that you still want to keep your ... estrangement ... from your colleagues, darling,' Rosemary was continuing innocently when a little green car turned in from the main road and drew up almost bonnet to bonnet with Gloria's.

Anja bounced out, calling, 'Hello, Neil!'

She reached into the car, displaying an attractively rounded backside garbed in a brief grass-green skirt, emerged clasping a large bouquet and trotted into the garden. 'For you; a welcome to Prior's Ford.'

'Thanks.' As he took the flowers she went on tiptoe so that she could pull his head down towards hers and kiss him on the cheek.

'And I see that you are making friends already!'

Gloria had insisted before they married on retaining her own surname for professional purposes, which made it possible for Neil to introduce her as Sergeant Frost, a colleague. 'And her mother, Mrs Frost.'

'Hello, hello,' Anja said cheerfully, while

138

Gloria stared at Neil, her eyebrows question marks above icy blue eyes.

'This is Anja Jacobsen, a local interior decorator. She helped me with the things for the house.'

'Really? Now isn't that interesting, Gloria? My daughter's just bought Number Nine.'

'Ah! So you might want my help? Here is my card.'

Gloria almost snatched the piece of pasteboard from the other girl's hand, today tipped with green nail polish. 'Mother, we *have* to *go*!'

'Not on my account, please, I have things to do.' Anja ran lightly back to her car, calling over her shoulder as she opened the driver's door, 'See you tonight, Neil.' She jumped in, started the engine, and blew him a kiss as she drove off.

'What a pretty girl. Scandinavian, is she?'

'Norwegian. She has a shop in the village. She's helped me tremendously.'

'You must visit the shop, Gloria,' Rosemary suggested. 'She could help with your move too.'

'I have my own ideas,' Gloria said coldly.

'Come and see round my house,' Neil invited. 'It'll give you an idea of what Anja can do.'

'How nice of you, dear, I'd love to...'

'I already have a good idea of what Anja can do, and we're running late. We must go.' Gloria headed for her car

'What a pity. Perhaps another time, Neil. It was lovely to see you, and I do hope we'll be seeing more of each other in the future.'

Anja, having driven to the top of the little

estate to turn her car, drove past, tooting her horn and waving.

'Mother!' Gloria almost shrieked.

'Coming dear,' Rosemary called and then as her daughter jumped into the car and started the engine, she added to Neil: 'She's jealous.'

'You think?'

'I know my own daughter, darling. Hang in there and don't lose hope. I haven't.' Rosemary winked and hurried to the car, which moved off before she had time to shut the passenger door.

Neil whistled as he carried the third case indoors and began to unpack it. If his mother-in-law was right and Gloria's reaction to Anja was born of jealousy, it must surely mean that she still cared for him.

He put a framed photograph of the two of them, taken on honeymoon, on top of the book-case, then found a vase he had bought from Colour Carousel – he had fallen for it because it was the same clear blue as Gloria's eyes – and unwrapped the flowers. An envelope had been tucked into them. It contained her bill, which was quite high, but as far as Neil was concerned she was worth every penny, especially if she was going to make Gloria jealous.

He made himself a cup of coffee and sat on the back doorstep so that he could survey his little kingdom as he drank it.

'Your friend, the one who is moving into Clover Park also, might be interested in the drama group,' Anja suggested that evening over dinner

140

in the Neurotic Cuckoo.

'Gloria? I doubt it.'

'She didn't look very pleased with you this afternoon. Are you lovers?'

He blinked at her, caught off-guard by the straightforward question, then said warily, 'We're colleagues, that's all.'

'Ah.' She raised an eyebrow. 'The way you looked at each other, and the way she looked at me, made me think there must be something special between you.'

'Oh no, nothing like that. She's got a lot on at the moment; she's just been made up to sergeant so she's having to work hard to prove herself.'

'That must be difficult.'

'Very difficult but I'm sure she'll get there. Gloria always gets what she wants.'

Once, he had been what she wanted, and she had reeled him in like a goggle-eyed fish with a hook in its mouth. Perhaps, Neil thought, it was his turn to try a bit of fishing, with Anja as the delectable bait. He might even enjoy it.

A sudden burst of laughter from the largest table drew his attention. They looked like a mixed bunch – possibly a family party, though it was hard to tell. There were three young men, and two older women, one of them particularly noticeable; small and with a shock of curly red hair. When she talked, which she seemed to be doing most of the time, her hands fluttered around like butterflies just below her pointed chin.

Although he was enjoying Anja's company,

Neil suddenly envied the group. It must feel good to be part of a happy crowd like that.

As Clarissa caught Alastair's eye he winked, and smiled at her. She smiled back, so filled with happiness that she could scarcely contain it all. Naomi had been right as always; following her revelation about them on the previous Sunday they had started to go about the village together, and although there were some stares and whispers most people seemed to accept them as a couple without apparent difficulty. And after Alexandra's shocked reaction, Steven's and Chris's total acceptance of the bond between herself and Alastair was as soothing as a good bread and butter pudding on a cold winter's night.

'What are you thinking about, Clarissa?' Chris asked.

'Me?'

'You were smiling to yourself so it must have been something good. Come on, share it with us.' Steven's partner was in his early thirties, a burly young man with cropped fair hair, a warm, happy nature and a square face that broke easily into a broad grin. He and Steven were a perfect couple, and Clarissa pitied her late husband, who had been too narrow-minded to feel comfortable with the fact that his only son was gay.

'If you must know, I was thinking that I'll never forget this moment, all of us together, and all happy.'

'Why shouldn't we be happy?' Amy asked.

'Aren't we all with the most fantastic people we know?' She raised her wine glass. 'Here's to the friends we never lose!'

'The friends we never lose,' they chorused.

Fifteen

'Ever done any amateur acting?' Neil White asked his estranged wife when they were on duty in the police car.

'Why on earth do you want to know that?'

'I've joined the village drama group. They're a nice bunch and I thought you might like to go along once you've moved in. They meet in the village hall, Monday and Thursday evenings. We've just started rehearsing for *The Importance of Being Earnest*. I'm playing Jack Worthing; it's the part I played in a school production when I was seventeen. A good play.'

'I didn't know you'd done any acting.'

'We weren't married long enough for me to tell you the story of my life.'

'We lived together for more than a year. I imagine we could have covered your entire life in a week.'

'As I recall, we wasted a lot of time arguing,' Neil said blithely. He was enjoying his new lifestyle too much to let Gloria bother him.

'As *I* recall, what really wasted time was being married in the first place.'

'So you don't want to join the drama group?'

'Not the drama group, the women's Rural, or

anything else. I'm too busy working and getting my house put to rights.'

'Need any help?'

'No thank you.'

'When are you moving in?'

'Not sure yet. So, is that Danish girl with the purple hair in the drama club too?'

'Anja? She is, as a matter of fact, and she's Norwegian. You should enlist her help with your new house. She's really good at it.'

'I'm sure she is,' Gloria said coldly, pulling down the visor and checking her blonde hair in the mirror. 'She seems to be good at so many things.'

'Don't tell me you're jealous of Anja?'

'Shut up and drive,' snapped Gloria.

'Remember the great times we had up here, Lewis?' Cam Gordon asked.

'That was a long time ago.'

The two of them, together with Jimmy Mc-Donald and Ginny, stood on the top of the hill behind Linn Hall, all dressed for hard, wet work in sturdy wellington boots, sweaters and jeans, and burdened with spades, forks, rakes and heavy duty gloves.

'Seems like yesterday to me. What a view!' Cam looked down on the roof of the Hall then beyond, to Prior's Ford.

Ginny's mind was focused on the work to be done. 'Once we get the rubbish shifted and the water running downhill as it should be instead of wasting its time up here, we could put in some water-loving plants. Eucalyptus is great for draining ground, and it looks pretty as well. But let's take it step by step. First we have to trace the original stream or burn or whatever you call it back to the Linn Hall boundary to make sure that it's only dammed here, within your property.'

'Lewis and I certainly made a good job of damming it,' Cam marvelled, eyeing the boulders and fallen branches piled across the original watercourse. 'It took us an entire summer holiday.'

'I'd call it more of a demolition job,' Ginny told him coldly. 'How far from here to the boundary?'

'About half a mile, isn't it, Lewis?'

'Might be a bit more.'

'Then we'd better start by heading towards it. We can leave the tools here, but bring the camera,' Ginny ordered. 'I want photographs of everything. Let's go.'

'Cool!' Jimmy disappeared into the thick undergrowth almost immediately.

'I wish we knew what it looked like when there were gardeners to tend the place,' Ginny said as they followed him. 'Can either of you remember what it was like when you played here?'

'I just remember a lot of trees. We should have brought machetes,' Cam panted as they fought their way along, their booted feet sinking at times into the marshy ground.

'And breadcrumbs to show us the way back,'

Lewis agreed. 'Remember the grotto, Cam?'

'Oh yes, it was great. It was everything from a besieged castle to a gang hut. Over in that direction, isn't it? I wonder if it's still there.'

'We'll find out once we've got the watercourse sussed out,' Ginny told them as the wall of branches and leaves before them rustled and then parted to reveal Jimmy's wide grin.

'This is brilliant; it's like being in a film about the uncharted jungle. Awooo!' he yodelled, and was answered by panicking birds.

'Ow!' Lewis said as a thin branch he was pushing aside whipped back to lash across his cheek. 'We're going to have our work cut out to clear this lot – is it really worth it? Who's going to want to climb all the way up here?'

'Lots of people, and it'll be worth it for the view alone. We'll create a stairway of big stepping-stones to make the climb easier, and have rustic benches in places where the ground's level enough so that people can take a rest and enjoy the scenery. Once this area at the top's recovered from your cute boyhood games–' Ginny paused to untangle herself from a long bramble feeler – 'we can have picnic tables. We'll have to cut back some of the big trees below to enhance the view. You're going to be so pleased with it once it's all completed, Lewis!'

To her relief it turned out that the main problems they faced were caused by the dam Lewis and Cam had created years before, together with the bushes and weeds that had taken advantage

147

of years of neglect.

'That's good news,' Ginny announced as Cam took photograph after photograph. 'I suggest that we start by clearing the blockage – not all of it at first, because there's no sense in letting too much water through until we're ready for it. I want to find out how the watercourse going down the hill copes. We'll probably have to clear the way here and there, work back from the pond in the rose garden to the top of the hill, then when we're sure that the water has a clear route all the way, we can dismantle the dam and start sorting out the marshy ground.'

'How long is that going to take, and how much will it cost?' Lewis wanted to know.

'If you can let me concentrate on it with four sturdy assistants to help, I reckon we could get most of it done before winter comes in.'

'I'll help,' Jimmy said at once.

'School starts in two weeks.'

'I can do evenings and weekends.'

'We'll ask your mother about the evenings because you'll have homework to do.'

'I reckon that our Norrie would help at weekends, and p'raps my sisters too, the ones that are still at school. 'Specially if they get paid for it,' the boy said hopefully.

'Again, we'll see what your mum thinks.' Ginny glanced at her watch then said reluctantly, 'Time to go back down. Cam, take photos all the way. I want to build up a good idea of what's ahead of us.'

'You've got a cracker of a girl there, mate,'

Cam told Lewis as they followed the other two. 'Worth her weight in gold. Anyone'd think she was born and bred at Linn Hall. She's daft about the place.'

'I know. We're fortunate to have her working here.'

Cam gave him a look that was half exasperated, half pitying. Lewis had always been a bit slow to notice things, such as the fact that Ginny Whitelaw was mad about him. And that she was more suitable for Lewis and Linn Hall than Molly could ever be.

Ginny and Lewis arrived back at the house to find Hector reading his newspaper and Fliss baking with help from Rowena Chloe, who stood on a chair with a dish towel pinned round her plump little body to protect her clothes.

'Daddy!' she screamed as soon as Lewis appeared, abandoning the piece of dough she had been happily slapping around and scrambling down, ignoring warning cries from all the adults, to rush to him.

'Hello, Trouble, are you making my dinner?' He picked her up and was immediately covered in flour.

'Yeth, caketh!'

'That's my favourite.'

'The postman brought an envelope for you, Ginny,' Fliss said.

'For me?' Ginny wasn't used to getting post. 'Are you sure?'

'Yes, but I'm really sorry about it, dear. I put it

on the dresser out of harm's way, I thought, but when my back was turned Rowena Chloe climbed on to the chair by the dresser and got hold of it. I think she was playing at being a postman, but unfortunately, by the time I saw what she was up to she'd posted it into Muffin's mouth. That's why the envelope's a bit chewed. I'm going to have to put the post on a high shelf in the pantry from now on.'

'Good idea,' Lewis said. 'This little minx of mine's more Tarzan than Jane. P'raps she's going to be a famous mountaineer.'

'I hope not, dear,' his mother said as she offered Ginny the damp and torn envelope. 'I worry enough now about the way she climbs everything she can find. I'd hate to think of her clinging to the side of a mountain; I'd never get a wink of sleep! I hope Muffin hasn't done any harm, Ginny.'

Ginny peeled the remnants of envelope free with a thumb and forefinger to reveal a large greetings card, covered with glitter. 'No damage done, it's only a birthday card from my mother.' The message was written in gold ink: *To my darling daughter, from Meredith Whitelaw. PS, I'm having a wonderful time!'*

'When's your birthday?'

'It's ... oh, today, actually,' Ginny realized with surprise.

'Why didn't you say? We could have made it special for you.'

'There's no need, really. My birthday's always been just an ordinary day for me.' That was true;

when Ginny was growing up her mother had rarely been at home for her birthday, and had depended on the current housekeeper to send a card and a gift, usually a large fluffy toy, in her name. Her absent father never remembered.

'That's terrible, Ginny,' Fliss was protesting. 'Everyone deserves a special day on their birthday.'

'But I've had a special day. We've had a wonderful time, climbing the hill and making plans for that area, haven't we, Lewis? And every day spent here with all of you is special as far as I'm concerned.'

'I tell you what,' Lewis said, 'how do you fancy dinner at the Cuckoo tonight? We could ask Jinty to look after Rowena Chloe for the evening.'

'You three go and I'll stay with the little one.' Dining out in public was an ordeal for Hector rather than a treat.

'We'll both stay with her. There's a programme on television that I'd really like to watch.' Owning a television set was still a novelty to Fliss, and she liked nothing more than being able to relax before the set in the evenings.

'It looks like just you and me, Ginny.'

'You don't need to, really!'

'I'd like to. I'll book a table for seven o'clock,' he said, and Ginny's personal cup of happiness ran over.

Sixteen

Dinner with Lewis – just the two of them, alone! And Ginny had nothing to wear!

She fled to her camper van in a panic, hoping against hope that she might just find something decent in her tiny wardrobe. But all it held was two pairs of jeans and a small selection of T-shirts and sweaters. She had only brought working clothes with her because all her time was spent at the Hall, with her social life confined to the occasional trip in the evening to the Cuckoo for a half pint of lager or a soft drink.

She groaned in utter despair. Why had her mother decided to remember her birthday this year of all years? There wasn't time to drive to a dress shop in Kirkcudbright. Then she recalled the only person in the village whom she could turn to.

Fortunately, Lynn Stacey was at home. 'Hello, Ginny, what can I do for you?'

'It's an emergency. We're around the same size, so can I borrow a dress in a hurry?'

'Of course you can. Come on up to the bedroom. What's the occasion?' Lynn asked over her shoulder as she led the way upstairs.

'It's my birthday and—'

'Is it? I wish I'd known. Why didn't you tell me?'

'Because I don't celebrate birthdays, never have. But this year my stupid mother remembered for once and sent me a card, and Rowena Chloe got her hands on it and posted it into the dog and the envelope got chewed up and then everyone found out...'

'I don't know what you're talking about. Sit down on the bed, take a few deep breaths and then try again,' Lynn advised calmly.

Ginny did as she was told then said, 'Sorry, but I'm in a bit of a panic. Lewis is taking me to the pub for dinner because it's my birthday and all I have with me are work clothes, so...'

'So you're looking for something to wear. Now I understand and I'm sure that mine will fit you.' Lynn opened the wardrobe doors and began to riffle along the hangers. 'Now then, I'd suggest trousers and a nice top because that's more you than a dress. Let me see...'

Half an hour later Ginny was wearing a black and white voile blouse in a patchwork pattern, over flared dark blue trousers, the outfit set off by a gold chain necklace. Lynn had even given her short hair a new look with the help of mousse and a brush, and found black strappy sandals that fitted.

'Is that really me?' Ginny asked in awe when she saw her reflection in the wardrobe door's full-length mirror.

'It certainly is. Sit down at the dressing table

and try this lipstick.'

'I never wear make-up.'

'A touch of lipstick won't hurt, and perhaps just a tiny bit of eye shadow to bring out the colour of your eyes. Some nice light scent, and then, Cinderella, you *shall* go to the ball!'

'It's not a date, Lynn, just a birthday meal in the local pub with my boss. And I wish he hadn't arranged it. I hate birthdays, always have.'

'That's because you've never had a proper one. You'll enjoy yourself, you really will. And I've loved playing the fairy godmother, much more fun than being a headmistress.'

Ginny was just climbing out of the van when Lewis emerged from the kitchen wearing a green and white open-necked checked shirt and grey trousers.

'Ginny? I scarcely recognized you in that outfit. Very nice! We'll go in my car,' he went on as she struggled to find a casual reply. 'All set?'

Looking back once she had returned to her camper van, Ginny could recall a three-course dinner with wine, but couldn't for the life of her remember what she had eaten. The food was unimportant compared to the pleasure of sitting opposite Lewis, being able for once to look at him directly without having to sneak quick glances. Drifting off to sleep, she recalled the way the light from the candle on the table had picked out red glints in his thick chestnut hair and made his grey eyes sparkle, the way his wide mouth lifted at the corners when he smiled and the way he tipped his head back slightly when he laughed. He had laughed quite a lot, and so had she.

It was late when they got back to Linn Hall. The kitchen windows were dimly lit, indicating that Fliss and Hector had gone to bed, leaving a lamp on for Lewis.

'Thank you for a very nice evening,' Ginny said politely as they stood together in the courtyard.

'No, thank *you*, for all the fantastic ideas you've had for the estate. There's a marked increase in the number of visitors this summer, and it's all down to the things you've suggested.'

'I've enjoyed every minute of it.'

'So you won't mind staying on into next year?'

'Try to stop me. I'm determined to get the lake and the rose garden pond restored to the way they used to be.'

'Good. Sorry we spent most of the evening talking shop.'

She almost said, 'Did we?' but stopped herself just in time. Of course they would have talked shop. What else was there to talk about? Although there had been the laughing, which was nice, even though she couldn't recall what had caused it.

'Well, see you tomorrow.'

'Yes. Goodnight, Ginny, and thanks for everything you've done for Linn Hall. Happy birthday,' he said, then bent, tipped her chin up, and kissed her on the lips.

It was fortunate that they were standing by the camper van by that time because the unexpected kiss, tame though it was, gave Ginny such a start that if she hadn't been able to grab the door handle her knees might have given way.

She hauled herself in and collapsed on to one of the benches, her heart pounding. It was the wine, she told herself, she wasn't used to wine and she must have had three glasses of the stuff. She'd have a hangover in the morning.

But when her eyes popped open at the usual time to find the van flooded with sunshine her head was perfectly clear. She was lying flat on the mattress with her arms wrapped tightly around the pillow, which, to her horror, bore traces of pale pink lipstick.

And when she looked in the mirror, she saw that the eyeshadow, which she had also forgotten to remove before going to bed, had given her blue panda-eyes.

'Oh – fish!' she said.

'So how was your date?' Lynn wanted to know when Ginny returned the borrowed clothes.

'It wasn't a date, it was Lewis being kind. And it was very nice, thank you. We got the chance to do a lot of talking about the work still to be done on the estate.'

'Did he tell you that you looked nice? Because you really did look nice. You scrub up well, Ginny Whitelaw.'

'Yes he did but he was only being polite.

Could you do me a favour? Mrs Ralston-Kerr and Jinty do my laundry for me and I don't want them to see this.' Ginny shook out the lipstick-smeared pillowcase. 'I'm not used to wearing make-up and I never wash my face before I go to bed. What's the sense in going to bed with a clean face when you need to wash it again in the morning? Could you launder this for me?'

'Of course.' Lynn took it from her. 'I don't suppose the lipstick got anywhere else, like Lewis's shirt collar?'

'Don't be daft!' Ginny's tone was withering. 'It was bad enough, getting it on the dratted pillow.'

'Drastic, but well worth Ewan's consideration,' Naomi said when she had finished reading the business plan draw up by Alison Greenlees.

'D'you really think it could be good for Tarbethill?' Jess asked nervously. 'She's talkin' about a lot of changes and I know that my Bert wouldn't have had anythin' to do with any of it, the same as Ewan.'

As always when she was caught up in a seemingly impossible dilemma, she had come to the Manse to seek Naomi's opinion. To Jess, the minister was the wisest, kindest and most trustworthy person in the entire village.

'I understand what you're saying.' Naomi put the papers down and held a large biscuit tin out to her guest. 'Take a chocolate digestive, there's nothing like chocolate for stimulating the brain. And have some more tea. Now,' she went on when Jess's cup was replenished, 'take a deep breath and then tell me what *you* think about Alison's suggestions. Not what Bert may have said, or what Ewan would say, but what you yourself think.'

'I'm not used tae business decisions; that side of things was always left tae Bert.'

'I know, but you were the only one who dealt with the hens, weren't you? You made sure that Bert ordered their feed and you looked after them and sold the eggs and kept the accounts for that, didn't you?'

'Hens are one thing and cows and sheep another.'

'How could you make more money from the hens, Jess?' Naomi wanted to know.

'I suppose we could buy in more birds and mebbe turn one of the sheds into a deep-litter house. Our Alice has one and she hatches some of the eggs out an' sells the chicks.'

'Could you do that?'

'Oh yes,' Jess said confidently, 'I like lookin' after the hens.'

'There you are then. That's an idea that Alison didn't come up with; you did. You were talking like a businesswoman then.'

'Was I?'

'You were. As I said, chocolate's great for stimulating the brain. Have another biscuit and keep talking. Concentrate on your opinion of Alison's ideas.'

Jess drew in a deep breath, then said in a rush of words, 'I've been turnin' things over and over in my head, and I know that we cannae go on the way we used to. Ewan cannae do it on his own with only Wilf tae help.'

'You're right.'

'I feel as if I'm betrayin' Bert and Ewan just by sayin' a thing like that,' Jess said miserably.

'Now you're wrong. You love them both and you want Tarbethill to keep going, in memory of Bert and for Ewan's sake, and his future happiness. That's not a betrayal, Jess,' Naomi pointed out gently. 'The farm's as much yours as theirs; you've devoted most of your life to it and you know as well as I do that if things don't change quite drastically Tarbethill could be lost. It can only be saved if it comes into the twenty-first century, like all the other farms. Clearly, Alison knows that.' She tapped the papers on the table between them. 'Ewan's intelligent; he knows it too, but he's in denial. He's hiding his grief and fear and despair beneath anger and he's working himself to death. You have to get him to concentrate on the present and the future, Jess, before it's too late for all of you, Alison included.'

'All that lassie wants is tae marry Ewan an' make him happy,' Jess said tearfully. 'An' it's all I want too, but it's as if he's built a wall round himself an' I don't know how tae get through it. Can't you try speakin' tae him, Naomi?'

'I doubt if he'd pay attention to me. I'm a minister, and while there are those who would say that I'm a shepherd looking after God's flock, that wouldn't cut any ice with your son at the moment.' Naomi picked up the business plan again and riffled through it before saying thoughtfully, 'No, I can't talk sense into him, and it's difficult for you. But I think we both know a man who can.'

'Are you talkin' about Wilf?'

'Not Wilf.'

'I cannae think of anyone else Ewan would listen to.'

'Oh yes you do, and you're going to show this plan to him and tell him you need his help,' Naomi said. 'I think that he'll be more than happy to give it.'

Seventeen

'This,' Cam Gordon said breathlessly as he and Lewis heaved at a large boulder, 'takes me right back to when we were kids.'

'Young vandals, more like,' Ginny corrected him. 'Come on, you lot, put some welly into it. We're almost there!'

'We're doing the best we can,' Lewis protested. Together with Jimmy and Norrie McDonald they were working on clearing part of the dam, every one of them soaked, muddy and thoroughly enjoying themselves. After three hours' work they had managed to clear some of the branches and smaller boulders damming the water that had once flowed downhill to supply the rose garden pond and the small lake beyond it, but had then been thwarted by the boulder wedged between what had been the banks of the stream. A sturdy plank retrieved from the material cleared out of the way had been pushed with difficulty down one side of the boulder and now the skinny McDonald boys were gripping its upper end in the hope of easing the boulder sufficiently from its muddy bed to allow Lewis and Cam to roll it aside.

'Ginny'll count to three, then you two put all

your weight on to the plank and try to lever the boulder up,' Lewis instructed.

'But be careful!'

'Ginny, we can't be careful *and* successful,' Jimmy argued.

'If anything happens to those boys, Cam, how could we face Jinty?'

'Nothin's goin' to happen to us,' Jimmy and Norrie chorused, while Cam said:

'But it's all right if the boulder pops out like a cork from a bottle and Lewis and I get crushed?'

'You were the ones who put it there. Jimmy and Norrie are innocent young boys.'

'How on earth did we manage to get it here in the first place, Cam?'

'I think we rolled it down the banking. It's easier to get a dead weight down the way than up the way, especially after it's had years to settle in.'

'I suppose.'

'Stop talking and start moving. One, two, and ... THREE!'

The McDonalds both leapt into the air, hanging on to the end of the plank while Cam and Lewis pushed as hard as they could.

'It's coming ... keep it up ... it's coming ... oh heck,' Ginny said as the boulder, with a loud squelching noise, was finally freed from the bed of the stream. Once freed it kept going, showering everyone with gouts of thick muddy water as it made for the lip of the stream and rolled out of sight to bound noisily down the hill.

The two boys fell backwards as the freed

plank shot into the air, the lower end narrowly missing Lewis.

'Omigosh!' Ginny clapped her hands to her face. 'You don't think that big stone's going to hurt someone, do you? Or smash into the stable building?'

Lewis spat mud out and wiped his mouth with the back of a filthy hand. 'It's a bit late to worry about that now, though I doubt it; it'll be stopped by all the undergrowth at the bottom of the hill, assuming it gets that far. Just as well, though, that we didn't try to shift it when the place was open to the public.'

'Look,' Jimmy pointed, 'the water's running downhill again!'

'Brilliant! Well done, gang. That's cleared as much as we need at the moment. The next step is to make sure that it's running down within the former watercourse and not spreading beyond the banks We might need to do some digging before we let it flow freely.'

'Hey, what do we look like?' Norrie asked, rubbing his hands over his face to spread the thick muddy water.

His brother did the same, then said, 'Commandos on a secret mission,' and they gave each other a high five.

'Now–' Ginny beamed at her filthy, sodden helpers, her own face as streaked with mud as theirs – 'let's start checking the watercourse all the way down to the bottom.'

'If you don't need us,' Jimmy said, 'we'll leave that to you and try keeping under cover all the way down. C'mon, Norrie!' And the boys vanished.

'I could murder a pint once we reach the bottom of the hill,' Cam said as the adults prepared to follow.

'I don't see the Fishers letting us into the pub looking like this. We're going to have to get washed in the stable block before we can even get a proper wash in the house. You can borrow some of my clothes, Cam–' Lewis slapped his friend on the back – 'and the first round in the Cuckoo tonight's down to me.'

While the struggle to clear the dam was being waged at Linn Hall the McNair brothers were walking together down through the fields to Tarbethill farmhouse, having spent the morning repairing a drystone wall. Since his father's death, Vincent had made a point of helping his brother and Wilf with the farm work whenever he could; Ewan had rejected his offers of assistance at first, but had finally had to admit to himself that an extra pair of hands, especially experienced hands, made a big difference.

Now he and Victor, like Lewis Ralston-Kerr and Cam Gordon, had almost regained the friendship they had known before Victor met Jeanette and decided to give up farming.

It was a hot day and the sun blazed down on them from the vivid blue sky. The animals in the fields they went through were enjoying a siesta and they themselves were more than ready for the midday meal Jess was preparing for them.

'I've been meanin' tae tell ye–' Victor finally broke their silence as they neared the farmyard – 'that me an' Jeanette are gettin' married on October sixteenth.'

'Oh aye?'

'Now that our house is ready there's no sense in waitin' any longer.' Victor and Jeanette were going to live in Clover Park. 'I told Mum the date when I arrived this mornin'. We're hopin' that you'll both be there.'

'I don't know about that. There's the farm...'

'There's Wilf, and I'm sure we can find someone tae give him a hand with the beasts for one day. Mum won't go without ye, Ewan, an' she's desperate tae be there.'

'Then Wilf can take her an' I'll get help with the beasts. I'm no' great at social things.'

'Nor me, but women like them an' women usually get their way, 'specially when it comes tae things like weddins. There's another reason I want ye there.' Victor gave his brother a sidelong glance. 'I want ye tae be my best man.'

'Me?' Ewan blurted. 'For pity's sake, man, why me?'

'Who else would I ask? You're my brother.'

'I don't know how tae be a best man!'

'It's easy. Jeanette's brother got married two years ago an' I asked him about it because I knew ye'd try tae wriggle out of it. You just have tae keep an eye on me tae make sure I don't take fright an' run away. You get me tae the church and stand by me and keep the ring safe for when I've tae put it on Jeanette's finger. That's all.'

Ewan halted, looking closely at his brother, then said flatly, 'Ye're lyin'.'

'How d'ye know?'

'I always know but I'm not tellin' you how.' Ewan started walking again. 'Ye're lyin'. There is more.'

'Well, there's a wee speech ye have tae make at the reception before ye propose a toast tae the bridesmaids.'

'I knew it,' Ewan yelped, and the nearest sheep raised its head and stared at them both with mild curiosity before slipping back into sheeplike meditation.

'I'll get her brother tae write a speech for ye, he's good at that sort of thing. Just one page. You can learn one page; look at all the pages ye learned for the drama club. Alison could mebbe help ye, the way she did with the play.'

'Shut up about Alison, she's not interested in me now that—' Ewan stopped short and took a running jump at a barred gate, vaulting it and setting off at a brisk pace down the lane leading to the farmyard.

'She is so interested in ye, though God knows why,' Vincent said when he caught up. 'I'm sure she could dae better than the likes of you ... or me. She's a right clever lassie, that one.'

'What are ye talkin' about? Ye scarcely know her.'

'I know her better than ye think, wee brother, an' if I didnae love Jeanette the way I do, I'd mebbe even be jealous of ye, havin' a girl like Alison.'

166

Again, Ewan smelled a rat. He stopped short and wheeled round to face Vincent. 'What's goin' on here?'

'Nothin',' Vincent said innocently, then, catching his brother's elbow in a firm grip: 'Nothin' here where we are; it's goin' on over there,' and he nodded at the yard.

Turning to look, Ewan saw that Alison Greenlees had arrived, briefcase in hand.

'What's she doin' here?'

'She's come for a business meetin'. No you don't,' Vincent said as his brother tried to pull free. 'You're needed.'

Alison was coming towards them, a tentative smile on her face, and Jess, Ewan realized, was standing at the kitchen door, watching them all.

'Ye've set me up, ye bastard!'

'It was the only way, wee brother.' Vincent urged him into the yard. 'Play nice, now. Hello there, Alison.'

'Hi, Vincent. Hello, Ewan.'

'Alison,' he said gruffly, trying to look everywhere but into her face.

'There you all are,' Jess called. 'Come on in, the dinner's ready. We're havin' it in the parlour today, so you two can hurry up and get washed in here,' she told her sons as they went into the kitchen. 'On you go while me and Alison take the food through. There's clean towels laid out, and clean clothes. And change your shoes, both of you.'

'What's goin' on?' Ewan demanded of his brother when the women had gone, laden with

167

big trays.

'Mum wanted it to be nice for Alison.' Victor stripped down to his underwear and turned both taps on at the big sink. 'Hurry up, I'm starvin'.'

'How come you seem tae know Alison so well all of a sudden?'

'Her parents invited me and Jeanette tae the Cuckoo for our supper last week. We'd a nice time, too. She's comin' to the weddin' with you and Mum.' Vincent plunged his head into the sink and came up spluttering and splashing water everywhere. 'That feels good!' He seized the large nail-brush on the draining board, rubbed it energetically on a big bar of soap and began to scrub his hands.

'So why would the Fishers invite *you* tae supper?'

'So's Alison an' me could go over the business plan she's worked out for Tarbethill.'

'You've all gone behind my back?'

'It was the only way, with you bein' so stubborn. Mind when we were kids an' I used tae dunk your head intae this very sink?'

'I'll never forget it. If Mum hadnae caught ye one time I'd have been drowned.'

'Well, if you don't hurry up an' get washed I'm goin' tae do it again,' Vincent said.

Eighteen

The meal seemed to Ewan to drag on for ever. Ravenous though he was, he scarcely tasted his food because he felt so confused. Part of him rejoiced in the knowledge that Alison was sitting just across the table from him while another part wished her a hundred miles away.

He tried hard not to look at her, but couldn't help giving quick, hungry glances at the silken sweep of her fair hair, her snub nose and the way her brown eyes crinkled at the corners when she smiled.

It was a relief when the meal was over and the dishes cleared away. For once, Jess left them soaking in the sink – though with a wistful backward glance – while Alison produced papers from her briefcase and spread them about the table.

'I've got things tae do,' Ewan protested.

'Wilf's managing. He's agreed to hold the fort for an hour,' Vincent told him firmly. 'Just you stay where you are. It's time you faced the fact that things have to change at Tarbethill if the place is to be kept going.'

'Mum and I can manage with Wilf's help!'

'You can't, Ewan,' Alison spoke up. 'It's far

169

too much for three people. You're working yourselves into the ground, and taking the farm with you.'

'We *could* manage, if you came back, Vincent.'

'D'ye think I don't know that? D'ye think I don't feel guilty for what I've done to you and Mum – and my father?' Vincent's voice broke on the last word and Jess reached out to put a hand on his arm. He sniffed, swallowed noisily, then forced himself on. 'I'll carry the blame for what happened to him to my grave, but if I had it to do again, Ewan, I wouldnae change things because I'm happy the way I am now, runnin' a garage for Alison's dad, and gettin' wed. Givin' my life tae Tarbethill would have made me miserable, so I did what I had tae do. I know you love the place more than I ever could but the way things are goin' you'll end up old before your time, and bitter from the sacrifice an' from watchin' Mum struggle on alongside ye. Let me have my say,' he added harshly when Jess tried to protest. 'What'll happen when she's gone an' you're past bein' able tae keep the place goin'? Who'll take over from you if you turn your back on marriage and a family? I'll tell ye who – builders!'

'Over my dead body!'

'Oh, it will be. Buildings like those built on the field Dad handed over tae me. That was supposed tae be a caravan park an' now it's a housin' estate. Even though I'm goin' tae live on it and even though I've made enough money from it tae marry, the knowledge of where the money came from sticks in my throat. I'll live with it, for it was my choice, but I don't want tae see the rest of Tarbethill goin' the same way. I don't want tae see the land kill you, and nob'dy left behind tae inherit it. That's what lies before ye if ye don't accept the need tae change – here and now!'

Ewan had been staring down at his hands, clenched tightly together on the table. Vincent was right in what he said. Who would inherit Tarbethill if he didn't have children to follow after him, as his father had, and *his* father before him? What was the sense of working to keep the place going if he was unable to leave it in safe hands once he had gone?

'Ewan?' It was Alison's voice. 'Did you look at my business plan?'

'No.' He threw his head up, glaring at her, having one more try, even though he knew that it was hopeless, at keeping his beloved farm the way it had been all his life. 'What d'you know about farmin' anyway?' he snarled, taking his frustration and misery out on the person he loved most in the world.

His anger cut into her like a dagger, but she was prepared for it. 'Nowadays, Ewan, farming's a business and I happen to know something about businesses. Since I came to Prior's Ford I've learned a little about farming as well, thanks to you and your parents. I've grown to love Tarbethill and I want to help you and your mother to keep it going. This–' she pushed some

171

sheets of paper, stapled together, across the table towards him – 'is the only real contribution I can make. Read it, please. Give me one chance!'

He glanced at Vincent, who looked back at him steadily, then at his mother, damp-eyed but trying to smile at him. She gave a little nod of encouragement as she had so often before; the time he finally managed to tie his own shoe-laces, on his very first day at school, and on the red-letter days when he mastered the art of hand-milking a cow and driving the tractor.

'Give me a minute,' he said, reaching for the papers.

He read them through once, then again with disbelief, not only because of the swingeing changes they suggested, but because they were so well laid out, so detailed and contained so much knowledge about the farm.

'Someone's told you a lot about us,' he said at last, looking directly at Alison for the first time.

'It was me, and before you explode, just listen for a minute,' Victor ordered. 'Mum's been so worried about you tryin' tae take Dad's place, and mine too, that she went tae Naomi Hennessey, and Naomi came tae see me. She doesnae mince her words, that woman. She told me straight out that even though I'd the right tae lead my own life, I still have a responsibility tae Mum and you and the farm. She told me about Alison's ideas and how it needed someone who knew Tarbethill tae tell if they'd work. Since you'd have nothin' tae do with them, Ewan, it had tae be me. So Alison and me went over them

172

together, and the lassie's got a good head on her shoulders. I think her ideas make sense.'

'But they're changin' Tarbethill from a farm tae a mess of bits an' pieces!'

'It would still be Tarbethill Farm, and the land would still belong to the McNair family, all of it,' Alison said. 'But turning it into bits and pieces, as you put it, would make it easier for you and your mother and Wilf to manage it.'

'Tarbethill's always been a dairy farm,' he told her obstinately.

'And perhaps it will be again, but from what Vincent's told me, for years the herd's been costing more money to keep than it's brought in. The supermarkets are killing off dairy farming all across the country with their insistence on buying milk too cheaply. Then there's the man-hours, milking twice a day; it's wearing the three of you out and you can't afford to pay for the extra help you need. If you sold off the dairy herd you could rent out the fields they're using at the moment.'

'She's right, Ewan,' Vincent said.

'Sheep are easier to look after and you could gradually increase your flock. The hens, too; one of the outhouses would make a good deep-litter house and provide more eggs to sell and maybe sell chicks as well. Your mother's willing to see to that side of things.' Alison glanced at Jess, who nodded. 'Selling the dairy herd would give you more time to develop the wormery. Once it's large enough you can sell compost, and fishermen would buy the worms for bait.

173

Those fields on either side of the lane would make ideal allotments. You only need to dig them up and partition them into sections, and you'd get a steady income from the rent to add to the income from the fields you let out. Sell off the machinery from the milking shed – more income – and perhaps you could rent that shed out as well. New, small businesses are always looking for accommodation.'

'You want us to fill the place with strangers?'

'You'd have the right to say no to anyone you didn't like. The busiest area would be the allotments, and they'd be down at the entrance.' Alison had suddenly changed from the woman he thought he knew so well – efficient, practical, but with an excitement in her voice and her eyes that made her all the more attractive. 'You have to make use of all your assets, Ewan,' she insisted. 'Look at the wonderful job you made of that little cottage on the lane. You saw that as an asset and you were proved right.'

'Even though me and Dad laughed at you for it. You did well,' Vincent chimed in.

Ewan looked down at the plan before him, then at his mother. 'What do you think?'

'We must make changes, son. It's the only way.'

'Dad wouldn't like it.'

'I know, but your Dad's time's by. You're the one in charge now, an' I'll stand by whatever you decide. I just want Tarbethill kept safe from the builders.'

'Time doesn't stand still, Ewan, even on a

farm.' Alison's voice softened. 'If you decide to turn those fields into allotments you'll clear the soil and turn it over with mechanical diggers. Your grandfather would have used horses and a plough, but that doesn't mean that you would, does it?'

'I'll think about it,' Ewan said, 'and have a talk with Wilf.'

'Do we have to go?' Allan Hunter asked his wife as they walked from Thatcher's Cottage to Mill Walk, the small private housing estate.

'It's kind of the MacBains to hold this party for us.'

'It's quite unnecessary of them, you mean. I didn't realize that buying the cottage obliged us to mingle with the locals whether we want to or not.'

'I know, but it'll be a one-off, I'm sure.'

He sighed, then said, 'I'd far rather be going to the pub for a quiet drink.'

'Me too,' Laura confessed. Then, brightening: 'Look, it's Amy Rose and that nice Clarissa Ramsay she's staying with, and Alastair Marshall. Thank goodness, it means we won't be arriving on our own.'

Allan frowned. 'You surely can't approve of an elderly woman living with a man young enough to be her son!'

'It's none of our business and as far as I'm concerned anything that makes people happy and stays within the law is acceptable. Hello, so glad to see the three of you,' Laura called out.

Cynthia herself threw the door open to greet the newcomers. 'Welcome, welcome, to our humble home,' she trilled as the Hunters stepped into the hall, then as Amy, Alastair and Clarissa followed, her face stiffened for a second before she managed another welcoming smile. 'You came together?'

'We met on the way,' Laura told her, 'and it sounds as though we're not the first.'

It was a lovely summer evening and the living room's French windows had been opened to allow guests, glasses in hand, to go into the garden. Gilbert MacBain was busy behind a bar set up in the corner of the room, and once the newcomers had their drinks Cynthia whisked Laura and Allan off to introduce them to Alma Parr, current president of the local Women's Rural Institute.

'She'll have our newcomers booked to give talks and judge competitions before the buffet's announced,' Clarissa murmured as she, Alastair and Amy wandered into the garden.

'I'm sure Laura will agree because she's a real nice person and she says herself that she wants to get involved in village life, but I don't see her stuffed shirt of a husband doin' anythin' he doesn't want to do,' Amy said dryly.

'To tell the truth, he reminds me a little of Keith, my husband. Although it was his idea to move here he wouldn't have anything to do with village life. I didn't even get to the church services while he was alive. I'm surprised that an independent woman like Laura Tyler married

176

someone like that.'

'And I'm surprised that an independent woman like you married the man you did,' Alastair told her.

'It was you who turned me into an independent woman, my love. I was a teacher then and Keith was the school principal. I was used to doing as he wished, and he was used to being obeyed.'

'Laura's husband was a different person when they met an' married, but movin' through the ranks and becomin' one of the top dogs changed him.'

'Is that what she told you, Amy?'

'It's more what she didn't tell me that was interestin'. Don't forget that I once lived with a cop myself an' I know how ambition and success can leech the humanity out of folks. I'm just thankful that my Gordon was content to stay on the beat,' Amy was saying when they came across the Pearces talking to Jenny Forsyth and her husband Andrew. 'Hello there. Oh, they've got beehives!' Amy took a gulp from her glass.

'It's Gilbert's hobby,' Jenny told her. 'The honey's very good; the village store sometimes has small jars of it for sale.'

'I hope it tastes better than this gin and tonic. I wonder if I can persuade Gilbert to put some gin into it. 'Scuse me, folks.'

As Amy headed back to the house she came face to face with Cynthia, followed, somewhat reluctantly, Amy thought, by the Hunters.

'Ah, there are Elinor and Kevin!' Cynthia

almost pushed Amy aside in her haste to get to the Pearces. 'You haven't been introduced yet. Elinor, you simply must meet Laura Tyler and her husband, Allan Hunter. Laura and Allen, my very dear friends, Elinor and Kevin Pearce.'

Just then Gilbert appeared, gin bottle in hand as he freshened up someone's drink. Amy Rose caught hold of his arm. 'The very man! Put a good slug of that into my glass, will you? I have sensitive taste buds,' she went on as he looked down his nose at her. 'It takes a lot of gin to get 'em to kick in, know what I mean? P'raps it's an American thing, huh?'

As he added a trickle of gin to her drink she happened to see the Pearces and the Hunters shaking hands. The two women were smiling and greeting each other warmly, but the men didn't seem to be at all pleased to see each other. They were both stiff and awkward, with only the minimum of eye contact, and only just touching hands before pulling apart.

It was, she thought, strange. Very strange indeed.

Nineteen

'Kevin is the local drama club's very talented director,' Cynthia gushed. 'We're doing Oscar Wilde's *Importance of Being Earnest* – a wonderful play! You must both come and see it in October.'

'I love Oscar Wilde's wit. I used to belong to a drama club,' Laura said, 'just small parts and backstage work, but I enjoyed it. Is there anything I can do to help?'

'We're in dire need of a props mistress, aren't we, Kevin?'

'I doubt if Laura would be interested in taking over such a mundane task, Elinor,' Cynthia chided.

'It's not mundane at all; I've done that before and enjoyed it, so count me in.'

'But won't you have moved back to your main home by the end of October?'

'We're planning to stay on here until the end of October. We're both in need of a few peaceful months, aren't we, Allan?' Laura turned to find that her husband, who had been by her side only a moment before, was no longer there.

'Allan? Where did he go?'

'He wandered off towards the bottom of the garden, where I keep my beehives,' Gilbert said.

'A fascinating hobby. He'll no doubt be interested in hearing about the ins and outs of it.'

He set off in hot pursuit while Cynthia said, 'It will be a thrill, Laura, to have you involved in our little thespian band. Won't it, Kevin?'

'Sorry – what?'

'Haven't you been listening? Laura's going to be our props mistress for the new play, isn't that kind of her? I have to warn you–' Elinor turned back to Laura – 'this play calls for a lot of props.'

'I like a challenge. The furnishings in Thatcher's Cottage are very basic at the moment and I love looking round charity shops and antique shops. With any luck I'll find items that'll come in useful for the play and then find a good home in our new cottage. Can I call on you in a few days' time, Kevin? I'll need to get a copy of the script and we should start discussing the sort of props you want as soon as possible.'

'Er ... yes of course.' He stumbled slightly over the words, passing a hand over his balding head.

Glancing at him, Elinor saw that his eyes seemed glazed. 'Is something wrong, dear?'

'No. Yes. I should have brought my Panama hat; the sun's a bit too strong.'

'But it's evening now and the sun's lost all its strength for the day.'

'Even so.' Kevin began to move towards the house, saying over his shoulder, 'I think I fancy a glass of iced water.'

'Oh dear, I hope he's not going to have one of

his headaches,' Elinor fretted.

'Does he suffer from migraines?'

'No, just headaches, but the way he behaves you'd think they were migraines. I have to go into the garden to cough when he's having one of his heads, no matter what the weather's like.'

'Dear Kevin,' Cynthia said fondly, 'his artistic temperament troubles him at times.'

'Was he an actor?' Laura asked.

'Amateur only,' Elinor told her. 'He was a journalist.'

'Though I'm sure he could have been on the professional stage if he'd chosen that as a career,' Cynthia chimed in. 'He's very good, and a wonderful director. We wouldn't have a drama club without him.'

'Do you act, Elinor?'

'Goodness no, I'm the wardrobe mistress; a seamstress to trade.'

'And what would we actors do without our wardrobe mistresses and our property mistresses?' Cynthia asked, taking each of them by the elbow. 'Come along, Laura, you must see our old-fashioned roses.'

'That's the last party I go to,' Allan Hunter said as he and his wife left for Thatcher's Cottage. 'I thought we'd never get away. You're making a big mistake, agreeing to speak to their women's group and get involved in the drama club as well.'

'I'm perfectly happy to take part in local activities, but you don't have to. We'll make it plain to everyone that you're too involved in your book to take on any commitments. And I'll make sure that you don't have to do anything you don't want to do.'

'I'll hold you to that. What a ghastly evening, and what a pretentious bunch!'

'Not all of them,' Laura protested. 'I'll grant you that our host and hostess are pretentious, and so's the man who runs the drama group, but he's perfectly harmless. He seemed to be a bit uneasy with you.'

'I didn't notice.'

Laura had enjoyed the evening and she was in a mellow, teasing mood. 'Perhaps you collared him years ago and he served time because of you. Then suddenly this evening he came face to face with the one man who could blow his cover, the dreaded Hunter of the Yard!'

'You're talking about *the* Hunter of the Yard, aren't you? The man who never forgets a criminal face?' Now that they were on their way back to the cottage he was beginning to relax. 'I don't recall that one.'

'He doesn't come over as the criminal type, does he? But he did seem to be uneasy all of a sudden.'

'For all we know he's always like that with strangers. Or perhaps he *is* guilty of something and coming face to face with Hunter of the Yard scared him. Wrong 'uns can always tell when they meet a police officer, even one who's retired and out of uniform.'

'I can't see Kevin Pearce as a lawbreaker. I

doubt if he could toss a piece of litter on the ground if his life depended on it. And being pompous isn't against the law.'

'It should be.'

'His wife's a sweet woman, genuinely fond of him, bless her. Anyway, most of the others are pleasant and I'm looking forward to spending time in this lovely little village. I feel,' Laura said thoughtfully as they arrived at the cottage, 'that I was guided here by fate.'

'Fate wanted you to give talks on cookery and help the drama group?'

'Why not? It just feels right to be here; as if I've been waiting for years to be summoned.'

'Good God, you're beginning to sound like some of the people we met tonight,' he said, and she laughed.

'No, I'm just seduced by the lovely evening weather and the blessed silence and the scent of flowers from all those cottage gardens. You never get to smell flowers in towns, even when you pass a florist's shop, because so many of today's flowers have lost their scent. The roses in the MacBains' garden smelled heavenly!'

'Fancy a good stiff brandy?' Allan asked, unlocking the front door.

'Lovely. Bring the drinks out to the back garden, will you? I'm going to walk round there. I want to listen to the river.'

'It'll certainly beat some of the claptrap I had to listen to at that party,' Allan said as he went inside.

As Laura wandered round the side of the

cottage, the high heels of her sandals clicking on the flagstones, she felt pleasantly light-headed, partly from the drinks she had had at the party and partly from an incredible sense of inner peace. Reaching the little patio at the end of the back garden she leaned over the old stone wall, listening to the soothing babble of the river below. Lives may come and go, generation succeed generation, but this river never ceased its journey, nourished by countless streams as it passed through town, village, and countryside on its way to the open sea.

'It must be lovely to be a river,' she said as she heard Allan put the brandy glasses down on the little table, 'always knowing where you're going, and that you'll get there, eventually.'

'Drink up,' her husband said, 'before the midges arrive.'

Clarissa, too, had enjoyed her evening, even though a few people such as the MacBains had avoided speaking to her and had given her disapproving looks each time they happened to catch her eye. And Alastair was jubilant because that day Lewis Ralston-Kerr had asked him if he would do a series of sketches of the Linn Hall gardens, recording the improvements.

'Lewis is planning to frame copies and sell them in the gift shop, and it means that I'll be coming back to the village most weekends.'

'That,' Clarissa said sleepily, kicking off her shoes, 'sounds perfect.'

'As long as you don't mind me staying here.'

'Even better than perfect. I'm going to have some hot chocolate. Want any?'

He kissed her nose. 'Sounds good. Did you enjoy the party?'

'I did, more than I'd expected. Nobody tarred and feathered me, or dragged me off to the village stocks as the scarlet woman of the village. You and Amy were right; we were a two-week wonder, and now they're waiting for the next scandal.'

'D'you know something?' Clarissa asked Amy over supper on Sunday. 'I'm not really bothered about whether people approve of me and Alastair or not.'

'Attagirl, you're learning. Why should any of us care about what folks think of us? As long as we've got friends we're OK.'

Clarissa nodded, then giggled. 'I was just thinking about what Keith would say if he knew what I've been up to.'

'From what you've told me he should be the last one to disapprove, seein' as he was playin' around with your best friend behind your back. At least you and Alastair are both free to be with each other. Nobody's bein' hurt.'

'Alexandra is.' Clarissa was suddenly serious.

'She'll come round, and even if she doesn't, she's a grown woman an' so are you. What you do's not her business. My feet are gettin' itchy, Clarissa. Stella's visitin' her friend's bed-and-breakfast place in Whitby early in October and she's asked me to go with her. I said yes, but I

185

feel like doin' a bit of travellin' on my own first.'

'I believe that Whitby's an attractive place.'

'It certainly attracts Stella. Remember last year, when she met a man who was stayin' there? I'm hopin' to meet him.'

'Will he be there again?'

'I haven't asked.'

'Very discreet of you.'

'I haven't asked because I haven't had to. She went quite pink when we were talkin' about the trip the other day. If this guy's as shy as Stella they'll never get together properly, so it could be a good idea for me to have a look at him. If he seems right for her, I could maybe give things a bit of a nudge along.'

'I'm convinced that you were a matchmaker in a previous life.'

'Could be. Before me and Stella go to England I'd like a couple of weeks on my own. You wouldn't mind if I head off?'

'Of course not. You know that you can use this place as a base any time.'

'At least I can go away knowin' that you and Alastair are finally together. My work here is done,' Amy announced.

Alastair phoned ten minutes later to report his safe arrival in Glasgow and say goodnight.

'Anything happened in the few hours since I left?'

'Amy's going off on her travels for a few weeks.'

'I wish I was due some holiday time. Remember that cottage by Loch Lomond?'

'I'll never forget it.'

'We'll go back there one day soon. In the meantime, are you free next weekend?'

Her spirits soared. 'Are you coming to Prior's Ford?'

'Actually, I've just been invited to my parents' place, and so have you.'

'What?'

'They want to meet you.'

Clarissa began to shake. 'Alastair, I can't!'

'Why not?'

'They're the same age as I am!'

'So?'

'What if they don't like me?'

'They like what they've heard, and if they take an instant hatred to you I'll immediately whisk you back home in high dudgeon. I'm looking forward to showing you off to them. You'll come, won't you?'

'I ... I suppose so.'

'Good. Do I hear a yawn?'

'It was a cry for help, actually.'

'Go to bed. Love you.'

'I love you too,' Clarissa said, and put the phone down, convinced that she wouldn't sleep a wink that night.

Twenty

The letter was a surprise. When she was off on her jaunts Molly sent postcards regularly, usually addressed to Lewis or to Rowena Chloe if the little girl was staying at Linn Hall. They didn't tell much, just a few scrawled words such as, 'Having fun, great weather, loads of love,' with most of the message section taken up by as many cross-kisses as she could squeeze in.

She had never sent a letter before, but Lewis recognized the handwriting on the somewhat crumpled envelope immediately, and the stamps were Portuguese.

He and Ginny had been working on the downhill watercourse all morning, so absorbed in the task that by the time they realized how hungry they were, they were late for the midday meal.

'Look at us, covered in mud! We're going to have to get changed before we can eat,' Ginny said as they made their way down to the house in time to see Duncan and the backpackers return to work. After using the outdoor cold-water tap they sat on the edge of the trough that had once held drinking water for the carriage horses and was now filled with flowers, to haul their boots off. Then Ginny headed for her camper van to wash and change while Lewis made for the kitchen, where Jinty greeted him with, 'At last! We've kept your dinner hot but it must be beginning to dry up by now. Where's Ginny?'

'Changing in her van, she won't be long. I'll need to get changed too.'

'Daddy!' Rowena Chloe yelled from her high chair, where she was watching Muffin's long pink tongue lick up the remains of her lunch from the stone flagged floor.

'No hugs just now, princess. Daddy's too muddy.' He blew her a kiss.

'This letter came for you.' Fliss handed the envelope over, a slight frown between her myopic brown eyes. 'It's from Molly, surely. I hope nothing's happened.'

'Thanks, I'll read it when I've changed.' He stuffed the envelope into his pocket and went upstairs to the big old-fashioned bathroom between his bedroom and his parents'. The bathroom, with its temperamental cistern, stiff squeaky taps and huge stained claw-footed bath was next on the list for upgrading, much to the three Ralston-Kerrs' delight.

Twenty minutes later, wearing a clean sweater and jeans and with his brown hair wet and roughly towelled, he stormed through the door leading from the rest of the house and walked straight past the kitchen table, ignoring shouts from Rowena Chloe, still trapped in her high chair.

'Lewis, your dinner...' Fliss called after him as

he reached the outer door.

'I'll eat in the pub!' He charged out into the courtyard, almost knocking Ginny over but marching on without a word. Rubbing her shoulder, which had banged painfully off the doorpost, she watched him disappear round the side of the house.

'What's up with Lewis?' she asked as soon as she went in. 'What's happened?'

'I don't know.' Fliss's face was pale, her eyes concerned. 'There was a letter from Molly. I gave it to him and he took it upstairs, then came barging down and out of the door without a word. It must be bad news of some sort.'

After she had eaten, Ginny, who had planned to return to the watercourse, went instead to help Duncan, who was grumbling over Lewis's unexpected and unexplained absence. Hector also volunteered his assistance, leaving Jinty and Fliss alone in the house, apart from Rowena Chloe.

Jinty watched Fliss worry in silence for a while before saying tentatively, 'I wonder if he's left that letter in his room? P'raps we should look.'

'In his bedroom? But we've always made a point of respecting his privacy, apart from when the bedlinen needs changing.'

'Mrs F, you're worried sick about him and there are times when privacy has to be thrown out of the window.' Jinty headed for the door that had once marked the borderline between the

190

below-stairs staff and the gentry. 'Come on, Rowena Chloe, we're all going a-noseying.'

'I don't think...' Fliss protested, then, ignored, she trotted behind them along the short passageway, past the narrow unused stairway leading to the former servants' quarters on the top floor, and through a second door into the large hall with its still-imposing staircase.

'Next year,' Jinty said as they ascended slowly in order to let the little girl climb on her own, one step at a time, 'you'll be ready to start work on the drawing room and study and library and dining room. I can't wait!'

'I can,' said Fliss, who loved the security of the kitchen and the butler's pantry, and was secretly terrified at the prospect of venturing into the larger rooms with their dusty velvet curtains and paintings of long-dead Ralston-Kerrs.

The wet, dirty clothes Lewis had taken off still lay on the floor of his room while the letter was on the bed, crumpled and abandoned in his haste to get out of the house.

Rowena Chloe, at home in this room, where her cot was in a corner, clambered on to the four-poster bed and began to bounce up and down while Jinty gathered up the clothing from the floor and put it into the linen basket. 'Straight into the washing machine with this lot, Mrs F. Aren't you going to read the letter?'

'It's ... not mine.'

'I know that you wouldn't dream of reading anything that's not yours, but Lewis is in distress and you need to find out what's wrong. Just

191

this once, you should read his letter. For all you know he can't bear to tell you what's in it, so he deliberately left it there for you to read,' Jinty added as Fliss continued to shake her head.

'You think so?'

'I do. If it's totally private you don't have to tell him you've read it, do you? I'll even empty the dirty clothes back on to the floor again if need be, so that he doesn't realize we've been here.'

Fliss picked up the single sheet of paper between thumb and forefinger as though fearing that it might sting her. Then, at an encouraging nod from Jinty, she smoothed it out and scanned the page.

The colour drained from her face and the page fell to the floor as she began to sway.

Muffin, who had followed them upstairs, pounced on the paper.

Jinty rushed to support Fliss and lead her to a chair while at the same time snapping, 'Drop that, Muffin!' in a voice that made the astonished dog obey, while Rowena Chloe stopped bouncing, her hazel eyes rounding with shock and her lower lip trembling.

'Daddy...?' she said in a small voice.

'Oh heck, sorry, precious, don't cry. I'm not angry with you, just Muffin. Are you going to be all right, Mrs F?'

'I'm ... I'm fine,' Fliss gripped the arms of the chair, resting her head on the high back. 'I'm not going to faint.'

'Take long deep breaths,' Jinty instructed,

192

scooping the letter up and putting it on Fliss's lap out of harm's way before gathering the little girl into her arms. 'There now, did nasty old Jinty give you a fright, pet? It's all right! Where are you going, Mrs F?' she added in sudden alarm as Fliss rose from the chair, clutching the letter, and made for the door.

'Downstairs. I think Hector keeps some brandy in the pantry.'

'So,' Jinty said ten minutes later, 'it's happened at last. We expected it, really. To tell the truth, I've been hoping it would happen.'

'Even so, it's still a shock. Poor Lewis.' Fliss took another sip of her husband's precious cognac. 'I hope Hector doesn't suddenly arrive in on us committing sacrilege like this,' she added. 'He thinks it's a hanging offence to drink good brandy from anything but the proper glass.'

They were all in the pantry, Muffin enjoying Lewis's dried-up lunch while Rowena Chloe was back in her high chair, being fed by Jinty with jelly babies as an apology for frightening her. Fliss had poured generous tots of cognac into two ordinary glass tumblers.

'You're going to have to tell him about the letter when he comes in.'

'Yes. Poor Hector.'

'Poor Lewis.'

The letter lay on the table between them, about ten lines written in Molly's schoolgirl hand with lots of loops. *'Babes,'* she had written, *'I have to*

193

tell you something. My best friend Janice is one of the people I came to Portugal with, and her brother Bob came along too. I've not seen him since we were at school. We used to go out together and it's been great seeing him again.

The thing is, babes, I've discovered that I still fancy him like mad. He still fancies me too and now he wants us to get back together and so do I. Sorry, Lewis, but I can't see myself living in Linn Hall and I don't think you can either. Bob and me have found good jobs here so we're staying on longer than the others. My mum and dad will collect Weena when they come back from Italy.

Sorry babes, but it's lucky I've changed my mind about us now and not when it was too late, isn't it? Molly. PS – xxxx to Weena from mummy.'

'No wonder Lewis blundered out the way he did. Talk about heartless! She didn't even have the guts to phone him.'

'I wish I knew where he is, Jinty.'

'Walking, probably, needing to be alone. Wouldn't you, if something like that happened to you?'

'What about Rowena Chloe? Are we going to lose her?'

'You still don't know if she's Lewis's daughter.'

'I hope she is because it would break his heart to lose her. And mine, and Hector's.'

'I know. It's a mess,' Jinty was saying when Hector called his wife's name from the kitchen.

194

'Oh no, drink up!' Fliss urged, but it was too late. The pantry door was flung open and Hector was looking in shocked disbelief at the scene before him: his wife and Jinty, tumblers in their hands, turning flushed, guilty faces towards him, while his precious bottle of cognac stood on the table between them, its contents noticeably depleted.

Ten minutes later he had read the letter and joined them, though insisting on drinking from a proper glass.

'What are we going to do, Hector?'

'First things first, dear. Where's Lewis?'

'Jinty thinks he needs to have time to himself.'

'You should probably let him be for the moment. He needs to come to terms with Molly's news.' Jinty glanced up at the clock on the wall and jumped to her feet, staggering slightly and catching at the back of the chair for support. 'Look at the time; the youngsters'll be in for their afternoon tea in half an hour and the dinner dishes haven't even been washed yet. I'm going to make black coffee for you and me, Mrs F, we both need it.'

When evening came with no sign of Lewis, Fliss and Hector began to panic.

'You start getting the wee one ready for her bed, Mrs F,' said Jinty, on the verge of returning to her own family duties in the village, 'and I'll phone Cam and ask him to look around, starting with the Cuckoo. Lewis has surely needed

195

something to eat by now, and something to drink too, no doubt.' She delved into the large bag she always carried and produced her mobile phone.

'Cam, it's Jinty. Have you seen anything of Lewis? He went off in a bit of a state early this afternoon and his parents haven't heard from him since then. They're starting to worry. Never mind what happened, just try to find him, will you? Start with the Cuckoo, and if he's not there, keep looking. And let his parents know as soon as you find him. No, he's not taken the car so he's probably quite near.'

She snapped the phone shut and smiled at her employers. 'Cam's just finishing his dinner then he's going to the pub. A pound to a penny Lewis is there drowning his sorrows, poor lad. I'm off home. Let me know as soon as you have news, and I'll do the same for you. And don't worry,' she added at the door, 'worse things have happened at sea.'

As Jinty predicted, Lewis had walked for miles until hunger began to gnaw at his stomach. Finding himself in a village far from Prior's Ford he had gone into a pub, only to discover, fortunately before ordering food, that he had no money with him. So he made his way back to his own village where he ordered a meal and a bottle of wine at the Neurotic Cuckoo.

Gracie was relieved when she saw Cam come into the public bar and glance around.

'Are you looking for Lewis?'

'Aye, he's missing from the Hall and his

mother's beginning to fret. Have you seen him?'

'He's in there.' She jerked her head in the direction of the dining room. 'Been here for ages. He had some food, not that he ate much of it, but he's drunk an entire bottle of wine and now he's having a pint. He's in a right mood; I've never seen him drink like that before. It's lucky we've not had anyone else in the dining room tonight.'

Lewis was hunched over one of the tables, an untouched bowl of trifle before him. When Cam sat down he looked up, scowling, then said, 'Oh, it's you.'

'I've been sent to fetch you home. Your mother's worried.'

'I'm old enough to be out on my own.' The words slurred into each other and Lewis's eyes had difficulty in focusing.

'Look at the state of you. How can I take you back home looking like that?'

'For one thing–' Lewis's forefinger stabbed hard at the tablecloth – 'my state's none of your business, and for another, who said I was going home?' A second stab of the finger landed in the trifle. He stuck his finger in his mouth, glaring at Cam as he sucked cream and jelly from it.

'I told her I'd get you home.'

'No right to do that. I'm sick,' Lewis said angrily, 'of people telling me what I should do!'

'So what do you want to do?'

'I want to strangle a man called Bob, tha's what.'

'Who's he?'

'I don't know! She's left me, Cam.'

'Your mother? She's up at the Hall, worrying about you.'

'Not her – Molly! Met someone called Bob. They're in Portugal together.'

'How d'you know?'

'A letter, thish morning. Doeshn't want to marry me any more. Doeshn't want to live in Linn Hall.'

'Ah. Let's go somewhere and talk about it. We could both do with some fresh air.' Cam got to his feet. 'Give me your wallet and I'll go through and pay Gracie.'

Lewis patted his pockets several times before admitting that he had forgotten to bring his wallet when he rushed out of the house.

Cam sighed, said, 'You'd better remember when you sober up that you owe me,' and went into the bar.

He returned to find Lewis sprawled over the table, trifle in his hair, snoring. 'Come on.' He hauled his friend upright and finally got him to his feet.

'Leave me alone! Leave me with my mishery!'

'You and your misery are coming outside with me.' Cam half carried him into the Crescent, where the fresh night air roused him slightly.

'You'd best come to my place and get yourself tidied up before you go home,' Cam said as the two of them began to weave their way along the pavement.

Twenty-One

'You've never done yourself up just to deliver the eggs before,' Jess said when her son came down from his room dressed in his only suit and with his normally curly brown hair dampened then brushed into submission.

'I'm...' He cleared the frog in his throat and tried again. 'I'm goin' to have a word with Alison.'

'About her ideas for the farm? What are you goin' to say?' she asked nervously when he nodded. 'Are you willin' to go ahead with them?'

'It's what you want, isn't it?'

'What I want is for everythin' to be the way it used to be, son, but that isn't goin' to happen. But I think Alison's ideas are worth tryin'.'

'So does Wilf. I don't have much choice, do I?'

Jess let out her breath in a long sigh of relief. 'I'm glad tae hear you say that. Ewan, that lassie cares about you, and about the farm. As she says, we'll still own the land and if things work out well you can start a new dairy herd one day.'

'Aye, I suppose,' he said, but without much hope.

* * *

Alison was polishing the tables in the pub's dining room when her father came to summon her.

'Young Ewan's brought the egg delivery, and he wants to see you in the kitchen,' he said, grinning. 'He's done up like a dog's dinner for some reason. A proposal, mebbe?'

'Nothing like that, it'll be about the business plan I did for Tarbethill. I'll just nip upstairs and comb my hair.'

'Your mother says she'll take over here to give you some privacy,' he called after her as she hurried out. Five minutes later she hesitated outside the kitchen door, taking a deep breath before going in. Ewan was staring out of the window, apparently fascinated by the view – a stack of beer kegs in the yard. He swung round as soon as the door opened, colour rising to his cheeks. Matching flushes, Alison realized, vexed, as she felt heat come to her own face.

'Alison.'

'Ewan, sit down. D'you want some tea?'

'Your mother already poured out two cups.'

'Oh so she did.' Alison would have welcomed the chance to bustle around the stove, but instead she had to sit down right away. So did Ewan, and they filled in several seconds making a show of insisting that the other take milk and sugar first before Alison ended it by briskly pouring milk and spooning sugar into both cups.

'How's Jamie?'

'Fine. He's playing with some of his wee school friends this morning.' Jamie was a pupil in the primary school now, and loving it.

'So–' Alison forged on – 'I take it you're here to talk about my ideas for the farm?'

Ewan swallowed a mouthful of tea and nodded. 'I doubt if it'll work, but Wilf and my brother and mother all think it will, so I'll have to give it a try.'

It wasn't exactly a vote of confidence, Alison thought, but better than a rejection. 'Good. When do you plan to start?'

'The sooner the better, I suppose.'

'The first thing is to take your dairy herd to the next auction. When's that?'

'Ten days' time. I'm no' happy about it. If my father knew he'd turn in—' He stopped abruptly.

'I know.' She dared to reach her hand across the table to cover his. 'It's an awful lot to ask of you, but while you've got the herd you'll not stop losing money. Selling them and the milking machinery will raise the funding to pay for the other changes.'

He jerked his hand free. 'Tarbethill's always been a dairy farm.'

'Victor said that too. He told me that the Tarbethill herd was always bred and raised on Tarbethill land, until the foot and mouth business put a stop to it. That's when the changes really began. The present herd's much smaller than before, isn't it? And all of them bought in. There haven't been Tarbethill-born cows for years.'

'I've said I'll do it, haven't I?' he snapped, getting to his feet. 'I'll have to go, there's work to be done.'

'Ewan, I want to be involved in every step of the changes.'

'It's not your worry.'

'Yes it is. You'll be following my plan; I need to make sure it's working, and pull the plug on it the minute I see it beginning to cause problems.'

'It's already causing problems – for me,' he growled, making for the door. Then he jumped and turned, startled, as Alison's fist suddenly banged on the table, making her mother's good china bounce and rattle.

'For pity's sake, man, will you stop being so *difficult?* Whether you like it or not we're going to see this thing through together. What's wrong with you? Scared that I'll start making advances, or look on a temporary business connection as an engagement?'

'Don't be daft!'

'It's not me who's being daft, it's you.' She got to her feet. 'To be honest, we could work together much more easily if we were man and wife, but you've made it very clear that you're not interested in me any more and I've got my pride, so you don't have to fret.' She picked up the papers and brandished them at him. 'I did this for your mother's sake, and your dad's too, because I like and respect her and I liked and respected him. And I did it for Tarbethill because I've grown to love the place and I don't want it to be sold off or left to fall apart or be built on. And yes, I'll admit that I did it for your

202

sake too, because I know that the only thing you love – the only thing you'll ever really love – is Tarbethill. I've come to accept that.'

'Alison—'

'Shut up!' she raged. 'If you want to know the truth, I can't be sure that you'll have the courage to throw yourself into this plan the way you must if it's going to work. So I'm determined to be right by your elbow every step of the way, to make certain that you do, and it does!'

Her voice began to waver on the final words, and she turned her back on him abruptly.

Ewan, appalled, stared at the slim shoulders shaking below the shining fall of fair hair. He wanted to go to her, to put his arms around her and tell her that she was wrong when she said that the only thing he loved was Tarbethill. But he knew that the farm needed him even more than he needed Alison. Like it or not, he was in no position to promise her the decent future she and her son deserved because Tarbethill, for the foreseeable future at least, had to come first.

So all he could do was stammer clumsily, 'I'm sorry, I didnae mean you to think that I don't appreciate what you're tryin' to do for us. If you're willin' to help pull the farm together that's fine with me.'

She shook her head, and for a moment he thought that she was going to order him out, then she ran both hands over her face before swinging round to face him, her eyes sparkling, not with joy but like hard, cold diamonds, and her soft, kissable mouth set in a tight smile.

'Good,' she said briskly. 'The first thing we must do is take the plan to your bank manager. You'll feel better if he approves it, and he might have changes or additions to suggest. He may even be willing to advance a loan once he sees it beginning to work. I'd like to go with you if that's all right.'

'I'll phone him an' let you know about the appointment,' Ewan said, and blundered out, leaving his tea scarcely tasted.

As Alison emptied and washed both cups the tears she had managed to hold back dripped into the sink. All she could think of was the way he had pulled his hand free of her touch, as though she were infectious.

The same memory was uppermost in Ewan's mind as he returned to the farm; the touch of her fingers on his and the way he had been forced to release himself before giving in to temptation and turning his hand over to clasp hers and never let go again.

Laura Tyler turned out to be an excellent addition to the drama club. She was one of the first to arrive for every rehearsal and one of the last to leave afterwards. She followed every rehearsal with close interest, laughing at all the right places and never failing to compliment the actors and actresses as well as Kevin, who blossomed under her unstinting praise.

'It's as if Meredith Whitelaw's back among us,' Jinty murmured to Elinor Pearce and Helen Forsyth as the three of them sat in a corner of the village hall, stitching costumes and watching the rehearsal. 'I could swear that your Kevin's grown a good inch since he walked in this evening, Elinor.'

'I noticed that too,' Elinor agreed dryly.

'But Laura's much more useful than Meredith was,' Helen said.

'Don't forget the way *she* upset poor Cynthia by taking over her lead part then leaving just before the play went on.'

'How could I ever forget? Kevin had to beg Cynthia to play the part after all and he was really upset when he got home that evening. I got the impression she and Gilbert made him grovel before she finally agreed. But Laura's not like that at all; she praises everyone, and she's the best property mistress we've ever had.'

'You're right. That feather boa she found for Cynthia is magnificent.'

Laura had taken to going far and wide to visit charity and antique shops, returning with all sorts of treasure trove such as ornaments to decorate the stage, pieces of jewellery for the actresses and clothes that Elinor, Jinty and Helen were able to alter for the play. When Kevin offered to reimburse her for her purchases she refused, insisting that the pleasure of poking around the shops in search of hidden treasure was reward enough. When Cynthia fell in love with the feather boa, a magnificent affair of floating purple feathers with a strong silken core, Laura promised to gift it to her once the production was over.

'She's a lovely person,' Helen said now as Laura's warm laugh rang out, 'and Prior's Ford's the better for having her here.'

'It's a pity her husband isn't more like her. He's a right stiff-necked man,' Jinty commented. 'I don't know what she sees in him; she surely deserves better.'

'Oh, you can never tell what some couples saw in each other when they first met,' Elinor told her placidly, the needle in her hand darting in and out of material with practised speed. 'Several of my friends were surprised when I married Kevin, and sometimes I wonder about that myself. But he's all right really. We rub along nicely and that's enough to keep me content.'

'You're doing this deliberately,' Neil raged at Gloria as he drove her back to Prior's Ford after work.

'Doing what?'

'Putting me on nights next week.'

'I'm doing my job as Operational Sergeant, that's all. And it so happens that you're required on late shift next week.'

'But you know that I've got two drama rehearsals every week.'

'Oh yes; how is the play going?'

'Very well, actually.'

'I can't wait to see it. I'm sure you'll be very good.'

'Not if I don't get enough rehearsal.'

'I thought you'd played that part before?'

'Years ago, and in any case the others need to be able to rehearse with me. When I'm at work the director needs to stand in for me and it throws them all, apart from making his life more difficult.'

'Oh dear. Still, into each life some rain must fall.'

'You're just being spiteful.'

'Watch it, Constable. You're only on late shift for one week at the moment, but I can toss a lot more rain your way if I want to. To tell the truth I'd quite enjoy seeing you with your own personal rain-cloud delivering regular downpours. Why are we stopping here?'

'It's where I live.'

'But I live up at the top,' said Gloria, who had moved into Clover Park a week earlier.

'One minute's walk away.'

'I'm tired. Being a sergeant's given me so much more responsibility. Thank you,' she said sweetly as Neil gritted his teeth and put the car into gear; then, as he drew up outside her gate some fifteen seconds later: 'So what have you got planned for this evening?'

'As it happens, Anja's asked me round to her place for dinner.'

'A cook as well as an interior decorator? Is there no end to her talents?'

'I might find the answer to that this evening,' Neil said, and she got out of the car without another word, slamming the door so hard that he was almost blasted, seat and all, out through the driver's door. Watching her jam her key into the lock with a hefty elbow action similar to those used by soldiers on bayonet practice, he wished that he hadn't let her rile him into that final sentence. Although there were times when he could cheerfully throttle his estranged wife, the thought of hurting her feelings was unacceptable.

As he showered and changed he pictured Gloria alone in her new house, cooking a meal for one while he enjoyed Anja's company, and when he finally set off on foot for the village, carrying a wrapped bottle of wine, he found himself wishing that he was heading towards Gloria's house rather than Anja's.

The dinner was delicious, the wine just right, the evening enjoyable, but when ten o'clock arrived and Anja made it clear that Neil could stay over if he wanted to, he made an excuse about having a report to write before bedtime, and left.

Anja was surprised, but not offended. Her Aunt Ingrid had told her that the British were not nearly as relaxed as the Norwegians about quite a lot of things, including the joys of casual, affectionate sex.

There was plenty of time, she told herself as she closed the front door.

Why, Neil wondered on his way back to Clover Park, was he doing this? Why was he walking back to his lonely bed when he could have been snuggling between the sheets, possibly silken, with Anja?

It wasn't a 'why', it was a 'who' – Gloria.

Turning in between the pillars flanking the entrance to the small estate he saw a light in an upstairs window of her house and wondered if she felt as lonely as he did at that moment.

Then it occurred to him that she herself might be between the sheets, probably Egyptian cotton, with another man.

It wasn't a pleasant thought.

Twenty-Two

The morning after Clarissa arrived home from her visit to Alastair's family, Amy Rose was on the phone. 'Is Alastair with you?'

'No, he had to get back to work, so he headed for Glasgow and I came home on my own.'

'So, how did it go?'

'It wasn't as terrifying as I'd thought it would be. Alastair's parents are very – what d'you call it? – laid back. In fact, they were wonderful. They behaved as if there was nothing unusual in their son falling for a woman the same age as his mother.'

'That's what I'd expect of his family, given what a nice lad he is,' Amy said comfortably. 'It was obvious to me that his parents would be just as you described them. So, d'you feel more relaxed about your relationship now?'

'Well, I've survived a meeting with the Marshalls, and most people here seem to be accepting us as a couple; I'm not being stared at or whispered about as often these days, as far as I know.'

'I told you it would be a five-day wonder.'

'Yes, you did.'

'But? I can tell by your voice that you're frownin'.'

Clarissa glanced into the hall mirror and hurriedly blinked the frown away. 'I'm not!'

'Are too, so there's a "but" buzzin' around your head.'

Clarissa sighed. 'I wish Alexandra could be more understanding. I've not heard a word from her since she stormed out of here. If only she'd stayed and given us a chance to talk things over.'

'Your late husband's daughter's approval isn't essential. Let her come round in her own time, and if she doesn't, so what?'

'I just hate falling out with family. It's ... it's as though I'm letting Keith down.'

'Oh, come on! You're his widow, not his representative towards her.'

'I suppose you're right,' Clarissa said doubtfully, and then, anxious to change the subject: 'How are enjoying your trip?'

'It's terrific. Just one disappointment so far; I spent an entire day on the banks of Loch Ness,' Amy complained, 'and that darned monster refused to show itself.'

'It gets the name of being a shy creature.'

'I had to make do with visitin' a gift shop and buyin' a little monster figurine and a pretty painted plate to show that I'd been to the area, but that's not enough to satisfy the folks back home. Ah well, onward and upward. I'm thinkin' of headin' for Skye next. Any interestin' gossip in your neck of the woods?'

'None that I know of, and that's the way I like it.'

'Let me know if anythin' exciting happens. Bye for now.'

'Bye.' Clarissa put the phone down and went into the living room to pick up the book she had been reading when Amy called.

After a moment she put it down again and wandered out to the back garden.

She had been telling the truth when she said that Alastair's parents and the rest of his family had made her feel welcome, but, strangely, the weekend visit had left her feeling vaguely unsettled, and she couldn't quite work out why. Perhaps, she thought as she dead-headed some roses, it was because she felt like an in-between. She was the same age as Sheila and Gordon, Alastair's parents, and yet they accepted her as Alastair's partner, just as they would have accepted a woman of his own age. Kind and well meaning though they were, Clarissa was left with an uncomfortable sensation, something like trying on a coat that didn't quite fit.

'We don't know what our Molly's thinking of, do we, Tony?' Val Ewing said almost as soon as she emerged from her husband's car to find Fliss and Hector in the courtyard.

'Do we what?' Her burly husband was still emerging from the driving seat.

'Know what our Molly's thinking off, finishing with poor Lewis and giving up the chance to live in a grand house like this. My poor Fliss, I'm so sorry!'

Val threw her arms around Fliss, who suddenly found herself in uncomfortably close contact with a soft, generous and heavily perfumed bosom. 'And as for Lewis, where is the poor lamb? In the kitchen?' She released Fliss and marched towards the open kitchen door.

Hector, who was standing directly in her way, hurriedly sidestepped and went to shake hands with Tony, wincing as his fingers were crushed in the other man's grip.

'Sorry, mate,' Tony said, 'about our Molly, I mean. It's typical, though; she's like a butterfly flitting from one thing to another. Always has been. You'd have thought having the kiddie would slow her down, but it hasn't.'

'Not at all,' said Hector, who couldn't think of anything else to say. Molly's parents always terrified him because they were large, loud and never seemed to stop talking. 'Come on in,' he invited, then jumped nervously as Tony bellowed:

'Stephanie, get a move on, will you?'

One of the car's rear doors opened slowly and Molly's younger sister emerged. 'Can't I just wait for you here, Dad?'

'Of course you can't. Where's your manners, girl? Come inside and be nice to Mr and Mrs Ralston-Kerr. So where's our wee princess, then?' Tony went on as he and his daughter followed Hector into the kitchen.

'Out in the garden with the girl that works here,' his wife informed him. She was already settled at the table, where Jinty was pouring mugs of tea. 'But where's Lewis, Fliss?'

'He's ... er...'

'Had to go to a garden centre in Dumfries to collect a lot of plants for the estate,' Jinty said swiftly. Both Hector and Fliss found lying very difficult and she knew that they were as likely as not to blurt out the fact that Lewis had gone to ground in Ginny's camper van, refusing to meet the visitors or to watch his beloved daughter being whisked off to Inverness by her other grandparents.

'But isn't that his car in the yard?'

'He's borrowed a friend's van. The plants are actually shrubs and that little car can't carry much. Tea, Mr Ewing?'

'Call him Tony, love.'

'We can't stay for long; I want to get back to watch football on the telly tonight.' Tony produced a flask from his jacket pocket and added some of its contents to his tea, then to Hector's. 'That'll put hairs on your chest. Anyone else want some?'

'I wouldn't mind,' Stephanie said, and was ignored.

'Molly's daddy gave her a right scolding when she phoned to tell us she was staying on in Portugal with Bob Carter, didn't you, Tony? But it wasn't any good, she's made up her mind. They were inseparable when they were at school, her and Bob. We even thought at one time that they were going to get married. You were dead against it, though, weren't you, Tony?'

'I didn't go for it at all,' her husband agreed.

214

'They were still only kids themselves but fortunately Molly had—'

'Second thoughts, didn't she?' his wife cut in.

Stephanie sniggered into her tea and Val glared at her before rushing on: 'Well, they were both only seventeen and it would never have lasted. Then Bob went off to work in Edinburgh and that was the end of that – until this year. They'd have made a lovely couple, our Molly and your Lewis, and now she's never going to live in this mansion of yours. It's so sad! Any chance that Lewis'll be back soon? I'd like to give him a big comforting cuddle, poor boy.'

'He said not to expect him back until the evening,' Jinty said firmly.

'And if we don't start back soon I'm going to miss the beginning of the match,' Tony warned his womenfolk. 'So we'd better collect Weena and her things.'

'Her little suitcase is all packed.' Jinty got to her feet. 'If you could fetch it from upstairs, Mr Ralston-Kerr, I'll bring Rowena Chloe from the rose garden.'

'I'll come with you,' Stephanie offered, leaping to her feet.

'If you ask me,' the girl said when she and Jinty were well clear of the kitchen, 'Lewis has had a lucky escape. He was never Molly's type and she'd have made his life miserable.'

'What makes you think that?'

'She's a flirt, isn't she? Always was, but Mum and Dad think the sun shines out of her you-know-what. Talk about love being blind! If you ask me – but nobody ever does, in our house – it was never Lewis she wanted, it was the thought of lording around as the lady of the manor that made her chase after him. She's been right fed up with the fuss he makes about the place, though,' the girl went on as they crossed the lawns. 'Molly's used to being the centre of attention and she didn't fancy playing second fiddle to a big house in need of a lot of expensive repairs.'

'D'you think this Bob's the one for her?'

'He'll do until someone better comes along. They were mad about each other when they were still at school, until the thought of being a gymslip mum scared her.'

'A gymslip mum?' Jinty stopped in her tracks. 'What d'you mean?'

'She had to have an abortion, didn't she? That's why Bob disappeared off to Edinburgh before Dad got his hands on him. It wasn't Molly's fault, of course; nothing's ever Molly's fault. I'm sick of it, I can tell you. As soon as I finish with school next year I'm off to university and they won't see me for dust. So where's this rose garden, then?' Stephanie said. 'We'd better get a move on.'

Lewis Ralston-Kerr had spent the night at Cam's house after being found slumped in the Cuckoo's dining room, returning home in the morning with a severe hangover. In the ten days since then he had scarcely spoken to anyone other than Rowena Chloe, choosing to spend every day working alone in remote parts of the garden. Now, sitting in Ginny's camper van with the curtains drawn, he heard everyone come out of the kitchen, identifying the Ewings' loud voices, his parents' quieter replies and the occasional comment from Stella, Ginny and Jinty. He could hear Rowena Chloe's sweet childish voice too; every time she spoke a knife seemed to turn in his heart.

At last the car engine roared into life then faded as the vehicle rounded the house and set off down the drive, every turn of its wheels taking the most precious little person in his world further from him.

Someone tapped on the camper van door and when he did nothing, Ginny called tentatively, 'They've gone, Lewis.'

'I know!' he snarled. 'Go away!'

She obeyed, taking refuge in the kitchen garden she had brought back to life when she first started working at Linn Hall. Usually when she was troubled, wandering along the gravel paths between neat beds of vegetables and inhaling the mixed scents from the herb garden soothed her, but not today. How could she be happy when she knew that Lewis was suffering?

'No, no, no!' Kevin Pearce snapped, 'you're almost cringing before Lady Bracknell, Neil. We can't have that!'

'But I'm afraid of her.'

'No, you're not; you love her daughter and you know that you're going to have to fight for her. You must tackle Her Ladyship with firm but polite determination. Can't you do that?'

'Yes, but it's not Lady Bracknell I'm afraid of, it's Mrs MacBain.'

'How very sweet of you, dear boy,' Cynthia cooed, 'but please don't worry. I may have a lot more experience of treading the boards than you, but I'm actually a very nice person.'

'I can vouch for that,' her husband Gilbert chimed in.

'He's like a parrot perching on her shoulder,' Jinty whispered to Elinor, who stifled a giggle at the word-picture. 'Always there to back her up and massage her ego.'

'A tribute to your acting, Cynthia dear,' Kevin agreed, 'but awe is not what I'm looking for at the moment. So let's try that scene again, this time with some firmness from Jack Worthing. Think yourself into the part, Neil. Have you ever loved someone so much that you simply had to make her your own?'

'Yes.' The word was out before Neil could stop it.

'Then work from that angle. Be determined! Right, everyone, back to work.'

To give Kevin his due, his ruse worked. With Gloria lodged firmly in his mind, both as the woman he still loved and the dragon that was Lady Bracknell, Neil sailed through the scene, so determined that there were times when Cynthia had to struggle to keep the upper hand. The result held everyone's attention and when the scene ended Laura Tyler led a spontaneous round of applause, while Kevin beamed.

'Excellent, both of you. Keep it that way.' He glanced at his watch. 'We'll leave it there for tonight and pick up where we left off on Monday.'

Elinor shrugged her coat on. 'If we go now I can catch a half-hour programme I forgot to record.'

'You go ahead, then,' Kevin said as the others started to leave. 'I'm staying behind to work out some new moves for Monday.'

'Sure you don't want my help, dear?'

'No, no, I'll be home soon,' Kevin told his wife absently, his eyes on the script and his mind already on the work in hand.

Elinor got home just in time to catch the start of her programme and when it ended she set out everything in readiness for their usual Horlicks nightcap before settling down with her library book to pass the time until Kevin's arrival.

The story was so absorbing that it held her attention for a full twenty minutes before she reached the end of a chapter, glanced at the clock and realized that Kevin had not yet arrived back from the village hall.

She peered out of the front door, but there was no sign of him.

Clearly he had become so caught up in what he was doing that he had forgotten the time. Tutting, she put her coat on.

As she reached the garden gate Cam Gordon hailed her on his way home from the Neurotic

Cuckoo, where most of the cast went for a drink after rehearsals. As Kevin always needed to unwind after the stress of rehearsals, the Pearces preferred home and Horlicks.

'Hello, Elinor, you're out later than usual.'

'Kevin's still not back from the hall; probably too absorbed in working out the new moves to realize what time it is. I'm going to fetch him.'

'I'll walk with you.'

'Aren't you going home?'

'Yes, but there's no hurry,' he assured her, tucking her hand in the crook of his arm. 'Good rehearsal, wasn't it? Poor Neil, blurting out that stuff about being afraid of Cynthia. He came to the Cuckoo with the rest of us and said he felt like a right fool. Not that I blame him. She can frighten me at times.'

'She was flattered, so no harm done.'

'When they finally got through that scene it looked really good, so all's well that ends well. Here we are, and the light's still on in the hall,' Cam said as they went through the gates. 'You're right, he's forgotten all about time passing.'

Kevin, as always during rehearsals, was sitting at the table in the middle of the hall, facing the stage. All that could be seen of him was his upper back and his head, slumped on his chest. Incongruously, the elaborate purple boa that Laura Tyler had found for Lady Bracknell was wrapped about his neck.

'What on earth are you wearing that for, Kevin?' Elinor called out, hurrying ahead of

220

Cam. She rounded the chair, looked down at her husband, then reeled back, her hands flying to her mouth.

Cam crossed the distance between them at a run and as he reached Elinor she turned and threw herself at him, almost knocking him off balance.

He steadied himself and put his arms about her. Her head burrowed in against his chest, and he realized that she was trembling violently. He started to tremble too, when he looked at Kevin, mouth sagging open, his face a horribly un-natural dark red colour and the fingers of both hands tangled in the purple feathers around his neck.

Twenty-Three

The people of Prior's Ford awoke to a beautiful morning. Only a few small white clouds offset the pure blue of the sky, and birds poured their music forth from trees stirred very slightly by a breeze.

Those living near the village green rose from their beds and drew their curtains to gaze with quiet content on their colourful gardens and the idyllic village beyond – only to be met by the sight of a police incident caravan outside the village hall and the comings and goings of a crowd of grim-faced strangers, some in plain-clothes, some in uniform, some clad in white space suits from head to foot. The centre of interest was focused on the hall, surrounded by great stretches of police cordon tape denying access to everyone but the strangers who had arrived overnight to take possession.

Phones began to ring from house to house, and the butcher's shop, the village store and the pub were soon packed with people seeking news. Word of mouth travelled like a mad game of Chinese Whispers, with fact and rumour being added together into a pattern that grew with each telling. 'Kevin and Elinor Pearce were killed in the village hall during the night ... a suicide pact, I heard ... the police are looking for a stranger spotted yesterday lurking in one of the Tarbethill fields ... did you hear about a man being attacked not a mile from here the other week? ... there's a serial killer on the loose out there...'

The pub was a popular gathering place that morning.

'Are you sure Kevin was murdered, Joe?' Robert Kavanagh asked. 'There're all sorts of daft rumours beginning to go round. Could it have been a heart attack?'

'Why would the place be full of police if poor Kevin died of a heart attack?' Cynthia MacBain wanted to know from behind the little handkerchief she kept dabbing at her eyes. Her husband's arm was around her shoulders, and brandy glasses were on the table before them.

'All I can tell you is what happened here last night,' Joe Fisher said patiently for the second or third time. 'Apparently Kevin stayed behind after the rehearsal and when Elinor went to remind him that it was getting late, she met Cam on his way home. The two of them went to the hall and found Kevin. Cam said a purple scarf thing was pulled tight round his neck and his face was...' Joe stopped short then continued slowly, 'Well, it didn't sound like a normal way to go.'

'A sort of scarf thing, did you say?' Cynthia's voice shook. 'Purple ... round his neck? It didn't have feathers, did it?'

'Come to think of it, that sounds like what

223

Cam described.'

Cynthia let out a scream and clutched at her husband. 'Gilbert, Lady Bracknell's beautiful feather boa's become a murder weapon! To think that I actually wore it at rehearsals – it's too much! I can never touch it again, let alone put it around my neck!'

'You won't be able to,' Jenny Forsyth pointed out, 'if it's a murder weapon. The police will have to keep it as evidence.'

'Another two brandies, please, Joe,' said Gilbert.

'Is there any news of Elinor?' Helen Campbell wanted to know.

'Elinor ... I'd forgotten about her.' Cynthia trumpeted. 'How could I? It was the shock. We must go to her at once, Gilbert!'

'No!' Joe said hurriedly. 'I mean, no need. Cam brought Elinor here, like I said, and then he went back to the hall. Young Neil White, being a policeman, went with him. Elinor just wanted to go home, so Gracie took her and stayed with her all night. Naomi's with her now, to let Gracie get a bit of shut-eye.'

'I would have thought that Elinor needed close friends at a time like this. Why didn't she telephone us? We would have been there like a shot, wouldn't we, Gilbert? Even during the night.'

'Of course we would, Cynthia. Like a shot.'

'And what's going to happen to the play now? Without Kevin we're a ship without a rudder. That wonderful man is – was – our leader in every way. Our inspiration. We cannot go on.

And yet,' Cynthia suggested, 'surely it's our duty to go ahead and give the performances of our lives as a tribute to the man who devoted *his* life to the drama group!'

'You don't think she's going to start singing "There's No Business Like Show Business", do you?' Helen whispered to Jenny.

'I'd not be surprised,' Jenny murmured.

By early afternoon the newspapers had got hold of the story and an army of reporters and photographers were descending on the village. As most of the activity was centred on the village hall uniformed police had to be drafted in to keep the traffic moving, and Lynn Stacey was having great difficulty in keeping her pupils' attention. During lunch and play breaks the children were glued to the railings, avidly watching all the comings and goings across the road, and even in the classrooms overlooking the hall their eyes were on the windows rather than their teacher.

Bob Green, chief reporter on the *Dumfries News*, was settled comfortably in Helen Campbell's kitchen, a mug of well-sugared tea by his elbow and a notepad on his lap. 'So tell me everything you know about Kevin Pearce and his missus.'

'There's not really anything to tell. They're a nice couple, and they've been living here for several years. Kevin directs plays for the village drama group and Elinor's the wardrobe mistress. She teaches sewing to the children in the primary school sometimes.'

'There must be more; ordinary folk don't get themselves murdered. There's a mystery lurking somewhere, Helen.'

'The only mystery's why anyone would want to kill poor Kevin.'

Bob sighed. Knowing Helen had given him a bit of a lead on the other reporters swarming into the village; he first met her when she became secretary of the local group set up to fight a plan to open the old quarry outside the village. Then, when he discovered that she wanted to become a writer he had persuaded her to start providing a Prior's Ford column for the paper. When the man who wrote the paper's popular agony aunt column under the name of Lucinda Keen moved on, Bob was instrumental in putting Helen in his place, something that only her closest friends knew about.

'Ah now, there's a question to start with. Was this man the intended victim or did the murderer mistake him for someone else? Have you had any agony aunt letters recently that might point to someone with a motive for murder?'

'Just the usual, about marriage and teenage problems.'

'Marriage problems ... D'you think that the wife might have been involved?'

'Elinor? Certainly not! She's a very sweet woman and she's ... was ... devoted to poor Kevin.'

'Genuinely devoted? If you ask me, there are more female murderers around than we realize.

Women can be good at hiding their feelings and biding their time until they get the chance to strike.'

'Not Elinor,' Helen said firmly, and Bob sighed, then closed his notebook and finished his tea.

'I'd best go and find out if the police have anything to say. Keep your ears and eyes open, Helen, and pay close attention to the agony aunt letters. There could be clues all over the place and I rely on you to pick up on them. When you do, get in touch right away, there's a good lass.'

As soon as he had gone Helen hurried over to Jenny's house to talk about his visit.

'First of all I end up as the village reporter, then an agony aunt, and now I'm an undercover policewoman snooping around for clues; all because I want to write fiction,' she ended despairingly. 'I want to create my own stories, not get caught up in real, horrible things happening to real people! What am I going to do, Jenny?'

'Bob's the reporter, so let him do his own reporting,' her friend advised firmly, spooning coffee into mugs. 'After all, he's paid to do that and you're not.'

'That's true. I feel better already,' Helen said gratefully, then: 'But no, I don't really, because what's happening here isn't fiction, it's real. Poor Elinor, what must she be going through?'

'I haven't been able to get her out of my mind since I heard,' Jenny agreed. 'It was bad enough for me when Andrew had cancer and I'd to live with the fear of losing him, but this – violent and

227

completely unexpected – is so much worse. Murder's something you read about in the papers, isn't it? Not something that happens to people you know. And why Kevin? He was a fussy sort of man but there was no harm in him.'

Helen nodded. 'Who on earth would want to kill him? Surely nobody living here.'

'Is it possible that someone from his past could have come to the village last night, found him alone in the hall and killed him, then left?'

'How would they know he was alone in the hall at that particular time?'

'Perhaps he stayed on after the rehearsal by arrangement, for a secret meeting with someone? Oh, listen to us,' Jenny exclaimed. 'We're beginning to sound like a scene from a Hercule Poirot film! Forget the coffee; let's have a large sherry and change the subject!'

'The children will be back from school soon. I don't want them to realize I've been drinking.'

'I have strong mints for after,' Jenny said as she produced the sherry bottle.

'Allan, something terrible's happened,' Laura said as soon as her husband picked up the phone in their Leeds flat.

'We've been burgled? Or is it the boiler that's burst? I knew buying that cottage was a mistake...'

'It has nothing to do with the cottage. Kevin Pearce was murdered last night in the village hall.' Then, as the silence seemed to be going on for too long: 'Allan, are you still there?'

'Yes of course I'm here. Who did you say was murdered?'

'Kevin Pearce, the man who runs the drama group I'm working with. You met him at that party we were invited to not long after we arrived. You seemed to take an instant dislike to him as I recall.'

'Oh yes, I think I know who you mean. What happened?'

'He stayed behind in the hall after the rest of us left, to do some work on the script, and apparently someone strangled him with a feather boa that I bought for one of the actresses. The place is filled with police and journalists.'

'Dear God, that's all we need. Come home at once, Laura.'

'I can't, the police are interviewing everyone who was at the rehearsal last night and it'd look suspicious if I left suddenly. They might think that I'd done it.'

'Don't be ridiculous, you scarcely knew the man, and you said you'd left the hall with the others?'

'I walked home with Jinty McDonald after the rehearsal; she lives in the council house estate so we parted company halfway down Riverside Lane. I walked on down to the cottage and phoned you to say goodnight, but you weren't in.'

'I'd arranged to meet a former colleague for a drink after the meeting; I needed his angle on a case we were on together. I checked the phone when I got in and heard your message, but you'd

229

have been asleep by then.'

'I'm booked to do a cookery demonstration to the Rural on Thursday. D'you think the hall will be available by then?'

'Probably, but I'd prefer it if you packed a bag and came here. The village is going to be crawling with police and reporters and gawpers.'

'I'm staying, and you're coming back tomorrow as arranged.'

'Now that I'm retired I don't really want to get involved in any more investigations.'

'You won't, Scotland's got its own police officers. I'll see you tomorrow afternoon,' Laura said firmly.

Clarissa got an entirely different reaction when Amy Rose heard the news.

'A murder? Are they sure?'

'Apparently they are. Poor Elinor. Who on earth would want to kill her husband? The police are doing door-to-door interviews; they were here earlier and I had my fingerprints taken. We all have to have our fingerprints taken because the hall was so well used. Not that I'm in it very often.'

'I'm coming back as quickly as I can, Clarissa.'

'You don't have to.'

'I've arranged to spend the first week in October in Whitby with Stella, remember? So I'd have to get back to Prior's Ford soon in any case. But now that there's been a murder...'

'The place is full of police, and I'm sure that

230

whoever did it will be putting as much distance between themselves and Prior's Ford as they can right now.'

'You think so?'

'It must have been a stranger, a tramp perhaps. Nobody living here would have any reason to harm poor Kevin.'

'You'd be surprised what can lie beneath the surface in some apparently placid minds,' Amy Rose said darkly. 'I'm on my way back, Clarissa.'

Twenty-Four

Ewan McNair was so caught up in his own problems that to him, Kevin Pearce's murder appeared distant and unreal. The police came to the farm and took his fingerprints and his mother's as well as Victor's and Wilf's, since they happened to be there at the time.

'Ye surely don't think my mother's a murderer,' Ewan said when he, his brother and Wilf were called in from the field where they were checking the dairy herd before taking them to auction.

'We've been told to do everyone who lives in the village,' Neil White told him. 'It's to find out if there are any unfamiliar prints in the village hall, and it seems that everyone's been in there.'

'I don't mind if it helps you, son,' Jess said. 'Not that I've been there for a while. We've got our own troubles at the moment. You were here before, weren't you, when...'

'Yes, I was, Mrs McNair. I'm truly sorry to bother you like this.'

'You're only doing your job. I mind how kind you and that bonny wee policewoman were to us. Is she working on this case too?'

Neil nodded. 'She's a sergeant now.'

'A clever lass, right enough. Would you and your friend not like a wee cup of tea and a pancake before you go?'

'Thank you for the offer but we've not got the time.'

'What's up?' Neil's colleague asked ten minutes later as the police car stopped halfway down the farm lane.

'We'd best eat these before we get back to the incident van or we'll lose them.' Neil opened the bag Jess had insisted on pressing into his hands as he left. 'They're still warm.'

The other constable took the buttered pancake handed to him and stuffed it into his mouth. He chewed, swallowed, and then reached for a second. 'They're fantastic.'

Neil nodded, his own mouth full.

It was Alison's business plan for Tarbethill Farm and her presence at the meeting in the bank that persuaded the manager to agree to a loan.

There was, however, a proviso. 'I would prefer to delay payment until you find out how much you make from selling the dairy herd and the milking machinery. Call it proof of your intention to turn the farm back into a self-supporting business. I know that this is a difficult time for you, as it is for most small farms nowadays, but my experience is that a change of direction can save the day, and I wish you well with your own project.' Then, as Alison and Ewan were leaving, the man added, 'Mr McNair, I admired your father, and it seems to me that you're a chip off the old block. You've got a difficult road ahead but I believe that you'll come through.'

Those final words helped a little. Ewan had to admit that Alison was right; the money raised by auctioning the dairy herd at auction and the milking machinery was badly needed. But money couldn't make up for returning home from the market without the beasts he had cared for and knew individually by name. Watching them in the auction ring, knowing that they were all going to new owners, hurt as much as seeing members of his family leave him forever. Without them, the fields and the milking shed were so empty.

'You can rent it out,' Alison said when the sale was over and she and Ewan stood at the shed door, staring in at the huge space.

'Who would want a place this size?'

'Someone starting up a small business, perhaps.'

'Strangers here on Tarbethill land?'

'If it brings in rent, then yes. The important thing is that it's still Tarbethill land, Ewan. The money you made today together with what you got for the herd guarantees the loan from the bank. You've begun to move forward and you have to keep going now.' Then, as she considered the size of the milking shed: 'How do you feel about bringing in more sheep?'

'It's a possibility.'

'If you plan to do it soon, this place would make a good lambing shed, wouldn't it?'

'I didn't think of that.'

'It's worth considering. And you need to look for local farmers interested in renting fields from you for their sheep or beef cattle. You can add a charge for keeping an eye on the beasts for them. And now's the time to start turning the fields on either side of the lane into allotments, so that they're ready for use in the spring.'

'What about planning permission or whatever's needed? A man can't make a move these days, even on his own land, without having to get permission from one jumped up pen-pusher or another.'

'Leave the paperwork to me; you and Wilf will have enough to do. And that big shed's to be turned into a deep litter house, remember, so that your mother can buy more hens to lay more eggs. I've promised to help her to get it ready; we're both looking forward to it. Ewan–' she caught at his arm as he began to turn away – 'the hardest part's over.'

'You think so?'

'Yes, I do. You've spoken to the bank manager and got him on your side, and you've taken the hard step of giving up dairy farming and selling off your beloved herd. Now you're ready to start rebuilding Tarbethill Farm. It's not your dad's any more, it's yours. You're taking it into the new century and I know that it's going to work out well.'

He gave her a long look before turning on his heel and walking away. The very thought of all the changes to be made exhausted him; at the

235

moment, all he wanted was to go back in time to the way it had been before Victor left.

Jess stood at the kitchen window watching her son walk away from Alison, his shoulders stooped, and watching Alison stand there unmoving until he was out of sight round the side of an outhouse. She saw the girl scrub tears from her eyes and straighten her own shoulders with a visible effort, and continued to watch, making no effort to move out of sight as Alison made for the farmhouse.

'He's grievin', lass,' she said as soon as the younger woman stepped into the kitchen. 'It's no' just his father that's died, it's a whole way of life. The only life he's known until now.'

'I just wish he'd realize that he can do it, and it's worth doing. Ewan's a farmer to his very core and I wish I could get him to realize that he's not turning his world upside down; he's only heading in a slightly different direction than before. He's not got much faith in me, but if you can show him that you rely on him and you've got faith in him that might help to get some purpose back in his life.'

'I'll be doin' that every minute of every day. I don't know what the two of us would do without you. You're bein' so good tae us!'

'I'm not,' Alison said. 'I'm being driven by sheer selfishness. I'm fighting for my future as well as yours. Mine and Jamie's future, here at Tarbethill with you and Ewan, where we belong.'

'I'd love tae see you and wee Jamie livin' here,

236

and other children too, yours and Ewan's. That's what this place needs tae bring it alive again. It's what Ewan wants too, but he just doesnae seem to grasp that.'

'He will, I promise you, but it has to be in his own good time.'

'Why don't you start bringin' the wee lad with you when you come over? I can look after him, and it'd do me a power of good tae see him. It might help tae pull Ewan out of his misery as well. He dotes on that boy of yours.'

'Good idea, I'll do that. What chance,' Alison asked, straightening her back and smiling at the older woman, 'can one man have against two determined women like us?'

Getting no reply when she rang the doorbell, Naomi strolled round the side of Willow Cottage to find Clarissa gathering vegetables while her temporary lodger hoed the rose bed.

'Hello, you two, am I interrupting?'

'Yes, and thank you for that.' Amy Rose straightened, one hand massaging the small of her back. 'I was beginning to hallucinate about a glass of sherry. Anybody care to join me?'

'Lovely.' Naomi settled into one of the garden chairs.

'Me too. I'll just take this armful into the kitchen. Naomi, could you use some veg? The runner beans are running out of control, and the same goes for the parsley and lettuce.'

'I'd welcome whatever you care to give me. Fortunately, Ethan enjoys vegetables as much as he enjoys burgers. Can I help in the kitchen?'

'You relax for once; Amy can see to the sherry while I sort out the veg. Won't be long.'

Ten minutes later the three of them were relaxing at the garden table, glasses of sherry and a plate of biscuits before them.

'This feels so wonderfully normal; for the past ten days I've felt as though I'm living in a nightmare,' Naomi sighed. 'I can't believe that something as dreadful as murder could taint Prior's Ford. Who on earth would want to kill poor harmless Kevin?'

'I know just what you mean,' Clarissa nodded. 'Murder is something you read about in fiction or in the newspapers; it never happens to someone you know. How's Elinor? We didn't know whether to call on her or not.'

'Coping amazingly well. She's always been a practical, self-controlled person and that's what's keeping her going at the moment. You know her sister's come from Moffat to stay with her?'

'Amy and I met her in the village store – a pleasant woman who comes over as very sensible, too – like Elinor herself.'

'Best to put visiting on hold for the time being but she'll need your company once she's living on her own again. She's insisted on continuing her work on Tricia Harper's wedding dress; she says that a girl's wedding day is the most important day of her life and she's not going to let Tricia down. That's giving her something to focus on, which helps.'

'Tricia and Derek Borland bought Ivy McGowan's home in the row of almshouses, didn't they? And they're getting married soon.'

'At the end of this month. It'll be nice to have another wedding in the village.'

'Any news from the police about how the murder investigation's going?' Amy Rose wanted to know.

'I think they're as baffled as we are. That nice young constable, the one who moved into Clover Park, told me that it's what they call a whodunnit murder. Apparently that means that at the moment it could have been absolutely anyone in the village, or even someone passing through and long gone.'

'Did he say whether they'd found any unidentified prints in the village hall?' Amy asked.

'Not as far as I know.'

'Just think,' Clarissa said with a shiver, 'the case may never be solved, and we may never know if whoever did it is still living among us, undetected!'

'Don't start to get spooked, the police still have a way to go before they give up.' Amy reached for the sherry bottle. 'Another all round, I think.' Then, topping up each glass: 'I know that you can't betray confidences, Naomi, but has anyone said anything unusual to you recently, or behaved differently?'

'If you mean has anyone come to me to admit that they killed Kevin, I can safely reveal that the answer's no. I'd be put into a difficult situation if that did happen. And I haven't seen anyone behaving unusually.'

'Come to think of it, I did,' Amy said. Then as the other two stared at her: 'But it was before Kevin died. At the party the MacBains held to welcome the Hunters to the village. I was there when Kevin Pearce and Allan Hunter met, an' it seemed to me that they took an instant dislike to each other.'

Clarissa raised her eyebrows. 'Why would they do that? They'd never met before.'

'Now that I recall it, I'm beginnin' to wonder – *had* they met before?'

'That's highly unlikely.'

'Maybe, but I think I'll mention it to one of the police officers, just in case. More sherry, Naomi?'

'I've already had one too many. Mind you, that one too many might help me to come up with a good sermon for Sunday. I think I sense a touch of the muse coming on even as I speak, so I'm off to my study. Thank you for your company, it's so good to experience normality in this dark time.'

'Come into the kitchen and I'll bag some vegetables for you,' Clarissa said.

She and Naomi had just gone into the kitchen when Marcy appeared round the corner of the cottage, a bag of sweets in her hand.

'There you are – you forgot to put these liquorice allsorts in your bag this morning, Amy.'

'Me and my memory! I love the stuff,' Amy

Rose admitted, accepting the bag. 'Would you like a glass of sherry?'

'I don't think Sam would be happy if I returned to the shop smelling of drink. I wouldn't mind something cold in a long glass though, if it's on offer.'

'Of course, sit yourself down. Clarissa's in the kitchen, packing some veg for Naomi. Could you use some?'

'I could if they're available. Thanks.' Left alone, Marcy settled herself in a deckchair, closing her eyes and resting her head back to soak in the sun. She was almost asleep when Clarissa and Amy came from the house, the former with a bag of vegetables, the latter with a tall glass of orange juice.

'This is lovely,' she said drowsily, pulling herself upright and accepting the drink. 'It's on summer days like this that I wish Sam and I could retire and just enjoy life for a change.'

'Have you heard anything new about the murder?' Amy asked. 'Working in the store means that you often hear things before the rest of us.'

'Only rumour and gossip. If you put it all together you'd end up with a dustbin full of rubbish rather than helpful facts. Sam and I are trying hard not to pass any of it on because it'll only muddy the water, so to speak.'

'I was just telling Naomi and Clarissa that I'm going to tell the police that I noticed Kevin Pearce and Allan Hunter reacting strangely towards each other at the MacBain party to welcome the Hunters. They'd just been introduced, and they seemed to take an instant mutual dislike to each other. It seemed to me as though they could scarcely bear to shake hands.'

'That's strange; I noticed something similar not long after that party. Mr Hunter was in the store with his wife, and while I was checking out their shopping I noticed Kevin coming in. When he saw them he turned round and went out again.'

'Did he come back?'

'Ten minutes after they left. He bought a couple of items and seemed his usual self.'

'So he'd stayed nearby to make sure that the Hunters were out of the way before he came back into the store.'

'You can't prove that, Amy,' Clarissa protested. 'For all we know he forgot what he was in for and had to go back and check with Elinor. Or he might have realized he'd left his wallet at home and had to go back for it.'

'I don't think so. My fingertips are tingling, just as they did when I saw the two of them together at the party.'

Clarissa and Marcy glanced at each other. 'Do your fingertips tingle often?' Marcy asked, keeping a straight face.

'They do when somethin's wrong. And there's somethin' wrong where those two men are concerned. And now–' Amy lowered her voice and leaned forwards – 'one of 'em's been killed.'

'Laura was with her husband in the store,' Clarissa pointed out. 'If he was trying to avoid

242

meeting one of them it could have been her.'

'No it couldn't. She's been workin' with the drama group and from what I hear, Kevin was quite taken with her.'

'Kevin loves to meet celebrities,' Marcy agreed 'D'you remember the way he behaved when Meredith Whitelaw was in the village, Clarissa? He followed her round like a besotted puppy. I wouldn't have been surprised if he had rolled over to let her tickle his tummy.'

'I still don't think that the police will give much credence to your tingling fingertips, Amy.'

'Clarissa, if my Gordon, rest his soul, was here he'd tell you different. More than once when he told me about a case he was on, my fingertips picked up on it. As often as not I'd come up with an angle the police hadn't thought of, and that's how the case was solved. I'm goin' to visit that incident room outside the school tomorrow,' Amy Rose decided.

Twenty-Five

Because Neil and Gloria lived in the village the CID Inspector in charge of the murder investigation had decided to make use of them both.

'I've cleared it with your Inspector on the grounds that if we're lucky the locals might just open up to you two, having seen you around the place,' he told Gloria after summoning her to his office. 'You've got a good head on your shoulders and I'm relying on you to help close this case as quickly as possible. I take it that the two of you will be able to work in tandem?'

'Of course, sir, though we've not been in Prior's Ford long enough to get to know the locals well.'

'Now's your chance. Living there means that you can mix with them while you're off duty as well as on. I'm told that young White's joined the drama club.'

'Yes sir, he has.'

'That's good, it means that he's keen on getting to know the locals.'

'I believe so, sir,' Gloria said primly, longing to add: *Especially a bimbo with purple hair*.

'That could be very useful, given that the victim's the man who ran the drama group. Visit the pub, the two of you; chat to people there and in the shops. Keep your eyes and ears open twenty-four seven. Find out all you can about Kevin Pearce, who liked or disliked him and why, especially the ones who disliked him. What's the general feeling in the village at the moment?'

'As far as I can gather he didn't have any enemies there. Everyone's convinced that it was someone passing through and long gone now. Nobody can make sense of it.'

'No suggestion of another woman in his life?'

'Nothing like that. His marriage seemed to be happy, and his wife's a pleasant woman. I can't see her committing murder.'

'A woman wouldn't have had the strength to pull that boa tight enough. It must have been a man. The slightest bit of gossip could turn out to be a lead, so dismiss nothing that you hear; run it all past me.' The DI leaned forward over his desk, fixing her with a stern gaze. 'We have to get this case cleared up asap, Sergeant.'

'Yes sir.'

'Because trying to solve a case that has an entire village-load of potential suspects could play merry hell with my budget. Know what I mean?'

'Yes sir.'

'And if my entire budget disappears up the Swanee, or floats down the Dee if you want to be local about it, then my department is going to have a very lean time. Get me?'

'Loud and clear, sir.'

'Good, because I don't want to have to say all that again. Now, go to it, Sergeant.'

'Sir!'

Neil was on duty when an eccentric-looking woman swathed in what seemed to be several layers of floaty, colourful garments arrived in the incident caravan.

'Hi, there, Officer,' she greeted him breezily, settling herself down in the chair opposite him. He was fascinated by her hair, a mass of curls that looked as though they had been left out in the rain and gone rusty.

'Good morning, madam, can I help you?' He had a vague idea that he had seen her before.

'I'm hopin' that *I* can help *you*, Sergeant.'

'It's Constable, madam. Constable White.'

'I'm guessin' that your mother didn't choose Constable as your first name?' She beamed at him, waiting for a reply.

'It's ... er ... Neil, madam.'

'Pleased to meet you, Constable Neil White.' A skinny arm reached out from the gauzy veiling and Neil found himself shaking a surprisingly strong hand with green polished nails. 'I'm Amy Rose.'

Beginning to feel that he was somehow losing control of the situation, he hurriedly retrieved his hand so that he could pick up his pen and note the name down. 'And your surname, madam?'

'You got it. Amy Rose. Mrs Amy Rose. My late husband Gordon Rose was a police officer over in America.'

'So you're American.'

'I was born as English as a cup of tea but my parents emigrated when I was a kid.'

'And your address, Mrs Rose?'

'You want my address back home in America, or...?'

'Here, please.'

'I'm stayin' at Willow Cottage with my friend Clarissa; that's Mrs Clarissa Ramsay. This is my second visit; I came over last year and had such an interestin' time that I'm back again. And guess what? I'm havin' another interestin' time. I love puzzles, Neil, be they crosswords or crime. My Gordon found me quite useful at times, when cases he was workin' on ran into brick walls.' Amy Rose delved into her capacious bag, produced a paper bag, and opened it. 'Chocolate nut cookie?'

'No thank you, madam.'

'Fresh baked to my own recipe.'

'Not while I'm on duty, madam.'

'So who's here to tell on you? Certainly not me, because d'you know somethin'? I love the way you say "madam". Makes me feel special. You can't tell me that a husky young man like you doesn't want a chocolate nut cookie. Come on,' Amy Rose coaxed.

As she had pointed out, nobody was watching, and a delicious smell was wafting from the bag she waved beneath his nose. Neil felt his stomach beginning to yearn.

'Well, thank you madam, perhaps just one.'

'I made 'em specially for you, so we'll each have one now and I'll leave the bag.'

The biscuit melted in Neil's mouth and tasted so good that if he hadn't been a sort-of married man who still cared for his difficult wife he might have proposed on the spot. Instead, he forced his mind back to business. 'Did you know Mr Pearce well, Mrs Rose?'

'I can't say that I did, but his wife's very pleasant. I met her when I spoke to the Women's Rural last year. I used to be a midwife and now I compose crosswords so they were interested in hearin' about both these things. After that, we chatted when we met each other in the village. But I certainly heard quite a lot about Kevin Pearce. He was kinda pompous, from what I gather. Some folks really liked him, others found him a bit much. But I never got the idea that anyone hated him. He was a journalist in England before he retired, d'you know that?'

'Yes, we know.' Suddenly Neil placed her – she had been at a nearby table with a crowd of people one evening when he dined in the local pub with Anja.

'Could have been killed by someone with a grudge from way back, I suppose,' she was saying now. 'D'you have any idea if he was one of the folks who got a poison pen letter last year?'

'There were poison pen letters received here in Prior's Ford?'

'Uh-huh. Quite a few folks got 'em and it might be worth your while findin' out if he did as well. If so, it might just hold a clue.'

'Was the perpetrator found out?'

'No,' Amy Rose said vaguely. 'The letters just stopped and that was the end of it. The ones I heard about were gossipy, not malicious, but it's still worth while findin' out if he got one, don't you think? Anyway, what I came to tell you was that a couple called the MacBains held a party not long back to welcome some newcomers to the village. They were special – not the Mac-Bains, the new folks – because the wife's a well-known cookery writer, a really nice woman, and her husband's a retired police officer who's writin' his memoirs.'

'Can you give me their names?'

'He's Allan Hunter and her professional name's Laura Tyler. They bought that nice little cottage down by the river as a holiday home. She's friendly but he's not keen on mixin'. What I was goin' to tell you is that I was there when they met the Pearces at this party, and I noticed that Kevin Pearce an' Mr Hunter seemed to take a dislike to each other right off. I mentioned it yesterday to Marcy Copleton, who runs the village store with her partner Sam, an' she said that she'd been servin' the Hunters not long back when Kevin happened by. As soon as he saw the Hunters he turned and went out again. Came back after they'd gone. Laura helps out with the drama group and Kevin got on with her well enough, it seems. So it looks like it was her husband he didn't want to bump into again. I thought it worth mentionin' to you. Have another cookie, one's just a mouthful.'

This time Neil took the proffered cookie without argument.

'There's folk here sayin' he was killed by some stranger passin' through an' long gone,' Amy Rose mused, 'but I don't see it myself. From what I've heard it doesn't sound as though he interrupted someone stealin', or a tramp plannin' to sleep in the hall overnight. I know from bein' a cop's wife that there's more murders committed by folks the victim knows than by strangers. It's my belief that whoever did it isn't all that far away from where we're sittin' right now. Well, best be gettin' along. See you again, Neil.'

As soon as she had gone he took another of the addictive cookies, just as Gloria arrived.

'What did that strange-looking woman want?'

Neil swallowed hurriedly and then took a coughing fit as a crumb went down the wrong way. He snatched at the bottle of water on the desk, and unfortunately his elbow hit the paper bag. It fell to the ground, landing upright. Gloria picked it up and peered inside while he gulped water.

'Don't tell me you're letting them feed you! You're a police officer, not an exhibit in a zoo.'

'She's American,' Neil finally managed to explain huskily between coughs. 'Visitor ... came with information...'

'And bribes?'

'They're what she calls cookies ... made them herself.' He sipped more water and finally managed to draw in a decent breath. 'They're very good, actually, and the information could be worth following up.'

He pushed his notebook over to Gloria, who took the seat recently vacated by Amy Rose and began to read.

'Laura Hunter – I've spoken to her. She was in the village hall on the night of the murder.'

'That's right, she's a member of the drama group.'

Gloria brought out her own notebook and riffled through it until she found the right page. 'Her husband was in their flat in Leeds that night, on business. I didn't know he was one of us.'

'Retired and writing his memoirs,' Neil offered, 'which sounds as though he might have been pretty high up.'

'Mmm. So this Mrs Rose seems to think that it wasn't the first time the husband and Mr Pearce met.'

'She seems to have a sharp eye for people. Quite a character too; her husband was a police officer and she claims to have helped him with some cases he was on.'

'God save us from amateur detectives,' Gloria muttered as she read on, one hand reaching into the bag for a cookie. 'What's this about poison pen letters?'

'Apparently there was a rash of them here last year. Mrs Rose said they were mainly filled with local gossip as far as she knew, but she wondered if Kevin Pearce might have received one he didn't talk about. Could be.'

'I suppose. I'll pass this on,' Gloria said, mindful of the Inspector's instructions to run even the slightest piece of gossip past him.

'Has anyone interviewed Mr Hunter?'

'There was no reason to. He'd just arrived back from Leeds and he's never been in the village hall.'

'What about this business of him and the victim seeming to take a dislike to each other?'

'People do, at times. It means nothing.'

'Two people noticed it, though – Mrs Rose at the party, and the woman who works in the village store.'

'You're chasing after a red herring,' Gloria said impatiently, but even so, mindful of the DI's words, she made some notes of her own before helping herself to another cookie. 'By the way, are you meeting your little Scandinavian friend later?'

'Not tonight.'

'Good. Be prepared to see less of her for the time being.'

'Why? Have you been interfering in my private life? What have you said to her?'

'Don't flatter yourself! Why would I be interested in what you get up to in your free time? The boss wants us to mingle with the villagers when we're off duty. We're supposed to win their confidence in the hope that they'll relax and open up to us, and that includes drinks and meals at the local pub. I'm booking us in for dinner at eight. You're going to have to put Miss

Scandinavia on hold for the time being. Sorry about that,' she finished sweetly.

Neil shrugged. 'No problem.'

When she had gone he permitted himself a smug smile. It was true what they said – every cloud had a silver lining.

Twenty-Six

Ewan McNair wasn't the only young man in Prior's Ford so wrapped up in his own problems that murder took second place to them. Several weeks after Molly broke off their engagement Lewis was still in a deep depression and holding everyone at arm's length.

'Do me a favour,' Jinty said when she met Cam in the village store. 'Try to have a word with Lewis.'

'What about?'

'What d'you think? Ever since the Ewings came to fetch wee Rowena Chloe home he's been hiding away from everyone, working on his own in far corners of the estate and coming in at odd hours to make himself a sandwich instead of sitting down to proper meals with the rest of us. And he refuses to speak to anyone, even about work. His parents are at their wits' end. It's as well the grounds are closed to the public for the rest of the year.'

'He's a fool. Molly's not the only girl in the world.'

'Maybe you could try to tell him that. The rest of us are pussyfooting around, scared to say a word in case it sends him into a worse temper than he's in already. None of the plans for the garden can go ahead; Ginny can't get any further with the waterfall because he won't discuss it and Duncan's getting more grumpy by the day. If anyone can make Lewis sort himself out it's you, Cam.'

'What makes you think that?'

'You used to be like brothers; what did you do then to get him out of a mood?'

Cam grinned. 'Goading him into a punch-up usually did it. He's never been able to get the better of me.'

'There you are, then,' Jinty said. 'Go for it – and the sooner the better!'

'I might just make things worse.'

'That,' Jinty told him, 'isn't possible. So just go ahead and *do* something!'

Between being fed by village women who pictured the handsome young police constable wasting away in the incident van, and socializing in the pub with Gloria every day, Neil reckoned that he'd have to find time to start visiting a gym if this case wasn't solved soon. Not that he was complaining, especially about spending more time with his wife.

Anja, however, was beginning to get jealous. 'Why do you have to be with that policewoman so much?' she asked, having found him alone in the incident van.

'It's to do with work. We need to exchange information.' He glanced nervously at his watch.

Anja, noticing, said, 'I came over to ask you to have lunch with me. At my house, where we can be alone. I've closed Colour Carousel especially.'

'Anja, I'd love to but I can't.'

'You're going to have your lunch with her again, aren't you?'

'As I said, it's business. She's a sergeant and that makes her my superior. I have to do as she wishes.'

'But why do you have to eat with her in the evenings as well, when you're not on duty?'

'In a murder investigation we can never afford to be off duty.'

'I can't even sit with you when we see each other in the Cuckoo,' she complained. 'That woman gives me the black eye every time I look at you.'

'The black eye?' He looked at her beautiful blue eyes, showing no sign of bruising. 'Are you saying that she hits you?'

'Of course not! If she ever tried I would hit back, I promise you that. She gives me the black eye like this.' She narrowed her eyes and glared at him.

'Oh, black looks!'

'Very black looks. I don't like her, but you do.'

'I have to like her, I work with her.'

'And she likes you.'

'Don't be daft, she can't stand me.'

'Men,' Anja said, 'are so like children. They never see what is beneath their noses.'

'Believe me, we do.' He got up and walked

256

round the desk. 'Anja, I have to go.'

'To her,' Anja pouted, then suddenly she went on tiptoe, grabbed his shoulders and kissed him. A long, hard kiss. 'That,' she said when she released him, 'is to make sure that you don't forget your Anja. Go if you must, but be careful!'

As soon as she had gone he rubbed at his mouth, and was relieved, when he studied his handkerchief, to see that there was no sign of lipstick. He emerged from the van to find Gloria standing on the pavement, watching the girl walk away.

'What did *she* want?'

'Nothing.'

'Giving you more tips on your interior decorating?' she asked icily, narrowing her eyes at him.

'Heard anything interesting?' she asked later, as they finished their pub meal.

'Only rumour and gossip, nothing that catches the attention. The locals are as lost as we are over this murder. It's boring, just sitting around.'

'Then you'll be glad to hear that you're not going to be bored any more. I passed that information you got on the poison pen letters to the boss, and he wants a couple of people to go through Kevin Pearce's paperwork, in case he got one. I spoke to Mrs Pearce this morning; apparently her husband was in the habit of keeping a lot of the articles he wrote during his years as a journalist. He also kept just about every other piece of paper he got, and sometimes clippings of other people's newspapers and magazine cuttings. He turned their box room into a study and it's got wall-to-wall filing cabinets. I said we'd go over this afternoon to collect the first lot and bring them back here for you to work on while you're waiting for the public to call in with vital information. I've arranged for WPC Nancy Hastings to help you.'

'Thanks a bunch!'

'No problem,' Gloria said sweetly. 'Just justify my faith in your ability by going through every single piece of paper in detail. Great oaks grow from little acorns, you know.'

'So this is where you've been hiding?'

'It's where I've been *working*.' Lewis kept plunging the spade into the hard ground, coming up with clods of earth that he threw aside before driving the spade in again with all his frustration, grief and anger behind it.

'Aye, working on your own for the past few weeks now. I suppose you know that Ginny needs your help with clearing out the watercourse from the top of the hill?'

'She knows what she's doing, and young Jimmy's working with her, isn't he?'

'You're the boss and she wants to be sure of your approval before she goes ahead. And Duncan wants to talk to you about half a dozen things. You are, after all, the young laird.'

'Oh, for pity's sake! Duncan's paid to look after the estate; if he isn't up to doing the job without me nursemaiding him every minute of the day he can get out and I'll find someone else to take over!'

'Fair enough, but it's not just the hired help that needs you, Lewis. I'm told that your folks never see you these days, not even for meals. Apparently you prefer to forage for food in the kitchen when nobody else is there.' Cam slipped the rucksack from his back and opened it. 'Your mother's fretting over you. She sent me out to search for you, armed only with sandwiches and a flask of tea. Look on me as your local Henry Stanley, Dr Livingstone. Personally, I thought you'd prefer this to tea...' Then, as Lewis kept digging, refusing to look up. 'It's a bottle of wine. I even brought paper cups.'

'Go away, Cam!'

'OK, if you're not hungry or thirsty I'll have it.' Cam settled down with his back against a tree and brought a packet of sandwiches from the rucksack. 'There's nothing I like more than to relax and watch some poor idiot toil beneath the sun.'

He sat in silence, chewing while Lewis continued to work, not even flinching when the clods began to land uncomfortably close. Three sandwiches and a cup of wine later he said conversationally, 'You must know that she wasn't worth it.'

'What?' Lewis was startled into looking at him.

'Molly; she was never going to marry you. Everyone knew that.'

'You don't know what you're talking about!'

'Oh, but I do. You forget that I knew her first.' Cam put a slight emphasis on 'knew'.

'Shut your mouth or...' Lewis drove the sharp edge of the spade hard into the ground.

'Or you'll shut it for me? I don't think so. I always won when it came to fisticuffs between us. When did the precious only son of the laird ever manage to beat the builder's boy? As I was saying when you interrupted me, I met Molly in Canada and we got to know each other very well, if you get my drift.'

'I told you to shut your mouth!'

Cam emptied the cup of wine and began to pack the rucksack. 'The thing is – and I should have told you this before – I remember telling her all about the village I came from and about my boyhood pal Lewis who lived in the big house with his parents, and about how back-packers like her worked in the house and gardens in the summer. What I didn't think to tell her was that the place was falling down around your ears at the time. But surprise, surprise, pretty little Molly turned up in Prior's Ford the very next summer and set her cap at the son of the big house. And he, being a poor university-educated innocent totally unused to the ways of women, fell for her hook, line and sinker.'

'Cam...!' Lewis warned between gritted teeth.

'You surely never thought she'd stick around once she realized that what you want more than anything is to put Linn Hall to rights and then live in the place for the rest of your life? I could never see our Molly becoming the wife of an impoverished landowner. If she hadn't already started persuading you to sell up once you own the place, so that she could enjoy spending the money, it was going to happen eventually. Most of the folk in the village had started saying that. You're just lucky that she lost interest and bailed out before you married her, pal. She's not marriage material, though I'll admit that she's really good between the—'

Cam had been reclining against the tree trunk, apparently relaxed, but when Lewis, finally enraged beyond bearing, threw the spade away and lunged at him he rolled swiftly to one side. Lewis landed clumsily on the ground, narrowly missing hitting his head on the tree, and Cam, already on his feet, reached down towards him.

'Ups-a-daisy,' he said cheerfully, and then stumbled back as Lewis's free hand, bunched into a fist, caught him on the side of the jaw.

'Watch it,' he warned before warding off another blow, then delivering one of his own. It caught Lewis on the cheekbone with enough force behind it to send him reeling off balance. Recovering, he charged at Cam, eyes blazing.

They had fought many times before; as children with flailing, windmilling arms and then, in their teens, copying boxers they had seen on television, but always as friends. Now all Lewis's pent-up heartbreak and shame was behind every blow. It was as though he needed to free himself of the intolerable hurt Molly had caused by channelling it through his arms and fists and into Cam, which was exactly what the other man had intended.

They crashed against trees, fell through bushes, rolled on the freshly dug earth with first one and then the other gaining mastery in a struggle choreographed by Cam, by far the better fighter of the two. He spent most of his time warding off Lewis's maddened attack, while delivering a sufficient number of blows to keep fury bubbling up within his adversary.

The fight only ended when they were both too exhausted to do any more than sprawl side by side, sucking in lungfuls of air. Several minutes passed before Cam said, 'Call it a draw?'

Lewis raised himself on one elbow, wincing. 'I thrashed you, you mouthy bastard!'

'Whatever. Fancy some wine?'

'Sounds reasonable.' Lewis got up and this time he was the one to hold out a hand, which Cam took gingerly, ready to retaliate if necessary. But he was glad to see that finally his boyhood pal was free of the misery that had weighed him down.

'I wouldn't mind another sandwich as well,' he said as he got to his feet. 'Your mum packed enough for two.'

Lewis found the rucksack and brought out its contents. 'They're squashed.'

'That won't spoil the taste. As long as the bottle didn't break.'

'No, it's all right.'

They finished off the sandwiches and wine

sitting side by side, their backs against a tree. Nothing was said until the food and drink was finished, then Cam was the first to speak.

'Feeling better?'

'I'm sore all over.'

'Me too, but I meant about Molly. She wasn't the right one for you, mate – honest.'

'P'raps not. I knew that Jinty disapproved – she doesn't hide her feelings – and she's usually right. But it hurt, Cam, the way she just dumped me.'

'It always does, but as one door closes...'

'What hurts most, to be honest, is Rowena Chloe. I couldn't bear to lose her.'

'We'd all hate to lose her, but didn't the Ewings say that she'd still come to stay at times?'

'Yes, but what if they change their minds?'

'Take things a day at a time.' Cam advised, getting to his feet. 'We'd better get back to the house. I'll need to borrow your bath before I go home.'

They brushed each other down as best they could, but it didn't make much of a difference. Lewis had a black eye and a huge lump on his forehead, while Cam's nose was swollen and one side of his face all bruised. They both ached from top to toe, but no bones seemed to be broken.

Together they limped through shrubbery towards the house, their friendship restored.

'What you were saying about Ginny wanting me to help with the watercourse down the hill,'

Lewis said. 'D'you fancy going there this evening to see what needs to be done?'

'No problem, as long as you buy us both a pint afterwards,' Cam agreed, seeing Lewis's renewed interest in the gardens as a sign that his heart was beginning to mend.

Twenty-Seven

'You look as though you could do with a change,' Amy Rose said as she and Clarissa had breakfast together.

'I'm fine.'

'Why don't you spend some time in Glasgow with Alastair?'

'The gallery's organizing a big exhibition, so I wouldn't see much of him.'

'You've not been yourself the past couple of days; you're not lettin' this murder business get you down, are you?'

'It's nothing to do with that. If you must know,' Clarissa admitted, 'it's Alexandra. I'd hoped to hear from her before this, but there's not been a word.'

'So what? You an' Alastair are happy, Steven an' Chris are happy for the two of you, the villagers are too busy talkin' about the murder to gossip over your business. Who cares about Alexandra?'

'I do. I hate this coldness between us. We've never been close, but I respect her.'

'So if the mountain won't go to Mohammed,' Amy Rose said briskly as she began to clear the table, 'why doesn't Mohammed go to the mountain?'

'You think I should confront her?'

'If it's goin' to make you feel better about things, yes. What's the worst that can happen? Face your demon, Clarissa. If she still refuses to accept the idea of you and Alastair together, at least you'll know you've tried, and you can stop worryin' yourself over her.'

'I don't know if I've got the courage. She's like her father; I could never win an argument with him.'

'But you're not the woman he married, are you? You're a heck of a lot stronger now.'

'Thanks to Alastair, and to you.'

'All we did was find the real Clarissa that lay buried beneath a lifetime of tryin' to please other folk. Come to think of it, it might not be a bad thing for you to test yourself against Alexandra. If she refuses to accept the new you, what have you lost? Nothin' at all. The loss is all on her side, an' at least you'd be able to say that you'd given her one last chance.'

'Perhaps you're right.'

'You're darned right I'm right. Spend the weekend with Steven and Chris – they'll help to cushion the disappointment if she's difficult.'

'I'd certainly enjoy spending time with them. I'll phone Steven later to see what he thinks.'

'Amy's right; if Alexandra's refusal to accept that you and Alastair are in a relationship's niggling at you, you need to clear the air, if only for your own sake,' Clarissa's stepson said on the phone that evening. 'And you're more than

266

welcome to spend the weekend with us.'

'I might back out of a confrontation at the last moment. I've got butterflies in my stomach at the very thought of seeing her.'

'I'll go with you, if you want.'

'The offer's tempting, but if I do this, I have to do it on my own.'

'She's not a monster, Clarissa, just an ordinary human being like the rest of us. Are you driving down?'

'Yes, I am. I thought I'd leave first thing on Friday morning and arrive early afternoon. I want to catch Alexandra as she returns from work, and get it over with so that I can enjoy the rest of the weekend with you two.'

'You know where the key's kept, just let yourself in and we'll see you when we get home. We'll take you somewhere really nice for dinner on Saturday. I won't tell Alex you're coming south – best for you to surprise her.'

'Perhaps I should have booked in at a bed and breakfast rather than stay with Steven and Chris,' Clarissa said to Amy Rose when she came off the phone. 'Then if I lose my courage at the last minute and flee back home nobody will know except you.'

'You won't lose your courage. You're stronger than you think!'

'Could you ... d'you want to come with me?'

'There's too much goin' on here at the moment. I need to keep my eyes an' ears open. It's surprisin' what people tell without realizin' it durin' a casual chat. In any case, this is somethin' you have to do on your own,' Amy Rose said. 'And go in fightin', girl!'

The marriage between Tricia Harper, the garage owner's daughter, and Derek Borland, who worked in his father's butcher's shop, was fast approaching, and both families were involved in a frantic last-minute bustle. The end house in Jasmine Row, formerly the village almshouses, had been redecorated throughout; the windows were now double-glazed and draped with looped-back floral curtains, central heating had been installed and Ivy's solid, wooden front door had been replaced by one that was almost all glass.

'Every trace of Ivy's been cleared away. I'd love to know what she'd think about what's happened to her house,' Hannah Gibb said as she and Cissie Kavanagh passed the smart new door on their way home after meeting in the butcher's.

'I doubt if she'd approve, being Ivy. It's sad in a way, but that's life. She had her day and now it's time for others to make their mark.'

'They've certainly done that. It'll be good for us to have some young people in the almshouses.'

'Perhaps there'll be a baby, in time.'

'That would be lovely. I wonder,' Hannah said thoughtfully, 'if one day, Tricia and Derek will become the oldest residents in the row.'

'Following in Ivy's footsteps?'

'Not entirely. Ivy had a ruthless tongue and I

wouldn't wish that on anyone,' Cissie said, and Hannah nodded agreement.

There was another wedding on the horizon: Victor McNair's marriage to Jeanette Askew in October. Although the wedding and reception were to be held in Kirkcudbright rather than in the Prior's Ford church, which she would have preferred, Jess was secretly beginning to get excited about it. After years of toil, worry and heartbreak, a happy event was approaching; a chance to get her hair done, wear her best finery, make a rare trip beyond the boundary of Tarbethill Farm and meet new people.

Oh, she would sob her heart out during the ceremony, as was surely her right as the mother of the groom, but the tears would be a mixture of joy and grief. Joy because her eldest was marrying the girl he loved, and the split between Vincent and Ewan was healing over, with Vincent spending more time at Tarbethill, helping his mother and brother, and grief because Bert wouldn't be by her side, scrubbed and in his best suit, complaining under his breath at the inconvenience of being away from his beloved farm.

There was hope as well. Alison had been invited to the wedding, and now she, too, spent most of her spare time at Tarbethill. Ewan was still stiff-necked about that, but at least he accepted her presence and didn't go off on his own to some far corner of the farm each time she appeared. With any luck there would be another wedding to attend in the future, bringing a ready-made little grandson with it. Hoping didn't cost a thing; if it had, Jess McNair would be in debt to the tune of millions of pounds.

Neil and Nancy Hastings quailed when Gloria led them into Kevin Pearce's study, where every possible piece of wall space was covered by shelves, all packed with neatly labelled box files.

'There's hours of work here,' Neil protested, while Nancy asked:

'How long are we expected to spend on this job, Sarge?'

'As long as it takes,' Gloria told them briskly. 'And no slacking; we haven't time to waste. I'd suggest starting with the earliest files, just in case, and taking ten at a time over to the van because there's not all that much room here. I'll keep checking in to see how you're getting on, unless you contact me first to tell me that you've found something interesting. Enjoy.' She threw the final word over her shoulder as she left them.

'It's going to take ages get them to the van in the first place!'

'Not necessarily. You pick out the first ten while I have a word with Mrs P,' Nancy said, and left, to return minutes later with a shopping trolley. 'I thought she looked like the sort of woman who would have one of those.'

'Clever you!'

'I have my uses. Now, where to start.' They

studied the box files.

'These can probably be left until later.' Neil indicated three files marked 'Drama Club'.

'I think we should take the latest "Miscellaneous" file because it covers last year, when the poison pen letters were being posted to people in the village, and for the other eight I suggest we begin with the earliest files and work our way forward.'

Clarissa had an easy drive south and arrived at Steven's flat in mid-afternoon. She unpacked her bag and made herself a coffee before returning to the car. Alexandra lived some seven miles from Steven, and Clarissa planned to reach her stepdaughter's home not long after she arrived home from the school where she was Head of Business Studies.

Driving along the tree-lined road she spotted Alexandra's car in the driveway. She parked where her car wouldn't be seen from the house and began to walk back, dialling Alexandra's number on her mobile phone. Her heart gave a great thump when the receiver was lifted and a familiar, crisp voice rattled out the number.

'Alexandra, it's Clarissa. We need to have a talk.'

There was a faint pause before Alexandra said coldly, 'About what?'

'About me and Alastair Marshall.'

'There's nothing to talk about!'

'I think there is. Are you on your own?'

'Yes, but I'm not going to discuss anything

271

over the phone.'

'Nor am I,' Clarissa said as she reached the driveway.

'I've no intention of going to Prior's Ford.'

'I don't expect you to. I'm coming to you.'

'I'm very busy over the next few weeks.'

'I'm only looking for the next two hours,' Clarissa said, and pressed the doorbell.

Alexandra always wore her long chestnut hair in a severe chignon at work, but released it to fall to her shoulders as soon as she got home.

'It would have been courteous,' she said stiffly as she led Clarissa into her immaculate lounge, 'to give me advance warning of this visit.'

'It would have been courteous of you to stay in Prior's Ford long enough to let us talk to you, instead of dashing off in a temper,' Clarissa shot back at her.

The look she got in return was just like the look Keith used to give her whenever she annoyed him. Come to think of it, it was the look he used on his students and his staff, the look that had once made Clarissa quail. But not now, she suddenly realized.

'I *beg* your pardon?'

'Alexandra, I'm not one of your students, I'm your stepmother. Don't give me that school-teacher glare. I wish you'd decided to take up a different career instead of following in your father's footsteps. Steven had more sense than you did and it's done him no harm at all.'

For the first time since they had met, possibly

272

for the first time in her life, Alexandra Ramsay was lost for words. Her beautiful face went crimson and her mouth opened and shut several times, while Clarissa sensed a sudden and most unexpected flood of confidence. 'Go in fightin', girl,' Amy Rose had advised, and she had. And it seemed to have worked.

'So, let's get down to business,' she said as she began to unbutton her coat. 'I've never liked you, Alexandra, but that may well be because I don't know you. Your father always visited his children on his own, and I've only recently realized why.'

'You don't know what you're talking about!'

'I do. Keith had reasons for everything he did. Although I felt uncomfortable with you – though not with your brother – I respected you, and still do, for your intelligence. You're so like Keith. I was in awe of you because I was in awe of him.' Clarissa draped her coat over a straight-backed chair. 'I intend to clear the air between us, Alexandra, even if it means we'll never meet again. I knew that if I gave you advance warning of this meeting you'd make sure it didn't happen. I need what the Americans call closure...'

'I don't,' Alexandra said harshly.

'...because I'm putting my life and my world to rights, and you come under the heading of unfinished business. I'm not leaving until I've said my say.'

'Then you'd better get it over with!'

'Whether or not you approve of my relationship with Alastair Marshall, it's the best thing

273

that has ever happened to me, so I've no intention of apologizing for it. He's made me happier than I've ever been, and certainly happier than I was during my marriage.'

'My father didn't force you to marry him. I knew he was making a mistake and I told him so, but he refused to listen.'

'You surely know that Keith never listened to anyone. He always thought himself to be in the right. I married him because he convinced me that I should. I'll admit that I was flattered by his proposal, though if I'd realized that marriage meant putting my entire life into his hands I would never have said yes. It was his decision that I should give up the job I loved as soon as we were married, because in his view it would not do for his wife to be a member of his staff. It was his decision that we move to Prior's Ford when he retired, but when we got there he refused to become part of the village, and as his wife – his possession, to be honest – I wasn't allowed to mix with my neighbours. But after his death things began to change. For one thing, I met Alastair at a time when I was so unhappy that I didn't know which way to turn. He was kind to me and I wasn't used to kindness. He saw beyond what I had become – Keith Ramsay's wife – and brought the real me back to life.'

Clarissa paused, but as Alexandra, who had sunk down on to one of the straight-backed chairs, just sat there, silent and stony-faced, she continued.

'I don't know how he managed it. It was as though he were a sculptor and I was a block of granite. That's certainly what I felt like at the time. I've heard it said that sculptors don't shape stone into figures; they chip into the stone to free the figure already there, waiting to be released. That describes the way I felt. Alastair released me and then he gave me the courage to go off abroad on my own. By the time I returned I felt whole again.'

'He's young enough to be your son. It's disgusting!' Alexandra said in a low voice to the hands twisting together in her lap.

'That's exactly what I thought when we began to grow close – not disgusted, because true love can never be disgusting – but I was astonished and frightened by the way I felt about him. I fought against my feelings and discovered later that he was involved in a struggle of his own. When he tried to talk to me about it I turned him away, time and time again, and it was only when he gave up and got a job in Glasgow that I came to my senses and realized that without him, my life would be empty again. I'm loved and *in* love for the first time in my life, and I will not,' Clarissa said fiercely, 'let our age difference or other people's disapproval spoil things!'

'The two of you must be laughing stocks in your village.'

'There was a lot of gossip at first and yes, probably a lot of sniggering, but our friends stood by us, and knowing that you have the support of good friends, even though they may be few, is much more powerful than a hundred gossips and finger-pointers.'

'You can't really believe that this romance of yours will last for the rest of your life!'

'It probably won't, but when you think of it, nobody can know for sure what lies ahead. I'm making the most of every day and leaving the future be until it becomes the present. In a way, I hope that what Alastair and I have right now doesn't last because I can't bear the thought of him having to look after me as I age, or grieving for me when I die. If – when – it does end, I'll have wonderful memories to keep me warm for all the time I have left. I'll have something to cherish, and that will be wonderful.'

Alexandra glanced at the gold watch on her slender wrist. 'I have to go out in half an hour.' Her voice was still frosty. 'I'd like you to go now.'

'Certainly. I've said all I wanted – needed – to say to you.' Clarissa got to her feet and reached for her coat.

Twenty-Eight

'Never mind,' Steven comforted Clarissa. 'Much as I love my sister, I know that she can be very difficult at times. She's still not happy about Chris and me living together as a couple, but once she realized that if I was forced to choose between the two of them I'd opt for Chris every time, she softened.'

'In an Alex sort of way,' Chris called from the kitchen.

'He's right. "Unbent very slightly" is probably a better way of putting it. But what does it matter to you? You never saw much of her, and now you're completely free to enjoy the life you've chosen for yourself – like me. And believe me, a chosen lifestyle's much better than one imposed by others,' Steven was saying when Chris put his head round the kitchen door.

'Dinner will be on the table in twenty minutes. In the meantime, who's for a gin and tonic?'

'Me,' Clarissa said with feeling.

Steven and Chris were good company, and by Sunday Clarissa felt completely relaxed. She was almost ready to start the journey home after a light lunch when the phone rang. Steven answered it, then tapped on the spare room door before coming in.

'Clarissa, it's Alex. She wants to speak to you.'

'Me?'

'That's what she said. Are you willing?'

'No, but I'm curious.' She followed him into the hall and picked up the receiver.

'Steven says that you're about to set off for Scotland,' Alexandra said. 'I wondered, have you time to call in on me first? There's something I want to ask you.'

'I can't stay long.'

'It won't take long.'

It being the weekend, Alexandra's shining nut-brown hair was curling about her shoulders and her slim feet were bare. She wore a dark green velvet trouser suit.

'Thank you for coming,' she said when she opened the door. 'I've made coffee.' Then, once they were settled in the lounge with their drinks: 'You said on Friday that my father had reasons for visiting us on his own, and that you knew them. What were they?'

'That's his business, not for me to talk about.'

'Did you by any chance suspect at any time that he might be unfaithful to you?'

Clarissa stared at her. 'How did you know that?'

'I visited Prior's Ford when you were abroad.'

'I know. You stayed in my house with Ginny Whitelaw, and helped the Ralston-Kerrs to cata-

278

logue generations of possessions. Alastair told me about your visit.'

'Did he tell you why I was there?'

'No he didn't, because it was none of his business, or mine. Anything you may have said to him would never go any further.'

Alexandra nodded. 'I wouldn't have spoken to him if I'd thought otherwise. It helped to talk. If he hadn't been there I expect I would have gone to your minister,' she added thoughtfully, tucking shining curtains of hair behind both ears.

'Who would also have respected your confidence. And so will I, though you may prefer not to confide in me, given that we're little more than strangers.'

'We have one thing in common – my father, and he's the person I'm going to talk about. You said that he and I were very alike, and we are, mainly because I worshipped him from childhood. All I ever wanted was to please him, make him proud of me. That's why I became a teacher – because it was what he'd wanted us both to do. When Steven decided to work in a building society then set up house with Chris I felt obliged to make up for what Father and I both saw as his failure. I know what you mean about trying to live the life that someone else wants you to live. It's hard. And what made it even harder for me was the fact that I knew that my father wasn't as perfect as he liked everyone to believe. That's what I told Alastair when I went to Prior's Ford. About the day I saw my father writhing about in the back of his car with one of

279

my teachers.'

'Oh, my dear, how long ago was this?'

'Three years before Mum left him. He told us and everyone else that she'd left because she wanted to be a career woman again, but I think it may have been because of other women. She and I have never discussed Father; not that I want to know what she thinks of him.' She drew a deep breath, then lifted her long-lashed dark blue eyes to meet Clarissa's. 'Is that what you were talking about on Friday?'

'Since you're being open with me, I suppose I should be open with you. After Keith died you and Steven took away a lot of his papers. Later, I began to clear out what was left, and found letters from a former colleague who also happened to be my best friend – or so I thought until then. It turned out that they'd been having an affair during most of our marriage. When he came south to see you and Steven he visited her as well. That's why I was never asked to accompany him.'

'Does this woman know that you found out?'

'I had to confront her because she was under the impression that we were still close friends. I phoned and told her what I thought of her, then I burned the letters.'

For the first time, Alexandra bestowed a genuine smile on her stepmother. 'Good for you.'

'I didn't do it straight away. After reading the letters I lost my mind for a while. I wandered out of the house and Alastair found me sitting on a stile in pouring rain, soaked to the skin. He thought I'd escaped from a psychiatric hospital, while I thought I was going to end up in one. He took me to his cottage to dry off, then took me home once I was able to tell him where I lived. He befriended me, healed me, saved me.'

'He's a very kind man, I'm aware of that.'

'My turn to ask you a question now. What sent you to Prior's Ford while I was abroad?'

'I suppose the desire to emulate Father went too far, subconsciously. I met a wonderful man and fell head over heels in love for the first time in my life. I may be intelligent, but when it comes to emotions it turned out that I'm hopeless. I discovered that he was married and had no intention of leaving his wife. And suddenly I realized that I was following in my father's footsteps. I was so ashamed of myself! I panicked and fled and ended up in Prior's Ford with some idea of staying at the pub until I'd had time to sort myself out. Then I met Alastair again, and I suppose I can say that I, too, was looked after and healed.'

'You're happier now, though – still seeing that nice man I met last time I came south?'

'Gerald – yes, he's still in my life. I think he's rather like Alastair; I kept pushing him away at first, checking him out to make sure that he was a bachelor. A widower, as it happens. A good kind friend who's willing to give me all the time I need to commit to something more than friendship. To tell the truth, you're here today because I told him the whole sorry story yesterday. He was incredibly understanding, and he pointed out that I have the habit of making mountains out of molehills. He said that I expect too much of myself and others.'

'So did Keith.'

'Gerald said that too. He advised me to concentrate on *my* life, and not my father's, or anyone else's, including yours. After speaking to him I had a new perspective on things and I realized that in some says we're quite alike, you and I.'

'If you mean once bitten, twice shy, I suppose we are,' Clarissa agreed. 'I'm glad we finally got the chance to clear the air. I can go back to Prior's Ford in a happier frame of mind, as far as we're both concerned.'

'More coffee before you go?'

'I'd better be on my way.' Clarissa got to her feet. 'Alexandra, I don't expect you to approve of my relationship with Alastair. To be honest, your opinion doesn't matter a whit. But I'd like to think that we can meet now and again on civil terms.'

'Me too,' Alexandra said. Her smile was slight but seemed to Clarissa to be genuine. At least, she thought later as she drove the car north towards Scotland and home, they had cleared the air without coming to blows. And for the moment, that was enough for her.

'Hello, Neil.' Cynthia MacBain gave a good facsimile of the royal wave as Neil and Gloria entered the Neurotic Cuckoo's restaurant, then murmured to her husband, 'You'd think they would bring packed lunches rather than waste time eating in here every day. I suppose we taxpayers foot the bill for the food they're ordering.'

'They probably have to meet regularly to exchange notes,' Gilbert suggested. He enjoyed a good police-procedural novel now and again.

'They could do that over a packed lunch, couldn't they? The sooner they find that murderer and let us all get back to our normal lives, the better.' Cynthia had seen the part of Lady Bracknell in Oscar Wilde's famous play as the pinnacle of her amateur dramatic career, and now her big chance was in danger, thanks to Kevin being strangled right in front of the stage she had so looked forward to appearing on, and with the lovely boa she had coveted. 'What was Kevin thinking of, letting some stranger walk in and kill him!' she pouted now.

'He couldn't help it, my dear. I know for a fact that he was as keen to stage that play as you were to be in it. You would have been magnificent!'

'D'you think we might manage to do it as our spring production next year?'

'If we can find another director.'

'Mmmm. Gilbert...'

'I'm not sure that I'm up to taking on a play like that,' he said hurriedly.

'There's plenty time; we can mull it over.'

'Right now the important thing is to find Kevin's killer.'

'If they find him,' said Cynthia through her

teeth, 'I'd like to wring his neck for ruining my chance to give my best performance ever!'

'He seems to have kept every article he ever published in a newspaper,' Neil was complaining to Gloria, 'and it's all dull as ditchwater. It's easy to see why he never made it to the nationals. Local court cases, reports of supposedly important events, interviews with local celebrities and the occasional visiting person of importance. Do we really have to go through them all?'

'You never know what you might find. Are they helping to create a picture of the man?'

'Yes, as the sort of person nobody would want to murder unless he was boring them to the point of madness. I can tell you that his hobbies were gardening and amateur drama because there are newspaper reports on plays he appeared in, then on plays he directed, and on a couple of flower shows where he won in the vegetable section. And a full report of him winning two Scarecrow Festivals, with photographs.'

'They all need to be looked at; you never know when something will catch your attention. Possibly something from his past.'

'So far it seems to be just the sort of dull past I would expect him to have.'

'Neil, someone hated that man enough to kill him, which seems to me to show that his past wasn't totally dull. He did something wrong, or he discovered something that was dangerous to know. I don't think it was a random killing, I

284

believe that his killer had a motive and it's our job to find out what that was. Motive, opportunity, evidence...' Gloria ticked them off on her fingers.

'Yes, Sergeant.'

'Don't be smart. Whoever had a motive knew that they'd have their opportunity when he stayed behind in the village hall that night. Someone who knew him, someone who knew the village and village life well. Someone who was there that night? Definitely someone who lives, or lived, here.'

'That's all very well, but so far we don't have a single thing to go on.'

'That,' Gloria said triumphantly, 'is why those files could be important. The answer almost certainly lies within them. What about his computer?'

'Nancy's been through it and there's very little there. The financial records seem straightforward; household expenses with no indication of blackmail, either on his part or anyone else's. The other files deal with the drama club's activities since he moved here and started the group. There's the beginnings of a pretty awful play; his wife says that a well-known television actress stayed in the village for a short while a few years ago, and Kevin had been trying to write a play for her. Meredith Whitelaw, she's called.'

'I know that name. Wasn't she in one of the soaps for a long time? And now she's in another one about expats living in Spain.'

'I don't recall you watching that sort of thing.'

'I don't,' Gloria said. 'My mother does. So Nancy's finished with the deceased's computer?'

Neil nodded. 'Nothing of interest there. She's going to start on the files with me this afternoon. I'll let her have a shot at the miscellaneous stuff while I try the newspaper ones.'

'Let's hope,' Gloria said, 'that you find something interesting soon. I'll see to the bill while you get back to work. I'll look in during the afternoon.'

Neil stepped out of the pub just as Anja emerged from Colour Carousel, beaming at the sight of him.

'Neil!'

'Hello, Anja, good to see you.'

'And you. I miss you.'

'Me too. I mean, I miss you.'

'Are you busy tonight?'

'Not entirely sure at the moment.'

'If not, I'll be eating at home around seven, all alone. I'm starting with marinated herring, followed by my favourite chicken dish. There will be enough for two.'

'Sounds good.'

'Then I hope to see you later. Look out, the black-eyed one is coming.'

'I'd best go.'

He had only taken another dozen steps when Gloria caught up with him.

'When I said that I hoped you'd find something interesting soon,' she said coldly, 'I didn't mean your little interior decorator.'

'As it happens, she's the most interesting thing I've seen all day,' Neil replied blithely.

Twenty-Nine

'If I have to read one more court report or one more interview with a local housewife who spotted the outline of Mary Magdalen's face on a potato just as she was about to peel it,' Neil snarled, 'I think I'll go berserk!'

'Tell you what,' offered Nancy, a kind-hearted young woman who had a secret crush on him into the bargain, 'I'll take over the newspaper files for the rest of the day and you can take the miscellaneous box. A change is as good as a rest.'

'A change to another case or even to some beat-walking would be very welcome.' He stretched, yawned, and rubbed his eyes. 'Thanks, Nancy, you're a pal.'

'P'raps that file will bring you luck,' she responded, and was more prophetic than either of them expected. Within an hour he had unearthed a sheet from a letter-pad with the words 'YOU SHOULDN'T BE SO EAGER TO FIND OUT A SECRET. IT COULD CHANGE YOUR LIFE FOREVER' printed on it in large, shaky letters.

'Bingo! I think I might have found a poison pen letter!'

Nancy read it over his shoulder. 'What does that mean?'

'I haven't the faintest. I'm going over to show it to Mrs Pearce and ask if she can shed any light on it.'

'Shouldn't you show the Sarge?'

'I don't know where she is.'

'You could call her mobile.'

'It's the damnedest thing, Nancy, but I can't for the life of me remember the number.'

'Can't remember your own wife's number?'

'Totally gone, Nancy, if you get my drift. Which is fortunate as I'm in the mood to do something for myself for once instead of having to go to Gloria all the time.'

'Oh, right!' Understanding dawned. 'I get your meaning. What if she turns up while you're away?'

'You don't know where I am. I didn't say,' Neil told her as he headed for the door, almost bumping into Gloria, on her way up the steps.

'Where are you off to?'

'Looking for you,' he said promptly.

'For me? Or for some little bimbo?'

'I wanted to show you this,' he said in a tone of hurt dignity. 'Come in and have a look at what I've just found among the papers.'

'But what does it mean?' she asked when she had read the page.

'"It could change your life forever" – or possibly end it?' Neil suggested. 'This could relate to his days as a journalist, possibly about a story he wrote that upset someone badly.'

'Badly enough to kill? And to wait a long time for revenge,' Gloria said doubtfully. 'He's been retired for years.'

'I understand that the Pearces moved here after they both retired. Perhaps the writer took a while to find him.'

'Is there an envelope?'

'Not with the note, though I'll go through the rest of the file to make sure. The handwriting's very shaky; someone unaccustomed to writing?' Neil wondered.

'Or using their non-writing hand,' Nancy ventured. 'It reminds me of when we were kids and we used to try mirror writing and writing with our left hands.'

'I'll show it to Mrs Pearce,' Gloria decided, 'to see if she recognizes it.'

'Rats!' Neil said when she had gone. 'That might have been the introduction to my moment of fame.'

When Gloria knocked on the living-room door she was answered with a muffled sound that could have been, 'Come in,' followed by a clear young voice saying: 'Come on in unless you're Derek. He's not supposed to see the dress until the wedding.'

A pretty girl in a bridal gown stood on top of the dining table while Elinor Pearce worked busily at the hem of the crinoline skirt. Turning to see Gloria, Elinor spat some pins into her hand and deposited them on a small plate.

'Sorry, Sergeant, I didn't realize it was you.

This is Tricia Harper; she's getting married next week and we're just putting the final touches to the gown.'

'Pleased to meet you,' said the bride-to-be. 'Have you found the murderer yet?'

'Not yet.'

'Our wedding reception's in the village hall,' Tricia chattered on. 'We were told that that's all right.' Then, with sudden concern: 'Isn't it? You've not come to tell me we can't, have you?'

'No, we've finished with the hall. I'm looking for your help, Mrs Pearce.' Gloria handed the page to Elinor. 'We found this in among your husband's papers. Have you seen it before?'

A frown puckered the woman's brow as she read the printed words, then read them again. 'I've never seen it before. What does it mean?'

'We don't know. Your husband never showed it to you, or told you about it?'

'Never. Careful, Tricia...' Elinor reached up towards the bride, who was in danger of falling off the table in her attempts to read the page.

'Oops, sorry. Is it a clue?'

'We don't know at this point.' Gloria took it back, to Tricia's obvious disappointment. 'I believe that last year some local residents received poison pen letters, Mrs Pearce. Did you or your husband receive one? Or did anyone show you one of the letters?'

'Neither of us received or saw one.'

'Same here. Nobody I know got one. To tell the truth, we all felt a bit left out,' Tricia contributed.

'We were both lucky, dear; poison pen letters can be very upsetting,' Elinor told the girl gently. Then, to Gloria: 'Naomi Hennessey spoke about them at a church service, and they stopped after that. She might well have read one. You should show that paper to her. She'll probably be in the manse, beside the church.'

'Thank you, I will. I know that you've already been asked this – you don't recall your husband seeming worried about anything recently?'

'Not at all. We don't–' Elinor winced slightly, then went on – 'didn't keep secrets from each other. Kevin was a perfectionist, and he often fretted about something, usually to do with the drama club, but nothing of any great importance.'

There was no answer when Gloria knocked on the manse door, so she went to the church. It appeared to be empty, but as she walked up the aisle towards what she thought may be the door leading to the vestry a large woman suddenly popped up from a row of pews.

'Hello, it's Sergeant Frost, isn't it? We met in Elinor Pearce's house.'

'Oh, Ms Hennessey, I didn't think there was anyone here.'

The minister began to ease her way towards the aisle, her beaming smile and her brightly patterned top seeming to light up the place. 'Everyone calls me Naomi. I was just doing a bit of dusting; the fancy carvings you get in churches can be real dust-traps. The parishioners here are very helpful, but they can't be expected to see to everything. What can I do for you?'

'We've found something among Kevin Pearce's papers and I'm wondering if it could have anything to do with the poison pen letters that circulated in the village last year. Can you spare five minutes?'

'With pleasure. Nice to get a break from work. Come and sit in the front row,' Naomi invited, emerging into the aisle. Once settled, she studied the paper Gloria gave her, then shook her head. 'It must have meant something to Kevin, since he kept it, but I've certainly never seen it before.'

'Does it resemble the poison pen letters going the rounds last year?'

'Not at all.' Naomi was clear on that. 'The letters I saw were handwritten, though nobody recognized the writing, and they were written neatly on lined paper. This page isn't lined and the writing's completely different; this is clumsily printed.'

'Did anyone ever find out who sent those letters?'

'I don't believe so. They stopped after I spoke about them from the pulpit; presumably the sender suddenly realized that he or she was causing great distress to decent people and decided that enough was enough. I imagine that everyone who received a letter got rid of it. Who would want to keep something like that around?' Then, glancing at her watch: 'Sorry,

293

I've got a casserole in the oven and I'd best get back to the manse to make sure it's not drying up.'

'That's all for the moment, thank you for your help.'

'D'you have any idea when Mrs Pearce can arrange her husband's funeral?' Naomi asked as they left the church together.

'That decision lies with the procurator fiscal, and depends on the outcome of this investigation. The normal procedure is to wait until someone's indicted for trial and after the defence have had a chance to arrange their own post-mortem. It can take months.'

'Poor Elinor – and poor Kevin. What happens if the murderer isn't found?'

'The body will be released once it seems unlikely that anyone will be charged. But again, that can take a long time. I can only assure you that we're as anxious as you are to bring this investigation to a close as soon as possible.'

'Are you sure that this is correct, dear?' Fliss asked Lewis as she and Hector, heads together, studied the papers their son had laid out on the table before them.

'Quite sure. I told you that opening the grounds to visitors in the summer would be worthwhile, and this proves me right.'

'I can't believe that so many people were interested in our shabby little estate,' she marvelled.

'Not as shabby as it used to be, my dear,'

294

Hector pointed out. 'You've worked wonders, Lewis.'

'I couldn't have done it without Ginny ... and Duncan and the youngsters, of course,' Lewis corrected himself. Then, smiling across the table at Ginny: 'You've been a godsend!'

She felt herself blush to the roots of her short black hair. 'I've had the best time of my life, working here.'

'I wish we could pay you more, dear,' Fliss apologized.

'I can get by on what you pay me, and I'm looking forward to staying on over the autumn and winter again. It means that we'll be able to clear the watercourse all down the hill and plant water-loving plants on its banks and by the lake in time to flower next year. By the time we – sorry, you – open the grounds to visitors again the lake and the pond in the rose garden will be filled. And I can't wait to explore the grounds at the top of the hill to see if there are any decent plants hidden beneath all that undergrowth. I'd like to clear that area and get some seats in place for people to relax and enjoy the view. We need to put shallow steps up the hillside too, Lewis.'

He nodded. 'It's all in the plan for next year. You were right about people being interested in seeing the estate as a work in progress; according to the visitors' book quite a lot of them intend to come back to see what's been changed.' Then, getting to his feet and stretching his arms above his head. 'Enough about work, I'm off to the Cuckoo for a quick pint before bed.

Coming?'

'He seems to be getting back to his old self,' Fliss said happily when the young people had gone.

'I hope so. Rotten business, that. Let's hope he finds someone less – whatever it was – than Molly.'

'Amen to that, dear,' Fliss said fervently. And then, after a pause: 'Someone who loves this place as much as we do.'

'Someone like Ginny,' her husband agreed.

'Someone like Ginny would be very nice, but let's not think about that,' Fliss said. 'I hate to look forward to things and then get disappointed. A cup of cocoa before bedtime, dear? Cocoa never lets one down.'

Thirty

'I shouldn't be takin' off at a time like this,' Amy Rose said as the visit to Whitby with Stella Hesslet neared. 'Not with a murder right on the doorstep. I should be here, watchin' and listenin' and pickin' up clues.'

'The police are still in the village every day,' Clarissa pointed out. 'They're keeping their eyes and ears open.'

'But they're trained to follow laid-down procedure and folks are wary about talkin' to them, even when they're not in uniform. It's different for people like me. I can mix with the villagers and get them to talk freely. And I'm very good at knowin' when people say one thing and mean another. If my Gordon was here he'd tell you that I'm *very* good at it. There's somethin' about this case, Clarissa, that's tuggin' at my mind and tellin' me I ought to stay here. It's like the poison pen letters last year.'

'Amy, you're not saying that you found out who sent them, are you?'

'Of course not,' Amy said swiftly, 'but I would have, if only a few more folks had gotten letters. I could sense somethin' then and I sense it again. D'you think Stella would mind if I called off on this visit to her friend?'

'She'd be very disappointed. Since meeting you she's come out of her shell and I can tell that she's looking forward to sharing her holiday with you. As for me, I'm glad you're going because I don't like the idea of you getting too involved in a murder. If the man who did it is still around – though I think he's long gone – you might become the next victim.'

'No way,' Amy said firmly. 'This wasn't a casual crime on the spur of the moment, it was a one-off killing for a special reason, so you needn't worry about the killer striking again.'

'You can't be sure of that.' Clarissa was beginning to feel exasperated.

'But I am. That's one of the reasons why I want to stick around, to find out why I'm sure. When I get the answer I'll be on my way to solving the case. There's this voice in my head – I sometimes think it's Gordon. I used to help him to solve crimes, and p'raps now he's tryin' to help me. Once a cop, always a cop, he used to say.'

'Please, Amy, just go to Whitby and enjoy yourself, and when you return you can tell me all about this man who seems to have caught Stella's attention.'

'I suppose you're right. Stella does need a man in her life and if he's as shy as she is they'll never get together without my help.'

'It's amazing how quickly you can switch between detecting and matchmaking.'

'It's called multitaskin' and I've always been

good at that. Which reminds me – is Alastair comin' to the village soon?'

'The weekend you're away,' Clarissa said, and went off to do some gardening, keenly aware that if it hadn't been for Amy's interference, she and Alastair might have never admitted their growing love for each other.

Neil almost missed the report cut from a newspaper page because it was at the very bottom of one of the box files, folded several times until it was little larger than a postage stamp. It was yellowed with age, and had to be unfolded carefully to avoid tearing the softened paper. After one swift read he spent a few minutes on the computer then said 'Jackpot!'

'You've found something interesting?' Nancy asked.

'I do believe that I have.' Gloria's phone was engaged so he grabbed the chance to phone Detective Inspector Cutler, who was in charge of the case. At last he had been given a chance to show some initiative.

'Sir, it's Constable White, phoning from Prior's Ford. I've just found an interesting article among Kevin Pearce's papers.'

'What's it about?'

'I think you should see it for yourself, sir.'

'As interesting as that? Very well, bring it over as soon as you can.'

'I'm leaving now, sir.'

'What is it?' Nancy wanted to know.

'No time to tell you, I've got a meeting with

the DI.'

'What about the Sarge?' Nancy asked as he put the receiver down. 'Shouldn't she be the one to deal with new evidence?'

'Her phone's busy and this could be important.'

'What if she comes in and asks where you are?'

'Tell her I'm off on important police work,' Neil said, hoping that he didn't meet Gloria on his way to his car. Five minutes later he was driving out of the village, his precious find tucked into the glove compartment. This article was different from all the rest in that it hadn't been written by Kevin Pearce. It was the story of a tragic incident in a Manchester suburb in the late 1950s when a young boy by the name of Patrick Hunter had broken his neck in a fall from a tree while bird-nesting.

Two older boys who witnessed the disaster were named as Kevin Pearce, and the victim's older brother, Allan Hunter.

'There's a newcomer to the village, sir,' Neil said when Detective Inspector Cutler had finished reading the article. 'His name's Allan Hunter – Chief Superintendent Hunter until he retired from the police service just over a year ago. His main home's in Leeds, and he and his wife recently bought a holiday home in Prior's Ford. They're there now.'

'You sure you've got the same Allan Hunter?'

'I checked on the computer and he was living

in Manchester around that time.'

'Who interviewed him after the murder?'

'I took a statement from his wife; she's Laura Tyler, a well-known cookery writer. She helps out with the drama club that Mr Pearce ran and she was at the final rehearsal. Her husband wasn't interviewed because that night he was in their home in Leeds.'

'Mmm.' Cutler read the article once more. It told the story of three youngsters, Kevin Pearce and brothers Allan and Patrick Hunter, who had been playing in a wood near to their Manchester homes. The Hunters were climbing a tall tree in search of birds' nests when Patrick fell. Allan scrambled down the tree and stayed with his brother while Kevin ran for help. Both boys were interviewed by the police, and an inquest found Patrick's death to be a case of misadventure.

'So Kevin Pearce and Allan Hunter knew each other once. Coincidences happen; a tragic accident long ago may not tie in with the murder we're investigating now.'

'There's an American woman staying at Willow Cottage at the moment, a Mrs Amy Rose. She came to the incident caravan a few weeks ago to tell me about a party held to welcome the Hunters to the village. She was present when the Pearces and Hunters were introduced, and she noticed that both men seemed to take an instant dislike to each other for no apparent reason. Then the woman who co-owns the village store told Mrs Rose about

301

an occasion when the Hunters were in the store. Kevin Pearce was about to come in but as soon as he spotted the Hunters he turned about and left. Then he came back a few minutes after they had cleared out of the place.'

'Since Mr Hunter's a person of some distinction I'd better have a word with him. Well done, White.'

'Thank you sir.'

Laura Tyler opened the door to Detective Inspector Cutler and Sergeant Gloria Frost and looked slightly surprised when they asked if her husband was at home.

'He's upstairs. I assumed that you wanted to speak to me,' she went on as she led them into the small living room, 'since I was involved with the drama group and I attended the rehearsal the night Kevin died. Allan wasn't even here; he was at a meeting in Leeds.' Then, as the DI merely gave a slight nod: 'I'll go and tell him you're here.'

'Attractive woman,' Cutler said as they heard her go upstairs. 'My wife's a great fan of hers.' He wandered around the room, hands behind his back. 'Constable White did well, coming across that old article. Can't be easy to concentrate on going through all that paperwork, but he clearly didn't let boredom get the better of him. I think that young man's got the makings of a sergeant. Still managing to work together amicably?'

'Yes sir.' If only Gloria had been available when Neil found the article, she would have been the one to present it to the DI. Part of her grudged his quick thinking and his success, while another part couldn't help but be pleased for him.

'Isn't that her?'

Gloria studied the framed photograph of a laughing dark-haired woman holding a long-bow. 'Her hair's got more silver in it now, but I'd say that's her.'

'Unusual to find a woman taking up archery, surely.'

'Not at all, sir,' Gloria was retorting somewhat sharply when Allan Hunter arrived, a handsome man of military bearing with cropped grey hair, cool brown eyes and a firm mouth. Although dressed casually in black trousers and a grey sweater over a blue shirt he managed to look, Gloria thought as he shook hands with the DI and gave her a brief nod, as though he were still in uniform. He may have left the police force, but the police force had not, and possibly never would, leave him.

His wife followed him into the room. 'Coffee?' she suggested, but Cutler declined.

'I don't think our business will take long, Mrs Hunter.'

'If you're looking for my assistance with this local murder you're out of luck,' Allan Hunter said brusquely. 'I'm retired.'

'I'm aware of that, sir. I understand that you only came to the village recently.'

'That's right. This is a holiday home; our main home's in Leeds.'

303

'I believe you met the murder victim at a party just after you settled in. Had you met before?' the DCI went on when Allan Hunter agreed.

'Not that I recall. Why would we?'

'Or since the party?'

'Again—' impatience began to creep into the man's voice – 'why would we? I've got no interest at all in socializing.'

'I'm the one who knew both the Pearces,' his wife put in. 'I volunteered my services to the local amateur drama club at that party. I've already been interviewed along with everyone else who was at the rehearsal the night Kevin was killed.'

'We're aware of that, Mrs Hunter. The thing is, sir, that this old newspaper cutting has been found among Mr Pearce's papers.' The DCI handed it over, encased in a plastic envelope. Watching Allan Hunter closely, Gloria saw him blink, then take a deep breath before starting to read it.

'Now I understand why you're here.'

'I take that you're the Allan Hunter mentioned in the article?'

'I am – or, rather, I was. It was a long time ago.'

'But it shows that you knew Kevin Pearce.'

Laura Hunter gave a startled gasp, while her husband said calmly, 'I did – once.'

'Can I see it?'

'I don't see why you need to be bothered with this, Laura,' Hunter said, but when she held her hand out, making it clear that she wouldn't accept a refusal, he gave the envelope to her.

'When you met recently, I understand that neither of you gave any indication that you had once been boyhood friends. In fact, we have witnesses who claim that you seemed to take an instant dislike to each other.'

'I'm perfectly willing to admit to instant dislike on my part; I loathed that man. He, I imagine, was alarmed when he recognized me.'

'Why would that be, sir?'

'Because he killed my young brother.'

Thirty-One

'Allan...!' The blood had drained from Laura Tyler's face. She moved to put a protective hand on her husband's arm. It was immediately shrugged off.

'If you're going to make a fuss, Laura, you'd better leave the room and let us get on with this ... discussion.'

'I'm staying.'

'Then stop interrupting. The officers have work to do.'

'Thank you, sir. Am I to understand that you're accusing Mr Pearce of murder?'

'Of bringing about my brother's death may be more apt, though as far as I'm concerned Pearce killed him. I suppose it's time for me to tell the truth, the whole truth and nothing but the truth.' Hunter's voice was calm, but his hands gripped the arms of his chair tightly as he told the story that had been buried in the back of his mind for years, yet never stopped plaguing him. 'I was ten years old, Patrick was six, Kevin Pearce was fourteen and leader of the local gang. He was a bully; all the local lads knew that, though as far as the adults were concerned he was pure as the driven snow. You could say that Kevin made the

306

bullets and got the rest of his gang to fire them.

'I was an adventurous kid; I craved excitement and I looked up to Kevin, we all did. Patrick and I came across him in the local woods that day, shooting at the wildlife with his catapult, and I plucked up the courage to ask if I could join his gang. He told me I'd have to pass an initiation test and I said OK, I'd do it there and then.'

'The test was to fetch him an egg from a bird's nest near the top of a tall tree. So I started to climb. It wasn't that difficult, though Kevin spiced things up by firing stones from his catapult at me as I began to get near my goal. I'd told Patrick to stay put and wait for me and I didn't realize that he was following me until I heard him yelling for help; he'd lost his footing and he was hanging on to a branch for dear life. I'll never know if Kevin had been firing at him too. If he had, then as far as I'm concerned it really was murder. I started back down at once and I'd almost reached Patrick when he lost his grip and fell. He hadn't far to go, but when I reached the ground it was clear even to me at that age that he was dead. He'd landed badly and broken his neck.'

'Was Kevin Pearce still there when you reached the ground?'

'Oh yes, the catapult was back in his pocket, and I remember that his face was white as a sheet, but he hadn't run away. He was waiting to make sure that I got the story straight,' Hunter said bitterly. 'The story being that it was my idea to take Patrick bird-nesting, and when

Kevin turned up and found us about to climb the tree he'd tried without success to stop us. He said that he and his gang would make me sorry if I didn't stick to that story, and I knew he meant it. So I did as I was told. My parents couldn't bear to stay on in the area after losing Patrick, so we moved away a few months later, and I thought that I was free of Kevin Pearce for the rest of my life ... until–' his voice was suddenly filled with venom – 'I had the misfortune to come face to face with him a few weeks ago.'

'Are you certain that your decision to buy the cottage wasn't linked in with the fact that he lived here?'

'Of course not!' The anger that had been building up as Allan Hunter recalled the events of years ago was turned on the DI. 'For God's sake, man, are you seriously accusing me of tracing Pearce and then buying this house just so that I could take my revenge for something that happened when we were kids?'

'I'm just looking at all the angles, sir, as you yourself would do in my place.'

Laura had been silent throughout, white-faced and with her hands knotted together in her lap. 'I was the one who found this cottage,' she said now. 'I was the one who insisted on buying it. My husband was opposed to the idea.'

'For the simple reason that I was perfectly happy living in Leeds and I saw no reason to buy a country cottage. If I'd wanted to kill Kevin Pearce over something that belongs to another life, something done that can never be undone, I'd have seen to it years ago.'

Hunter paused, and then said evenly, 'I said earlier that he'd killed Patrick, but deep down I know that if anyone was responsible for my brother's death, it was me. I hated Pearce and I didn't want to have anything to do with him, but that's because he brought back memories I've been trying to bury ever since that day.'

'You could have been concerned in case he spread the story around the village.'

'I doubt if he'd have done that. From his reaction when we came face to face at that damned party he was as appalled as I was. Neither of us wanted to rake up the past, or to see each other ever again. And as you already know, I wasn't even here on the night he died. I was at a meeting in Leeds and when it finished I spent the night in our flat there. I'll give you details of the people I was with.'

'I phoned the flat to say goodnight after I came back from the rehearsal,' Laura confirmed, 'then I went out to post a letter I'd forgotten about. I saw a few people on my way to and from the post box, but nobody who looked suspicious. It's all in my statement. Allan drove back here on the following day.'

'One more thing, sir. We found this anonymous letter among Mr Pearce's papers.' The DI handed over another plastic envelope. 'Do you know anything about that?'

Hunter gave it a brief glance before passing it to his wife. 'It means nothing to me and I've never seen it before. Pearce was a journalist, wasn't he? Leopards don't change their spots and bullies seldom change. I imagine he may have made a lot of enemies during his career. If you've quite finished with me–' he got to his feet – 'I'll give you details of the people I was with on the night of the murder.'

'I'm so sorry, Allan,' Laura said when husband and wife were alone again.

'Why should you be?'

'I should never have insisted on buying this place when you were against it.'

'You couldn't know that we'd land in the middle of a murder case, or that someone I'd hoped never to meet again lived here.'

'I wish you'd told me about your brother.'

'It happened a long time ago and it wasn't something I wanted to talk about ... until I was forced to.'

'Did his death have anything to do with you joining the police force?'

'Are you inferring that I saw every criminal I caught as a substitute for Kevin Pearce?'

'It sounds silly when you put it like that,' she admitted. 'I was thinking more of some form of revenge.'

'Revenge against a boy I never expected to see again? Definitely not. If I'd joined the force because of him I'd have been a lousy officer.'

'So you don't believe in revenge?'

'You're in a strange mood today, Laura.'

'Am I? I think it must be because of the shock

of hearing about your brother, and having to stand by and watch you being interrogated by officers of the law.'

'Interviewed, my dear, not interrogated. And where's the sense in seeking revenge for Patrick's death? It won't bring him back to life, and as I said, the fault was as much mine as Pearce's – probably more mine. I'm not glad the man's dead – of course I'm not – but at least his death has forced me to talk about Patrick for the first time. Perhaps it's given me closure, as our American friends would put it. I think I'll open a bottle of wine for lunch.'

'Then I'd better make something special.'

'Good. I'm going back to work.' He made for the door, then halted and turned. 'Why did you lie to the inspector, Laura?'

'Lie?'

'You said that we'd said goodnight to each other on the phone that night when I was in Leeds. As I recall, I was still out when you phoned, and when I got your message I didn't call back because I knew you'd probably be asleep by then.'

'I said that I'd phoned you. I didn't say that we actually said goodnight to each other, did I?'

'Come to think of it, you didn't. Was that a clumsy attempt to protect me?'

'Of course not. All I meant to do was confirm that you were staying at the flat that night, and not here.'

'I see. White wine suit you?' he asked.

* * *

The marriage of Tricia Harper and Derek Borland on a beautiful late September afternoon was just what the villagers needed, still reeling as they were from the horrors of the past few weeks.

Only the most dedicated gardeners decided against being at the wedding, which meant that the flower-filled church was packed well before the bride was due to arrive. Even Elinor Pearce was there, at Tricia's insistence.

'You've made me such a beautiful dress, Mrs Pearce, and I'd love you to see me walking down the aisle. Mum wants you to sit with her – please?'

'The church, then, dear,' Elinor agreed, 'but if you don't mind I'll not come to the reception.' Her sister had been sent back to her own family under protest, with Elinor announcing, 'I have to learn to be a widow and the longer I put it off, the harder it will be.'

The police presence in the village had lessened, but Gloria and Neil were still seconded to the case. While the villagers celebrated a marriage they were in the incident van, going through more files brought from the Pearce house.

'Did this man keep every single article he ever wrote?' Gloria said wearily, breaking an hour's silence.

'Probably not, but he certainly wrote a lot. You don't have to read every word,' Neil explained, pleased that she now knew how much he and Nancy had suffered over the past ten days or so.

'Just check the headline and then let your eyes bounce down the lines, like abseiling down a mountain. It's amazing how you can pick up the sense of the story that way.'

'My eyes don't bounce.' She pushed her chair back and got up, stretching her arms above her head.

'Bouncing and getting it over with, or reading every line and going mad. Your choice.'

'I'm going for a walk round the green. You continue abseiling.'

She returned ten minutes later, carrying a tray. 'The pub's open, so I got us some coffee and sandwiches. The bride's just arrived. I don't think much of her dress, too bulky. She looks like one of those dolls people use to cover spare toilet rolls.'

'As long as she likes it that's all that matters.' Neil helped himself to a sandwich, recalling the figure-hugging gown Gloria had chosen for her wedding. The perfect gown for a figure well worth hugging, he thought, then had to force the mind-picture away.

'Are you going to the reception in the hall tonight? It's an open invitation,' she asked, totally unaware of what was going on in his head.

'Of course. It's a great chance for newcomers to meet and mingle.'

'And watch and listen. I presume that you'll be taking your little Scandinavian friend?'

'Anja doesn't need to be taken, but as far as I know, she plans to attend.'

'I thought she would,' Gloria said.

* * *

Neil just happened to be glancing from his bedroom window as Gloria walked down from her house that evening. He took the stairs in a couple of bounds, grabbed a jacket from the hallstand on his way past, paused briefly at the door to slide his arms into the jacket sleeves and was strolling nonchalantly down the path by the time she reached his gate.

'Oh, hi, on your way to the hall?'

'That's right.' She wore a purple dress originally bought for her trousseau, short-sleeved and with a flared skirt that seemed to flow about her slim legs with every step. A soft white wool jacket was slung around her shoulders and her fair hair had been released from its usual combs to frame her face. 'What have you been up to?' she asked as he fell into step by her side.

'Nothing. Why do you ask?'

'You seem a bit short of breath.'

'No I'm not.'

'You should have asked me to phone just before I left my house. Then you could have strolled out calmly to meet me rather than erupt breathlessly from the door. Or is it the thought of spending the evening with your little blonde and purple friend?'

'Oh shut up,' Neil said.

Thirty-Two

It was hard, that evening, to believe that anything as terrible as murder had recently touched the village hall. Naomi, determined to make the place as welcoming as possible, had made arrangements with the local Women's Rural well in advance, and as soon as the newly-wed couple left the church for photographs on the village green, followed by a wedding breakfast at the Neurotic Cuckoo with family and close friends, the women of Prior's Ford sprang into action.

Wedding hats were removed and stored safely in the vestry, aprons were tied over best dresses and while one group began to strip the church of wedding flowers now destined for the hall, another collected even more flowers and vases begged from gardens and borrowed from every house. A third group set up trestle tables to hold the evening's buffet and as soon as the tables were ready a fourth group began to put out the food while the hired musicians set their instruments up on the stage and started rehearsing. By the time the bride and groom arrived with their invited guests the hall was looking magnificent.

Anja was already there when Neil and Gloria

arrived. 'Neil,' she shrieked, making a beeline for him. She wore a short white lacy dress, sleeveless and low-cut, over tight-fitting black and gold patterned leggings. Elaborate silver earrings swung from her pretty ears, her slender wrists were encircled with gold and silver bracelets and there were rings on almost every finger.

'Good grief,' Gloria murmured. 'Be careful, Constable; are you sure she's over the age of consent?'

'Very funny! As a matter of fact, she's twen...' Neil started, but she had already disappeared into the crowd. He kept catching glimpses of her, dancing, talking, laughing, and mingling with surprising enthusiasm.

They met up during Strip the Willow, an energetic Scottish dance where Gloria had the misfortune to be partnered with a particularly vigorous young villager. They were supposed to link arms and spin round sixteen times before separating; Gloria was then required to dance her way down a row of men, linking arms for a half-turn with each, but her partner spun her round with such speed that when he released her she cannoned into Neil, who was first in the row.

Seeing her approach at speed he managed to brace himself and catch her as she slammed into his chest. For a moment they clung together, looking into each other's eyes, then Gloria wrenched herself free and whirled back to her exuberant partner, who was stunned thereafter to find himself being firmly controlled by a woman who, though feminine in every way, had a grip of iron and knew how to get the better of any man when she wanted or needed to.

When the musicians took a break and everyone made for the bar and buffet in the lesser hall, Neil searched for Gloria, but there was no sign of her and he realized that she must have left. Anja was sitting at a table in the lesser hall with the bride, bridesmaids and several other village girls. She made a disappointed face at him as he passed. He shrugged his shoulders and smiled before moving on, straight into the path of Amy Rose.

'Ah, there you are, Neil, I've been lookin' for you. There's someone I want you to meet. He used to be a cop, Chief Super, I think, so here's your chance to impress him.' She caught at his arm and dragged him to a table by the buffet. Two women and a man were already at the table.

'This charming young man is Constable Neil White, who's come to live in the village. He's helpin' to solve our murder at the moment. Neil, this is my friend Clarissa Ramsay, and here are two other newcomers to Prior's Ford: Laura Tyler Hunter, the famous cookery expert, and her husband Allan Hunter, who was a police officer before he retired.' Then, as soon as they had all shaken hands: 'Go get yourself somethin' to eat an' drink, Neil, then come back here to talk with us.'

He did as he was told, wondering, as he carried a loaded plate and a half-pint of beer back to the table, how such a small woman could get people to do whatever she wanted of them. With Gloria, it was something to do with the way she could pin people down with a look; with Amy Rose, it was somehow different. Whatever it was, he was getting the chance to meet an ex-Chief Superintendent, and, hopefully, get a few tips on how to deal with a murder case.

By the time he rejoined them the three women were absorbed in a conversation, heads together, while Allan Hunter, ignored and bored, was glancing around the room. He seemed quite pleased to see Neil.

'I take it you're based at Kirkcudbright.'

'Yes, sir. My ... my sergeant and I both happened to move into the new housing complex, Clover Park, recently, and our boss decided that since we lived in the area we should be seconded to CID to work on the local murder.'

'That makes sense. Good experience for you.'

Neil took a gulp of beer and set the glass down. 'That's what I thought, but to tell the truth, I've been slogging through paperwork most of the time. More dull than interesting.'

'Dull is part of the job. Were you the one who came across my name in an old newspaper cutting? It shows that you're being meticulous,' Hunter went on smoothly as Neil, who had just bitten into a slice of quiche, almost choked. 'I've been duly interviewed and cleared, but I presume you've heard that. A word of advice, Neil – don't try to keep secrets if you work in the police service, you're bound to be found out in the end. But on the other hand, it's a good thing that Pearce kept all or most of his cuttings because one of them may unmask the murderer. So keep on being meticulous, no matter how boring it is.'

'I intend to, sir.'

'Good man. I met your sergeant; she came to the house with DI Cutler. Although she didn't get the chance to say much, I was impressed by her. Efficient and ambitious, I'd say.'

'Spot on, sir.' The beer, not his first that evening, was beginning to help Neil to relax. 'She made Sergeant in record time.'

'So I'm right about her being the ambitious type.'

'Definitely.'

'Then another word of advice, if I may,' Allan leaned forward, lowering his voice. 'I happened to be watching Strip the Willow earlier – more of an ordeal than a dance, to my mind, but the Scots seem to enjoy that sort of thing – and I noticed the way you caught her when her partner tossed her into your arms. You resembled a football player who'd just scored the winning goal.'

'Sir?' Neil squeaked, his face reddening.

'I'm not in the service now, Neil, so you don't have to call me "sir". Allan will do. I'd say you've fallen for that pretty sergeant, but you'd be well advised to look elsewhere for a lifelong companion. I say this because I was led by single-minded ambition when I joined the force and although it paid off, now that I'm retired I'm beginning to realize that being married to an ambitious police officer wasn't easy for my wife at times. More often than not, to be honest.'

'Thank you for the advice, si— Allan, but it's a bit too late. We're already married,' Neil confessed. Then as the older man's eyebrows shot up: 'That is, married but separated.'

'And both working from the same station?'

'Senior management knows the situation, and as long as we get on well together at work they're willing to keep both of us. Our colleagues don't know that we're apart, though. The fact that we both bought houses in Clover Park without realizing it helps. When we work the same shift we can travel in one car. I'd be grateful if you kept this to yourself. Nobody in the village knows the truth.'

'Of course. What caused the split, if I may ask?'

'It was just as you said earlier. Gloria was more interested in making sergeant than in us building a life together.'

'I see. Pity I didn't manage to give you advice before it was too late.'

'To be honest, it wouldn't have made any difference to me, though probably Gloria would have listened to you with interest.'

'Are you ambitious?'

'I like the job and I want to be good at it, but I'm not as hungry for promotion as she is; though I certainly wouldn't turn it down if I got the chance.'

'Wise man. If I was your senior officer I'd certainly encourage you to go onwards and upwards. Working on this case could do you a lot of good, so keep your eyes and ears open. But one final suggestion,' Allan Hunter said as the musicians started to play in the other room. 'Don't let the job take you over completely. It will if it can, but that may cost you more than you're prepared to pay.'

Hours later, having walked Anja home and once again declined her invitation to stay the night, Neil discovered lipstick smeared at Gloria-height over his shirt. He stripped it off and tossed it into the new laundry basket, then changed his mind, took it back out, folded it carefully, and tucked it at the back of a drawer.

While most of the villagers were enjoying the wedding reception, Jess McNair was sitting by the range in the farm kitchen, knitting a jersey for Alison's son Jamie. Now that she only had one man in the house instead of three, darning and mending took up less time, leaving her free to start knitting again.

At that moment, her one remaining man was sitting at the table, poring over the plans he and Alison between them had drawn of the Tarbethill farmland. Jess glanced over the top of her spectacles at him, noting with relief that the worry lines that had begun to make him look older than his twenty-nine years were easing.

Now that Alison's plan was under way, the

321

dairy herd gone and the milking shed emptied of its machinery, he was beginning to look forward instead of clinging to the past. The two top fields had been rented out to a neighbouring farmer who might well have bought the land had the McNairs been forced to sell it off, but was now content to rent it. He was moving his beef cows into them, and paying Ewan to watch over them.

The first of the two fields to be turned into allotments was being ploughed, and already several people had shown interest in the scheme. Now that the plans on paper were becoming physical reality and the changes starting to bring in desperately needed money, Ewan was beginning to accept that he, not his father, was now the owner of Tarbethill Farm.

And it was all down to Alison Greenlees. If that clever lassie can work her magic on Ewan the farmer, Jess thought to herself, surely in time she'll be able to do the same with Ewan the man. There could be a new generation of bairns toddling about the courtyard of Tarbethill Farm yet!

Ewan, stretching his arms and resting his eyes from the paperwork, suddenly noticed that his mother was smiling broadly at nothing at all while the knitting needles in her hands moved so fast that they were a blur.

'What are you grinning at?' he wanted to know.

'Me? I wasnae grinning!'

'You were nearly laughin' out loud. Somethin'

was amusin' you.'

'I was only thinkin' about that deep litter house I'm goin' to get,' Jess lied. 'I can't wait tae get more chickens tae look after. When'll the shed be cleared so's Alison and me can get it scrubbed out?'

'Why the hurry?'

'You're doin' your bit tae set Tarbethill right again an' I want my chance tae do the same.'

'I'll ask Wilf to start on it tomorrow.'

'Good. We'll have a cup of tea before bed.' said Jess, laying aside her knitting.

Thirty-Three

Amy Rose arrived in the police incident van on the day following the wedding reception. 'Morning, Neil, I brought some brownies for you to try.' She opened the paper bag she carried, releasing a mouth-watering aroma. 'Have one.' Then, taking a brownie for herself: 'So how did you get on with Allan Hunter last night?'

Neil, unable to resist the brownies, had to chew and swallow before answering. 'Very well. He's a nice man.'

'I've come to think so. Some folk round here reckon that he feels he's too good for the likes of them, but I've come to believe that it might be down to bein' cautious about strangers – probably to do with his job. Mebbe there's a touch of shyness there too. Have another brownie, they're best eaten fresh. I've discovered that although first impressions are usually right, there are times when you need to step back a bit from a person and think again before you decide for sure what they're really like. The important thing is, did he give you some helpful tips about your job?'

'He did.'

'Good. Don't forget them. I think he was impressed by you, too. I've come to tell you,' Amy went on briskly, 'that I'm off to Whitby later today. I promised ages ago to spend a week there with Stella Hesslet. She visits a friend in Whitby every year and last year she met a man there. I want to check him out because, although it would do Stella the world of good to have a man in her life, she's not got much experience in knowin' good from bad.'

'Right. Well, have a good time.' Neil hadn't the faintest idea why his visitor was discussing the local librarian with him.

'If he's the right one for her I'll move things on a little and if he's not – well, I'll deal with that if it happens.'

'I'm sure you will.'

'The thing is, I'm not happy about bein' away from the village when there's a murder investigation goin' on.'

'I think you can safely rely on us to keep working on the case while you're away, Mrs Rose.'

'I've told you, Neil, the name's Amy. Bein' called Mrs Rose makes me feel like my mother-in-law an' we never got on, her and me. I know you're here, Neil, and so's that pretty blonde sergeant that carries a torch for you, but as I've said before, it's good to have someone like me around to ask the sort of questions that you can't.'

'I think we'll manage. Just concentrate on enjoying your time in—' Neil stopped short, then asked cautiously, 'What did you say?'

'Whitby. It's in England.'

'I know where it is. What did you just say about the serg—' Neil stopped abruptly again, this time as Gloria arrived.

'Neil, have you – oh, good morning.'

'Mornin'. I was just deliverin' some brownies to Neil. A husky young man like him needs to keep his strength up. Help yourself, honey, there's enough to go round; fresh baked this mornin'. See you both next week,' Amy said cheerfully.

'I wish you wouldn't encourage that woman to keep popping in with food for you,' Gloria said irritably when they were alone.

'Believe me, she doesn't need encouragement. But she's a great baker. Have a brownie.'

Gloria peered inside the bag suspiciously, then succumbed.

'Anything to report?'

'Nothing at all. You left the village hall early last night.'

'That sort of thing isn't really my scene.'

'I'd a long talk with Allan Hunter. He seems like a decent sort.'

'He's all right, I suppose.'

'Is he still a possible suspect?'

'No. His alibi for the night of the murder's solid.' Gloria finished the brownie and wiped her mouth carefully with her handkerchief. 'So how long did you stay last night?'

'Not all that long. I was in bed by eleven.' He waited for a moment, then said, 'No questions as to whose bed I was in?'

'Not my business.'

'My own, as it happens. Alone.'

She ignored the comment. 'I'm off to a meeting with the DI. Be sure to let me know if anything useful happens while I'm away. I'll be back early afternoon.'

Once he was alone Neil finished off the brownies, pondering over Amy Rose's comment about Gloria carrying a torch for him. It couldn't be true – or could it? No, it couldn't and no sense in hoping otherwise. But there was always Anja. Since Gloria was going to be away until the afternoon he'd look in at Colour Carousel to find out if Anja was free for lunch.

He crushed up the brownie bag, lobbed it neatly into the waste-paper bin, and settled down to going over the meeting with Allan Hunter for the umpteenth time. It wasn't every day that a constable got the chance to listen to words of wisdom from someone like Hunter, and Neil intended to imprint every word on his brain.

'Is all this really necessary? Surely only fit people will want to climb the hill,' Lewis said.

He and Ginny were making their way up to the top of the dammed waterfall. Progress was slow because Ginny paused every few yards to scribble notes about areas in need of stepping stones, seats for weary visitors to rest on, and places where she wanted to put in plants.

'You're surely not going to deny less fit

people the pleasure of seeing the fantastic view from the top,' she objected.

'They may not want to make the effort to see the view.'

'Look at the other side of the coin, Lewis – some of them will yearn to be able to get to the top, fit or not, and we should make it as easy for them as we can. Big flat stones to form a natural staircase, with fencing that blends in with the surroundings but is also strong enough to give support. Seats they can rest on, interesting and fragrant flowers to look at, not to mention the sound of water running down the hill – one of the loveliest sounds in the world.' She looked around, her inner eye seeing a place of pleasure and beauty rather than the rough, neglected hillside. 'We mustn't deny older, less fit people the choice. And there'll be a picnic area at the top to make it all worthwhile. I know exactly how we're going to achieve it and I promise you that it'll be worthwhile. Get it organized now and I reckon we could have it in place by next summer.'

She gave him the half-determined, half-pleading look he had become used to. So far Ginny's plans had worked out, and his instinct told him that once again she was right.

'OK, we'll do it your way,' he said, and she beamed at him before moving on.

They were nearing the top when the rain started, a gentle drizzle at first, but getting stronger by the minute. Lewis suggested going back down, but Ginny would have none of it.

'We've come too far to give up now, and I'm dying to see this stone grotto you told me about. Now's our chance. Come on, we'll be under the trees once we get to the top.'

By the time they reached the summit it was raining in earnest, big heavy drops splashing into the already waterlogged dammed area. 'If this is what you mean about the pleasure of hearing running water,' Lewis puffed as they made for the shelter of the trees, their wellington boots throwing up gouts of water with each step, 'I for one could do without it.'

'But isn't it fun?' Ginny said happily. 'Like being a kid again, but without adults around to tell us to stop splashing.' Then, lifting her face to the downpour: 'It's lovely!'

'It's wet! And,' Lewis said as they reached the trees and were dripped on from the canopy of leaves overhead, 'we're not getting much shelter.'

'I bet you and Cam had fabulous times up here when you were kids. It must have been heaven. I wish I could have been with you.' Ginny ran her hands through her wet hair, then rubbed them over her face. 'I wasn't allowed out when it rained in case I got a chill. And I couldn't splash in puddles either. Oh look, there's your grotto!'

They had reached a clearing dominated by a small round flat-roofed ivy-clad stone summer-house with a small glassless window to either side of the gaping door-frame.

'Come on.' Lewis took her hand and pulled

her inside. 'It's just a little bit drier in here.'

'It's wonderful!' Ginny stood in the middle of the single room, circling slowly. The light was dim on this sunless day, with a greenish tinge. 'And look at this—' she dropped to her knees, brushing dead leaves aside – 'mosaic flooring, with a lovely pattern. What a fantastic little hideaway!'

'You can use the stone walls and the ivy to climb to the roof. It made a great clubhouse for me and Cam.'

'It's going to make a wonderful feature. We'll clear the undergrowth and create an avenue leading to it from the top of the waterfall. And we'll have other paths so that visitors can walk through the trees and bushes, right to the edge of the estate.'

The grotto was dry but chilly, and Lewis began to shiver. 'Let's get back down and talk about it over a hot drink,' he suggested, and Ginny got to her feet reluctantly.

'You were so lucky to have this place to play in,' she said wistfully as they headed back to the top of the waterfall.

'It sounds as though your childhood wasn't much fun.'

'It wasn't. Being looked after by housekeepers and never getting the chance to get out on my own and make friends.'

'Poor you.'

'Poor me,' she agreed. Then, suddenly cheerful again: 'But meeting you and being allowed to work in the Linn Hall estate's garden more than made up for it. I'm going to miss this place so much when all the work's over, but think of the CV I'm building up.'

'And the reference you're going to get. You'll be able to get work anywhere. But that won't be for quite a while yet.'

'I hope not. Can this area be my next project?'

'It's going to take a long time. Are you sure it wouldn't be better just to open up the waterfall and leave it at that?'

'Quite sure,' Ginny said. 'It's going to look terrific when I'm done with it.' The longer it took, she thought, the better. She wanted to be part of Linn Hall for as long as possible.

'If you undertake it you'll need to use the McDonalds and some of the backpackers. Duncan and I have enough to do.'

'Jimmy'll love this just as much as I do. I'll spend the winter planning it. I'd like to get rid of some of the trees and replace them with eucalyptus to drain the ground. Eucalyptus looks beautiful and smells nice, too. And ... hang on...' She halted, then plunged off into the undergrowth.

'Ginny, come on, I'm drowning here!'

'Come and look at this, Lewis – quickly.'

Not another murder, Lewis hoped as he struggled after her. Please, not a body in the undergrowth or stolen goods stashed away by some burglar. He had enough to worry about without getting caught up in the result of criminal activity.

'Oh my God!' Ginny was saying over and over

again when he reached her. She was on her knees, heedless of the cold wet mud soaking through her sturdy jeans, caressing the leaves of a plant crowded against the trunk of a tree.

'What's wrong?'

'Nothing's wrong, nothing at all. Do you know what this is?'

He peered at the plant. It looked insignificant to him. 'Not the faintest.

'Then let me introduce you.' Her voice was shaking with excitement. 'This is a Cypripedium Tibeticum, and I think it's going to play an important part in your future.'

'Is it?'

'Oh yes, because it doesn't belong here. This is a very beautiful, dramatic plant when it's in bloom, and it comes from the Himalayas.'

By now, Lewis was too cold and wet to think straight. 'How did it get here?'

'I think we can safely assume that it didn't book a trip through a travel agency. It was collected by a botanist, probably your great uncle or whatever he was, and brought here, along with the other plants that Jimmy McDonald's grandfather told him about years ago.' She threw her arms out to indicate the entire area. 'It's my guess that his collection of exotic plants, the collection we've been looking for, is right here on the top of the hill, hopefully still thriving like this little darling. And once we've located them the Linn estate is going to be inundated with visitors dying to see them.'

'Are you sure?'

'Really! This could be the saving of your ancestral home.'

'I can't believe it!'

'Believe it!' Ginny began to get up, but slipped in the mud and if Lewis hadn't caught her arm she might have fallen on top of the plant that according to her was going to make Linn Hall's fortune. She scrambled clumsily to her feet, using his body as a support.

'Let's go further in to see what else is there.'

'No, let's go down and tell Mum and Dad what you've just told me.' They were still clinging together, grinning at each other like idiots. 'Ginny Whitelaw, I bless the day I met you. You're worth your weight in gold!' Lewis said, and then he bent his head to hers.

Her mouth was wet, yet warm, and quick to respond. For a moment they stayed as they were, locked in each other's arms, sharing the kiss, then they both realized what was happening, and broke contact, almost hurtling back from each other.

'Well ... that's ... great news,' Lewis said awkwardly, avoiding eye contact. 'I can't wait to tell my parents.'

'Yes, we should get down to the house at once,' Ginny agreed in a rush of words, and they both headed for the way down as though their lives depended on getting away from each other.

Thirty-Four

'Clarissa, it's me.'

'Hello, Amy, how are you enjoying Whitby?'

'Very nice. You don't happen to have the police incident van's phone number, do you?'

'No, why would I have that?'

'I should've taken a note of it before I left Prior's Ford. I meant to, when I went to say goodbye to Neil, but then his sergeant came in and I didn't want her to start askin' why I wanted to keep in touch with him.'

'Why *do* you want to keep in touch with him?'

'Never mind that, just write this number down, will you?' Once Clarissa had done as she was told and read it back to Amy to make sure that she hadn't made any errors, Amy hurried on, 'Please take it to the van as soon as you can. But if he's not alone go away and try again later. And when you give him the number ask him to call me right away.'

'What's going on?'

'Urgent police business. Must go, I'm supposed to be servin' breakfast to the guests,' Amy said, and rang off.

It was eight o'clock and Clarissa was still in her dressing gown, but by nine she was on her way to the incident van where, to her relief, Neil White was on his own, going through papers in a box file.

'Yes, madam, can I help you?'

'This sounds rather strange, but my friend Amy Rose asked me to give you this phone number. She wants to talk to you as soon as possible. Does that make any sense?'

He took the note, glanced at the number, then said, 'It might.'

'Oh, good. You'll phone her, then?'

'Yes, I will. And thank you.'

'Not at all,' Clarissa said, and escaped to the normal outside world.

Three minutes later Amy Rose was asking, 'Are you alone?'

'Yes, I am.'

'Good. If anyone comes into the van, end this call and phone me later. Are you still lookin' through Kevin Pearce's papers?'

'Almost finished.' Hell, Neil thought, was probably an eternity of looking through Kevin Pearce's endless newspaper cuttings.

'Have you found anythin' from the North Yorkshire area?'

'Not so far. I don't know if he ever lived or worked in that part of England.'

'So here's what you should do,' Amy said briskly. 'First, go and ask Elinor Pearce if Kevin ever lived in the Scarborough area.'

'Why?'

'Because it's the biggest place near Whitby and if he did work with a newspaper in that area, it could be in Scarborough.'

'But—'

'Just listen, Neil. Did you know that Laura Hunter comes from Whitby, where I am at this minute?'

'I wasn't aware of that, but I don't see—'

'Just *listen*, Neil. The folks here are proud of her – local girl made good sort of thing. Yesterday I got talkin' to a woman who knew her when she lived here, only she was Laura Young then, and she said how sad it was about her mother.'

'Laura Hunter's mother?'

'Uh-huh. Apparently Laura's father died of cancer when she was a teenager and it hit her mother real hard. She went off the rails a bit afterwards, got all confused and then she was caught shopliftin' and taken to court. She got off with a caution because of the way her husband's death had upset her so badly. The judge said there were mitigatin' circumstances, which was true, and asked for her name to be kept out of the papers to give her time to get over her grief, but one paper printed the whole thing, name and photograph. She'd everyone's sympathy here but it was too much for the poor soul and she killed herself. Laura was distraught, the woman said, but it was too late to change things, the damage was done. Laura left Whitby not long after that because she couldn't bear to stay on there. What I'd like to know is this: who wrote that article? If anyone can find out, it's you.'

'You can't think that it was Kevin Pearce!'

'It's a long shot, but surely worth lookin' into.'

'Mrs Rose ... Amy ... it takes strength to strangle a man from behind. A woman couldn't have done it.'

'Did you know that Laura was an archer, and she could pull a longbow well enough to win competitions? That takes strength, doesn't it?'

Neil hesitated. Don't miss anything, the DI had told him and Gloria more than once. Note every tiny detail.

'I suppose it wouldn't hurt to check it out.'

'Good. And listen, don't pass what I've told you to your sergeant; deal with it yourself. That way, if it's a wild good chase nobody needs to know, but if it turns out to be worth the diggin' up, why shouldn't you be the one to get the credit? I'm talkin' about an article in the late nineteen-seventies, by the way.'

'Yes, we did spend some time in Scarborough shortly after we married,' Elinor Pearce said half an hour later. 'Not much more than a year. Kevin was an assistant editor in one of the local papers and when the editor retired he expected to take over the post, but they brought someone else in. He was so disappointed, because the editor had been poorly for months and Kevin had been standing in for him. It was unfair of them not to promote him.'

'Would that be around the late nineteen-seventies?'

'That's right. We moved away from there in nineteen-eighty.'

'You're sure that we've seen all his files?

There aren't any others?'

'No, they were all in his study.'

'Thank you, Mrs Pearce, sorry to have troubled you,' Neil said. He and Nancy had almost finished looking through the files but it would be easier and faster to fetch his laptop from home now that he had a place and a time to focus on.

Just under three hours later he phoned Detective Inspector Cutler's office.

'Would it be possible to call on you in half an hour, sir? I've got some interesting information that you need to see,' he said.

Allan Hunter raised his eyebrows when he opened the door of Thatcher's Cottage to Detective Inspector Cutler, Gloria Frost and Neil White.

'More questions? I thought we'd cleared things up on your last visit.'

'We did, Mr Hunter. I'd like a word with your wife this time.'

Laura, leafing through a magazine in the small living room, welcomed the visitors with her warm smile and immediately offered coffee, which was refused.

'The last time we were here, Mrs Hunter, your husband told us that he and Kevin Pearce once knew each other. But you didn't mention that you, too, had met Mr Pearce years ago.'

'What? That's impossible!'

'I only saw him twice, Allan,' Laura said calmly.

'When and where, Mrs Hunter?'

'The first time was outside a courtroom almost forty years ago. My mother,' Laura went on, talking to her husband rather than to the police, 'had just been let off with a caution on a charge of shoplifting. The magistrate was a decent man; he acknowledged that she was suffering from depression and exhaustion after years of seeing my father being slowly destroyed by cancer. His death came as the final straw, and the shoplifting offence was the result. The magistrate asked journalists present in court not to reveal my mother's name, and when we left the court I too asked the journalists not to print the story. Kevin Pearce was one of them.'

'Mrs Hunter,' Detective Inspector Cutler interrupted, 'I have to tell you that as a possible suspect in a murder enquiry, you don't have to say any more at this stage.'

'Suspect?' Allan Hunter almost shouted. 'What are you—'

'It's all right, Allan. Let the police officers get on with their job. I understand what you're saying, Inspector, but I would prefer to tell the whole story here and now.'

'For God's sake, Laura,' her husband said urgently, 'do as the man says!'

'Leave things to me, please, dear. I've been carrying this weight around inside me for so long that I can't bear it any longer. Let me free myself of it, please.' Then, as he subsided, shaking his head: 'Kevin was the only journalist to run the story, complete with my mother's name and address. People who knew her were kind and understanding but the humiliation was too much for her and she ... killed herself.' She swallowed hard, then went on, 'I saw him for the second time when I went to the newspaper office to confront him. Apparently the editor was ill and Kevin, the assistant editor, was making the most of being in charge. He claimed that he had every right to do his job as he saw fit and there was nothing I could do about it. Even if he had been penitent it wouldn't have brought my mother back. So I had no option but to let the matter drop, but I never forgot or forgave him.'

'You took a long time to find him, Mrs Hunter,' Cutler commented.

'I wasn't really looking for him. As I said, there was no point.'

Neil cleared his throat, then ventured, 'The note already shown to your husband, Mrs Hunter, the one about secrets...'

'Oh yes, I'd forgotten about that. I sent it to Kevin's office not long after that second meeting, in the hope of worrying him. Perhaps it did. Perhaps that's why he kept it. I was surprised, Inspector, when you handed it to Allan. As I was saying, I gave up on taking revenge on him, but not a day has passed since then without me thinking of him, and hoping that someone somewhere had destroyed his life as he destroyed my mother's. Archery helped. Every time I loosed an arrow at a target I was aiming for Kevin Pearce's heart.' She gave a faint smile. 'That may be why I won so many competitions. But constant festering hatred is exhausting, especially when there's nobody to share the weight of it. Then, at the beginning of this year, I happened to read a magazine article about the growing popularity of scarecrow festivals, and there was Kevin, in a group photograph. Winner of the scarecrow festival in Prior's Ford. The man who had driven my mother to her death was alive and well. It was like being given the key to a locked door. Seeing that face smirking at me from the page made me realize that my chance to avenge my mother had come at last. It was like an eternal itch that could finally be scratched. That's why I found this lovely little cottage, so that I could re-enter Kevin Pearce's life, and end it.'

'He didn't recognize you when you met again?'

'Of course not. I was a teenager when we first met, and my name then was Young. I meant nothing to him. When I started writing recipe books I took my mother's maiden name. He didn't care a jot about Laura Young, but Laura Tyler, who wrote books and had been on television, was a different matter altogether. He loved knowing her, and he was thrilled when she became part of his precious drama club. Age hadn't improved him; he was still the self-centred man who cared about nobody but himself.'

'When did you decide to kill him?' Cutler asked.

'The moment I discovered that he was alive,

well, and living here in Prior's Ford. If he'd changed, become a more pleasant person, I might not have done it,' Laura said thoughtfully. 'But to be honest I'd probably have gone ahead no matter what. I knew that I'd be found out eventually, but that didn't matter – it still doesn't.' She turned to her husband. 'I got such a shock when I discovered that you'd also been involved with him long ago, Allan, and been damaged by him. I would of course have confessed had there been any possibility of you being accused. He was the one I wanted to hurt, never you.'

'So you're admitting that you killed Kevin Pearce, Mrs Hunter?'

'Laura...!' Allan Hunter said, and was ignored.

'I am, Chief Inspector, and I don't regret it. I knew when he decided to stay behind in the hall that night, on his own, that the time had come. Fortunately, my husband was in Leeds so I had to make the most of the opportunity. Instead of putting the feather boa in the props box I left it in the hall. I was the one who bought it and I knew that its silk core was strong enough to do the job. And I was strong enough to use it, thanks to the archery. I walked part-way home that night with Jinty McDonald, and when we separated I came on here and then went out again, planning to say if anyone I knew saw me that I was going back to the hall to put the boa away safely. It's very old, and quite expensive. Poor Cynthia MacBain; I told her that I would make her a gift of it once the play was over, but

I don't expect she'll want it now.

'I got to the hall without meeting anyone I knew, and Kevin didn't even hear me because I was wearing trainers and he was intent on the script. I picked up the boa on my way to where he sat, and it was around his throat before he realized that he wasn't alone. And there, Inspector, endeth my tale. Now it's your turn.'

Cutler nodded, then said, 'Laura Hunter, I have to tell you that you're under arrest for the murder of Kevin Pearce.'

'Why didn't you tell me about you and Pearce before?' Allan Hunter's voice was little more than a choked whisper.

'Why didn't you tell me that *you'd* known him, Allan? Even the closest of couples have their individual secrets. In a way, I've avenged your brother as well as my mother. Isn't it strange that two of Kevin's victims should meet and marry? But I'm sorry you have to go through this, my love. If you want to disown me I'll understand fully.'

'Of course I'm not going to disown you! I'm going to do everything I can to help you!'

'In that case, could you fetch my coat? I expect the Chief Inspector will want to take me to the police station now,' Laura said gently. Then, turning to Neil as her husband blundered from the room: 'I'm so sorry, Neil, to spoil your chance of doing *The Importance of Being Earnest*; you're a very good actor. Let's hope that they find another director, and you get to play the part.'

Thirty-Five

'The real tragedy is,' Amy Rose said, 'that Laura Tyler let what happened to her mother destroy not only her own life, but so many others. When all's said and done, poor Kevin didn't deserve to die for that article he wrote years ago. It's like a row of dominoes, set up to be knocked down, one after the other. Kevin's dead, Laura's going to spend years in prison, and Elinor's and Alan Hunter's lives will never be the same again.'

It was a balmy mid-October day and Amy, Clarissa and Naomi were sitting in the back garden of the manse, drinking tea. A basket filled with cooking apples stood in the middle of the garden table.

'Do you think Laura might be able to plead insanity?' Clarissa wondered. 'Waiting for all those years to get revenge surely must have had a detrimental effect on her mind.'

'I don't know. Her barrister might think it worth pursuing. But in a way, that might be even worse for her poor husband,' Naomi said. 'Or can having a wife who killed because she was insane be less harrowing than a wife who killed because she knew exactly what she was doing?'

A sudden shiver gripped Clarissa. 'Stop talking about it, please!' she begged. 'Whatever the reason, and whatever was in Laura's mind, it won't bring Kevin back.'

'*Cooee*, Naomi,' a voice called from the side of the house.

'In the back garden, Cynthia!'

'Our fruit trees are laden with apples this year,' Cynthia MacBain said as she came round the corner, basket in hand, 'so we thought you might ... oh, you've already got some.'

'Hello, Cynthia. My single tree's done well this year too,' Clarissa said. 'I expect it's the same with everyone who had apple trees.'

'Tea, Cynthia? I was about to make a fresh pot.'

'That would be lovely.' Cynthia sank down on to a garden seat as Naomi went into the house. 'Have you heard that Thatcher's Cottage is up for sale again? Gilbert and I,' she swept on when the other two nodded, 'were just saying this morning that the Thatchers lived there happily for more than half a century, then the new people came along with their disruptive twin daughters, and had to leave in disgrace – and now the Hunters. That poor little cottage; you don't think that it's been taken over by evil spirits, do you?'

'Not for a minute,' Amy told her firmly. 'It's not the cottage's fault that the wrong people decided to live in it.'

'To think that Gilbert and I gave a party to welcome that woman to the village, and all the time she was plotting to murder poor dear

345

Kevin, who wouldn't hurt a fly.' One of Cynthia's hands flew to her throat. 'And murder him with that lovely feather boa she had promised to me! Did you know that Elinor's decided to go and live with her sister in Moffat?'

Clarissa nodded. 'We heard. And I have to say that I liked Laura from the start, and in a way I still like her.'

'Clarissa!' Cynthia squealed as Naomi reappeared from the house, carrying a tray.

'There's Laura the person, and there's Laura the murderer,' Clarissa tried to find the right words to explain herself. 'It's tragic that she killed Kevin, but that doesn't make her a cold-blooded serial killer, does it?'

'I don't know how you can *say* that!'

'I can,' Amy butted in. 'Being a murderer is just a part of Laura. Deep down, there's a decent person who took a wrong turning in life, and is going to have to pay for it. I think she's strong enough to cope with her future, though. Elinor, too. I just hope Allan Hunter can as well.'

'I think I agree with you.' Naomi poured a cup of tea for Cynthia, then asked, 'More tea, Clarissa? Amy?'

'Naomi, do you think that Thatcher's Cottage could be haunted?' Cynthia wanted to know.

'No, what makes you think that?'

'I was just saying to Clarissa and Amy that we've had two bad lots living there since Doris died – the Alstons and then the Hunters. None of them people we would want to live in this village. Who knows what we might get next?'

'I can't wait to find out,' Amy said, her eyes bright with interest.

'Perhaps, Naomi, you should exorcize the cottage while it's empty, just to be on the safe side.'

'I don't do exorcisms.'

'But surely you know someone who does?'

'I can't say that I do, Cynthia. After all, that cottage is at least a hundred years old, and I don't think that two short recent occupations could seriously cause damage or disrupt its peace.'

'Naomi's right,' Amy put in. 'Who knows what old and hidden secrets an exorcist might disturb and let loose on the village?'

'Ohhhh!' Again, Cynthia's hand went to her throat.

'I think we should be going, Amy,' Clarissa said firmly. 'Thank you for the tea, Naomi.'

'What about the apples? I don't think I could deal with two baskets.'

'Why don't you keep Cynthia's offering, Naomi, and we'll take Clarissa's back,' Amy suggested, reaching for the basket. 'I just love to stir Cynthia up,' she said as she and Clarissa left the manse.

'What are we going to do with those apples? I really can't use them.'

'But I think I know a man who can,' Amy told her cheerfully.

Neil, on his way to a house at the top of Clover Park, wasn't quite sure that he was doing the right thing, but didn't know what else he *could* do. Especially with the basket of cooking apples. It wasn't as if he were a cook, or a baker, or whatever you called someone who could turn apples into something edible but in a different way.

'I wouldn't know what to do with them,' he had told Amy Rose when the American arrived at his door an hour earlier with the apples.

'Easy – you give them to someone else,' was her answer. 'Someone like that sassy blonde sergeant of yours. Can I come in? Hmm, nice place,' she went on as he stepped back to give her access to the hall. 'Where's your kitchen?'

'Straight through.' He followed her into the kitchen, where she put her basket on the table.

'I don't think the sergeant would know what to do with them either, to be honest.'

'That doesn't matter, Neil. What matters is the giving. As I said to you earlier, that sergeant kinda likes you...'

'She doesn't. I happen to know that for a fact.'

'...and you more than kinda like her.'

He felt his face grow hot and knew that there was no point in denying it. 'Yes I do, but that's as far as it can ever go.'

'Don't be such a loser! Faint heart never won fair lady. I'm tellin' you, you're in with a chance!'

'You don't understand Gloria.'

'It's you that doesn't understand women, but that's natural. Women are like an ancient language as far as men are concerned; they hear it but don't understand it. They need to *learn* how to understand it!'

He felt even more confused. 'And where do the apples come in?'

'Haven't you ever read your Bible, young man? It all started with an apple.'

'And look at the trouble that caused.'

'Oh, come on,' Amy scoffed. 'Think of the fun it gave Adam and Eve. They wouldn't have got anywhere without that apple. So give the basket to your sergeant as a present, and see what comes of it. It's my guess that she's waiting for you to make the first move – I'm not sure she's knows about first moves any more than you know about women. I've got to go – I'm headin' back home in a few days' time. It was nice knowin' you and you did a good job with that murder. With any luck you'll do a good job with the apples too.'

'But—'

'My mother used to say that if you want somethin' really badly you'll get it, but you have to work at it,' Amy remarked, heading past him towards the front door. 'Be lucky!'

This, Neil thought as he carried the basket through Gloria's gate, was his first move. No doubt the second move would consist of him heading back to his own home at speed with Gloria throwing apples after him. But he'd tried everything else and perhaps it was time for some dangerous living.

Gloria was wearing a dressing gown; her face had a freshly scrubbed glow about it and a towel was wrapped around her head. Her eyebrows shot up when she saw him on her doorstep.

'What are you doing here?'

'Someone gave me these apples; I thought you might like them.'

'You know that I'm not into cooking or baking.'

'Your mother is. They're for her, really.'

'Oh, all right then.' She took the basket from him. 'I'm going over there this afternoon as it happens.'

'Say hello from me.'

'I will.'

'Well – goodbye.'

'Neil,' she said as he began to turn away.

'Yes?'

'You did a good job on that murder, finding out about Laura Tyler's mother and the link with Kevin Pearce.'

'Thanks.'

'How exactly did you work it out?'

'Are you having dinner with your parents?'

'No, just a quick visit.'

'Have dinner at the Cuckoo with me tonight and I'll tell you all about it.'

She considered the offer, then said, 'Or you could have dinner with me, here, where we could talk without being overheard.'

'You mean it?'

'Of course.'

'I'll bring wine.'

'And I'll raid Mum's freezer for something decent to eat. About seven thirty?'

'OK,' he said casually, and turned away before she could see the stupid grin that insisted on plastering itself across his face. It was a start. And he used to be quite good at French and Latin at school.

He just hoped that Woman wasn't more difficult than Latin.

'Why don't you and Alastair come over to me for Thanksgiving?' Amy Rose suggested as Clarissa helped her to pack. 'Even if it's just for a week, we could have fun.'

'It's an idea. I'll phone him tonight to see if he can get time off at short notice.'

'If he can't, you come, and bring Stella with you.'

'With all the excitement of the murder, I didn't get to hear much about this man friend of hers. What's your verdict on him?'

'He's OK. A widower, grandfather, lonely; he could be just right for Stella. So that's your love life settled, and Stella's on the right road. And a murder's been solved. It's like the old days when Gordon was alive. But now it's time for me to be getting home. My work here is done,' Amy announced, closing her case and locking it. 'An' I'm itchin' to discover what's been happenin' across the water while I've been gone.'

'I'm going to miss you!'

'An' I'll miss you. But hey,' Amy Rose said cheerfully, 'I'll be back!'

1	2	3	4	5	6	7	8	9	10
11	12	13	14	15	16	17	18	19	20
21	22	23	24	25	26	27	28	29	30
31	32	33	34	35	36	37	38	39	40
41	42	43	44	45	46	47	48	49	50
51	52	53	54	55	56	57	58	59	60
61	62	63	64	65	66	67	68	69	70
71	72	73	74	75	76	77	78	79	80
81	82	83	84	85	86	87	88	89	90
91	92	93	94	95	96	97	98	99	100
101	102	103	104	105	106	107	108	109	110
111	112	113	114	115	116	117	118	119	120
121	122	123	124	125	126	127	128	129	130
131	132	133	134	135	136	137	138	139	140
141	142	143	144	145	146	147	148	149	150
151	152	153	154	155	156	157	158	159	160
161	162	163	164	165	166	167	168	169	170
171	172	173	174	175	176	177	178	179	180
181	182	183	184	185	186	187	188	189	190
191	192	193	194	195	196	197	198	199	200
201	202	203	204	205	206	207	208	209	210
211	212	213	214	215	216	217	218	219	220
221	222	223	224	225	226	227	228	229	230
231	232	233	234	235	236	237	238	239	240
241	242	243	244	245	246	247	248	249	250
251	252	253	254	255	256	257	258	259	260
261	262	263	264	265	266	267	268	269	270
271	272	273	274	275	276	277	278	279	280
281	282	283	284	285	286	287	288	289	290
291	292	293	294	295	296	297	298	299	300
301	302	303	304	305	306	307	308	309	310
311	312	313	314	315	316	317	318	319	320
321	322	323	324	325	326	327	328	329	330
331	332	333	334	335	336	337	338	339	340
341	342	343	344	345	346	347	348	349	350
351	352	353	354	355	356	357	358	359	360
361	362	363	364	365	366	367	368	369	370
371	372	373	374	375	376	377	378	379	380
381	382	383	384	385	386	387	388	389	390
391	392	393	394	395	396	397	398	399	400